LOVE BY SURPRISE

There were voices in the corridor outside the door. Someone growled: "I know he's in there!"

"Dash it all, it's too late," the handsome gentleman with Ada hissed, pulling her rudely to her feet.

Ada gaped at him openmouthed. "What—?"

They could hear the rattle of the doorknob. "Forgive me," the man muttered, brazenly taking her into his arms, "and whatever happens, for God's sake don't give me away!" Then, before Ada could utter another sound, he pressed his lips against her mouth in a strenuous—in fact, Ada thought, very *immoderate*—kiss.

A SPLENDID INDISCRETION

ELIZABETH MANSFIELD

Elizabeth Mansfield

A Splendid Indiscretion

BERKLEY BOOKS, NEW YORK

A SPLENDID INDISCRETION

A Berkley Book / published by arrangement with
the author

PRINTING HISTORY
Berkley edition / January 1985

ISBN: 0-425-07454-4

A BERKLEY BOOK® TM 757,375
Berkley Books are published by The Berkley Publishing Group,
200 Madison Avenue, New York, New York 10016.
The name "BERKLEY" and the stylized "B" with design
are trademarks belonging to Berkley Publishing Corporation.
PRINTED IN THE UNITED STATES OF AMERICA

Prologue

He'd already brushed the snow from his shoulders and was stripping off his gloves as he crossed the threshold of the inn's parlor, but he froze at the sight of the lady standing nervously before the window. "Julia! What on earth—?"

He had entered the inn in perfectly good humor, looking forward to the dinner he would be served in the private parlor (Yorkshire ham covered with the inn's famous raisin sauce, homebaked bread and a brew that attracted drinkers to the taproom from miles around) and the good night's sleep he'd have in the inn's pleasant back bedroom (the room that Goodell, the innkeeper, always managed to have available for his use), but Julia's unexpected presence caused his pleasant mood to evaporate at once.

The innkeeper at his side, who had just opened the door for him, was as startled as he was. "I beg pardon, yer lordship," he mumbled in embarrassment. "Me missus didn' tell me she'd let th' private parlor."

Ivor Griffith, Viscount Mullineaux, merely waved him away, his eyes fixed on the lady's face. "Close the door, Goodell, if you please. And don't disturb us until I call."

The innkeeper withdrew, closing the door carefully behind him. Mullineaux stared for a moment at the woman across the room. She was a creature of remarkable beauty, but Mullineaux had no need to take note of her lovely light-haired coiffure, her translucent skin, the exquisite slimness of her waist or the swell of her deliciously shaped bosom. With these attractions he was yawningly familiar. He took note only of the thick maquillage she'd applied to cover the crinkles at the corners of her large blue eyes, the blacking she'd used on her lashes, the near vulgarity of her daring decolletage, and the tension that was evident in the way she clenched her ringed fingers and bit her full nether lip. "How did you know I would stop here?" he asked coldly.

She crossed the room and threw herself against him. "Oh,

1

Griff!" she breathed into his shoulder. "I've been waiting for hours."

"I asked how you knew where to find me, ma'am."

She wound her arms tightly about his neck and looked up at him with a smile that was both mischievous and nervous. "Aubrey Tait told me you generally stop here on your way to Mullineaux Park."

Lord Mullineaux's mouth tightened. "When I next meet Aubrey I shall wring his neck," he muttered, thrusting her arms down.

"Don't blame him. I wheedled the information from him. I *had* to find you, Griff, don't you know that?"

"I don't know anything of the sort. I warned you from the start that this . . . this liaison would be short-lived."

"But Griff, I *love* you! You can't—"

"Love? You don't know what love is. You offer love as if it were a little sugary confection you can take from a silvered tin and present to whomever pleases you at the moment. Whenever the weather is gloomy, or there are no balls for which you can prepare, or poor Alcorn starts to bore you—"

"My husband *always* bores me."

Mullineaux ignored the interruption. "—that's when you look around for a diversion. And everyone knows what your favorite diversion is: finding yourself a new suitor, someone to whom you can offer one of the sweets from your little tin. Love, indeed! Love, my dear, is more than a deuced container of bon-bons."

"Griff, don't be horrid. You know that what you're saying isn't at all true."

"No? I suspect that Harrington and Lord Cloverdale and that idiot Nigel Lewis would fully agree with me."

"How can you compare those incidents with . . . with what we've had together?" the woman asked, her voice trembling. "I've never felt for *anyone* what I feel for you!"

Mullineaux raised an eyebrow icily. "Stop it, Julia. You knew from the first that this would be nothing but a light flirtation. In fact, you agreed that love would have no part in—"

"I? When did I agree to such a ridiculous arrangement?"

"Are you trying to pretend you don't remember? Then let me remind you. The scene took place in the little sitting room down the hall from the Bromwells' ballroom. You had taken me there after twisting your ankle on the dance floor during the waltz. But you hadn't twisted your ankle at all, had you, Julia? It was only one of your little ruses. However, I didn't know that, then. I was dizzy and half disguised on Bromwell's excellent madeira, and, as I recall, I had just released you from a somewhat uninhibited embrace. But instead of slapping my face and calling for Lord Alcorn to come and avenge your honor, you smiled at me tantalizingly and suggested an assignation."

Julia's eyes fell. "I do remember. You refused me. You thanked me but said that you were weary of love involvements at the moment."

"Yes, just so. Do you also remember what you answered?"

"I said, 'La, Lord Mullineaux, what's wrong with a gay little flirtation?'"

"No, not quite. What you said was, 'Love has nothing to do with this, Lord Mullineaux. I promise you *nothing more* than a gay little flirtation.'"

"But, Griff, how could I have known how I would feel? That was three months ago!"

His Lordship looked at the woman disdainfully and then walked away. He said nothing more until he'd crossed to the fireplace and kicked some life into the fire with the toe of a boot. "This discussion is neither here nor there, ma'am," he said, his eyes on the low flame. "The fact remains that your husband is beginning to suspect the worst, and I, since I have no wish to face him over pistols at dawn, realize it is time we call it quits."

"No, no!" She ran to the fireplace, pulled him round and clutched at the collar of his greatcoat. "You mustn't leave me now! You *can't!* My heart will crack in two!"

He loosed her fingers and stepped back out of her reach. "Hearts don't crack so easily, my dear." His voice was low and not unkind, but there was a finality in the tone that she couldn't miss.

She stared at him with stricken eyes. Now that she was about to lose him, he seemed more desirable than ever. Imposingly tall and well built, he had glossy chestnut hair (now falling appealingly over his forehead); eyes of ocean grey that could darken frighteningly when he was angry, like the ocean itself; a strong, thick-lipped mouth; a face slightly elongated by a square chin; broad shoulders (now emphasized by a caped greatcoat that hung open to reveal a wide, waistcoated chest and narrow hips clad in tan chamois riding breeches); and a pair of beautifully shaped legs, their muscular calves not hidden but emphasized by his high top-boots. The fact that she was now about to lose him filled her with panic. "What do you know about hearts?" she cried, wringing her hands while trying desperately to think of ways to attach him again. "Sometimes I think you don't have a heart. Please, Griff, listen to me. Though it amuses you to deny it, I know you care for me. It's Alcorn you're thinking of, isn't it? You feel guilty. But there's no need to think of him. We can run away and never see him again. We needn't see anyone we know ever again. We can go to the continent to live. The *haut monde* of the continent . . . they all understand about these situations. They will accept us with open arms. We can have new friends, new surroundings, a new life. We can have each other! We can live in Paris or Venice and be *happy*."

His eyes were fixed on her face, glinting with a forbidding anger she hadn't seen before. "Do you know what you're suggesting, ma'am?" he asked in a voice of ice. Like most of the men of the Corinthian set, who found it admirable to engage in the most competitive sports, the most excessive gambling and the most passionate amours without exhibiting a trace of emotion, he had trained his face to be impassive, but at this moment his eyes revealed much of his inner revulsion. There was no question that, whatever he might once have felt for her, he felt nothing now but disgust. "Have you no conscience? Have you given no thought to the pain and shame you'd be causing Lord Alcorn to suffer? Have you no feeling for your husband at all?"

"Why should I concern myself with—?"

Her question was cut short by a sudden pounding on the door. "Griff? Griff? Are you in there?" someone was shouting from outside the room.

"Good God!" Mullineaux threw Julia a puzzled look. "Is that *Aubrey?*"

He strode to the door and threw it open. In the corridor stood a stout, youngish fellow with red cheeks, two quivering chins and a pair of brilliant black eyes. His chest was heaving with exertion, and his breath came in gasps. "Ah, there you are!" he panted in relief. "Afraid I'd be . . . too late."

"Too late for what, you bobbing-block," Mullineaux said

curtly, stepping aside to admit the breathless fellow. "What the devil are you doing here, and why the devil did you tell Julia where to find me?"

"Never mind all that," Aubrey said, dropping into a chair and pulling out a huge handkerchief from a breast pocket. "Better run for it at once."

"Run for it? What are you talking about?"

Aubrey removed his high beaver and mopped his brow. "Rode all the way from London in the saddle," he said, explaining his breathlessness. "Made it from Knightsbridge to this Oxfordshire backwater in under three hours." He grinned up at his frowning friend proudly. "Wager even *you* couldn't have done better."

"Yes, yes, you gudgeon, it was deuced good riding. But why was it necessary to follow me . . . and in such haste?"

"Alcorn. He found some sort of note from his lady there and flew into a frenzy. Came to White's looking for you, pistol in hand. He's out for your blood, Griff. Came to warn you."

Julia gasped. Mullineaux spun about and glared at her. "Good God! What did you *say* in that note?"

"Nothing about you . . . I *swear* it! I only said that I was leaving him."

Mullineaux strode across the room and grasped her shoulders furiously. "Do you take Alcorn for a fool? A wife should know her husband better. Everyone in town is probably aware that I'm off to Wales. Did you think your husband would not notice the fact that you timed your departure to coincide with mine?"

"It never . . . I didn't think—"

He thrust her away from him in disgust. "No, of course you didn't."

Julia watched him in alarm as he turned his back on her and began to pace about the room. Aubrey was equally alarmed, for he knew there was little time for pacing. But neither Julia nor Aubrey had the courage to interrupt his lordship's cogitations. After a few moments of pacing, Mullineaux stopped at the chair that held his things and picked up his beaver.

Julia expelled a worried little breath. "Griff? What shall we d-do?" she asked helplessly.

"We?" He gave her a mirthless, sardonic snort. *"We* shall do nothing. *You,* ma'am, will remain here to face your husband, and I—"

She whitened. "Face Alcorn? But . . . why?"

"Why? Because you've made a cuckold of him once too often, and it's time to make amends."

"But I don't *want* to make amends," she said, trying to play the suffering heroine but sounding more petulant than tragic. "I want to go to Paris . . . with *you!*"

Mullineaux clapped his hat on his head, picked up his gloves and cane and came up to her. "I am not going to Paris, my dear . . . not with you or with anyone. I am going to Wales."

"That is ridiculous. What can you possibly wish to do in Wales, all alone? There is nothing to do there but look at the trees."

"I shall have a great deal to do there. My grandfather willed his library to me, hoping that when I combine it with my own, it will become one of the country's great collections. I intend to go through the catalogue to see which volumes are to be crated for shipment."

Her eyebrows rose in disbelief. "Is *that* how you intend to spend your time? It sounds a crashing bore."

"Not to me. I shall enjoy every moment."

"How nice for you. But what about me, Griff? What shall happen to me?"

"I've been trying to tell you. You say you want to go to Paris, isn't that so? Well, you may some day get there, if you play your cards well. If you use your head, you may yet prevail upon *Alcorn* to take you."

"Alcorn? Ha! How can you believe that Sir Giles Alcorn would *ever* take me abroad? You're quite off the mark." She pulled a handkerchief from her bosom and sniffed pathetically into it. "You don't know him, Griff. He'll be *livid!* He'll *never* forgive me."

"Oh, yes, he will, if you use the wiles on him that you've used so successfully on your numerous admirers. Go upstairs to the bedroom, lock the door, put on the most demure night-clothes you can find in your bag—and if you haven't anything demure, ask your abigail to lend you one of hers; I suspect that all abigails carry a supply of dowdy kerseymere night-dresses along with them—and climb into bed. Then, when Alcorn arrives and bursts in, fall into his arms and explain that you've run away—alone!—because you feared you'd lost his love. Come, come, Julia, don't look at me that way. You know just how to carry it off. All you need do is convince your husband that you truly love him, and in no time at all he'll be conveying you to the continent for a second honeymoon."

Julia looked up from her damp handkerchief, her eyes expressing clearly her lack of conviction. Facing her husband was the last thing she wanted to do. Of course, she'd known when she'd set out this morning from London that she was gambling her future on a liaison that had lost its glow, but desperation had made her reckless. Now she knew without a doubt that Lord Mullineaux was not going to run off with her. She'd lost the gamble. There was nothing left for her but to try to patch up the rift in her marriage. Perhaps Griff was right, she thought. Perhaps she could do it. But Alcorn had a quick temper and a sour nature; she would have a difficult time of it. "Second honeymoon, indeed!" she muttered bitterly. "More likely, he'll convey me to his mother's country seat, where I shall spend the rest of my life listening to her scolds and living like a *nun*."

The thought of the flamboyant Lady Julia Alcorn living like a nun made Mullineaux and Aubrey exchange quick grins. But Aubrey, aware of the passage of time, could not permit this scene to continue much longer. "Rubbish, my dear," he said, getting up and putting a friendly arm about Julia's shoulder. "You'll have him eating out of your hand in a week, see if you don't. Meanwhile, I think you should run upstairs and ready yourself, for there isn't a moment to be lost. Alcorn's carriage was hard on my heels when I set out, you know."

Lord Mullineaux watched with knit brows as Aubrey guided her firmly to the doorway. "Can your abigail be trusted to remain silent?" he asked.

"Yes," Julia replied glumly. "The girl is completely devoted to me." She looked back over her shoulder to take a last, meaningful, tragic look at her erstwhile lover. "G-Goodbye, Griff," she murmured brokenly. "I shall n-never forget you."

When the door closed after her, Aubrey glanced at his friend dubiously. "Do you really think Alcorn will believe that she came here alone?"

"No, I don't. But there's always a chance, I suppose. When a man loves a woman, he wants to believe the best of her." He fell silent for a moment, trying to imagine how he himself would react if he were in Alcorn's shoes. Soon he shook himself from his reverie. There was no time for rumination. He glanced over at his friend, a smile of fond affection suddenly lighting his face. "Thanks for coming, Aubrey, old man. It was an act of courage to gallop so many miles in this deuced weather for my sake, and I won't forget it. But I think you'd better start back to town at once. It won't help matters if Alcorn finds you here."

"What do you mean, *I'd* better get back to town? Aren't you coming with me?"

"No. I'm on my way to Wales, remember?"

"Good. The best solution is to run for it. Not that I believed for a moment that trumpery tale about a library collection. Griff Mullineaux going off to look at books! What a hum! But Wales is as good a place as any in which to rusticate. That's just what I would do . . . make myself scarce for a while."

"I'm glad I have your approval," his friend muttered drily.

"But, Griff, suppose he catches up with you? Take my word, he'll force a duel. Won't be any reasoning with 'im, the state he's in. Not that I don't think you're a sure shot, old fellow, but Alcorn ain't a duffer. Bound to be some blood shed . . . and all sorts of trouble with the magistrates afterward. And that would be in the *best* of circumstances."

Lord Mullineaux eyed him ruefully. "If that's the best, what do you think can be the worst?"

"The worst would be a situation in which you'd take a notion to delope."

"Of course I'd delope. Do you think, after what I've done to him, that I want to *shoot* the poor fellow?"

"There, you see?" Aubrey's usually cheerful, red-cheeked face clouded in alarm. *"Knew* that's what you'd take it in your head to do—aim into the sky. There's no sense in that course, Griff. The worst might happen. He might very well *kill* you!"

"Quite so. He might at that."

"Then, good God, man, what do you intend to *do,* eh?"

Mullineaux clapped him on the shoulder and propelled him toward the door. "I shall do exactly as you advised," he said with a reassuring grin. "Run for my life."

Chapter One

Jasper Surringham, Bart., eagerly picked up *The Times* from the hall table and turned immediately to the financial page. The newspaper had been delivered only moments before and was already four days late. Delivery of the London papers was always slow to Gloucester, and since the snowfall had blocked the road to Bishop's Cleve for more than a day, delivery had been even slower. Jasper, engrossed in the long-delayed news, crossed the hall to the library while keeping his nose buried in the pages. Thus he failed to notice a thin sheet of pattern-paper that had floated to the floor from the long table where his niece was absentmindedly pinning together the parts for a new blouse. His slippered foot trod upon the pattern-paper, the paper slid forward (carrying Sir Jasper's foot with it), and he found his legs flying out from under him. With a sharp intake of breath, he landed clumsily on the polished oak floor, his tailbone and elbow painfully jarred.

The sound of his gasp and the impact of his body on the floor would ordinarily have captured the attention of anyone seated nearby, but Jasper's niece Ada was not ordinary. She was deep in thought, and when her mind was thus occupied, it took a great deal of noise to rouse her. Her uncle's fall would have gone completely unnoticed were it not for the fact that the abrupt movement of his body disturbed the air and caused the pattern-pieces on the table to fly up. Ada, distracted by the unexpected movement of the papers, looked up at them in mild surprise. "My goodness," she murmured to the pieces of tissue, attempting to catch them as they floated past her, "why are you flying away so abruptly?" She addressed the papers with a smile. "Do you think you're birds, flying off to the south for the winter?"

She succeeded in catching only two of them. The rest eluded her, some wafting serenely to the floor and others dancing up over her head and out of reach. The more she flailed about in her attempt to catch them, the more air currents she created, and the more the tissue-thin papers sailed about the room.

Jasper, wincing in pain, lifted himself up on an elbow and glared at her, furious because she was aware of neither his presence in the room nor the havoc she'd caused. "Bubble-headed female," he muttered.

She didn't look round from her task of catching the pattern-pieces. "Uncle Jasper? I didn't hear you come in."

"No, of course you didn't," he retorted sarcastically, "since I came in so *quietly*. For heaven's sake, what're you doin', jumpin' about so?"

"There must have been a sudden draught," she explained, still not looking at him. She was busy trying to capture a curved piece of paper—the pattern for the collar, she realized—that kept winging out of reach like a teasing bird.

"Yes, there was a draught," her uncle declared acerbically. "I was the one who caused it."

"Oh, I don't think so, uncle. You needn't worry about it . . . I'll catch hold of them all in the end."

"Oh, you will, will ye? Too bad ye couldn't catch *me* in the end."

"What?" The collar pattern having been captured, she now got down on her hands and knees and crept under the table to salvage the pieces that had come to rest on the floor. After collecting the last piece she turned round on all fours and crept out, coming face to face with her still-supine uncle. "Uncle Jasper, is something wrong?" she exclaimed, startled.

"Wrong? What makes you think there's something wrong?"

"You're . . . you're on the floor!" the bewildered girl exclaimed.

"Oh, you noticed that, did ye?"

Ada sat back on her heels and eyed him reprovingly. "I know I'm bubbleheaded and absentminded and not always aware of the details of my surroundings, but even *I* take notice when my uncle greets me from a position flat on the floor. May I ask what you're doing down here?"

"Ain't it obvious? I wanted to examine the condition of the ceiling from a new angle."

"Oh, *Uncle*." His niece, long familiar with Sir Jasper's sarcastic wit, his acerbic manner, and his yeoman-like speech (all of which served to mask a heart as soft as a plum pudding), shrugged and turned her attention to counting the pattern-pieces in her hands. "Here's the sleeve . . . and this is the cuff . . . but

I wonder where the yolk has gone . . ."

"You don't believe I merely wanted to examine the ceiling, eh? Then let me say that I wanted to see the world from a different viewpoint. A change o' perspective, so to speak."

". . . and the collar. Can the collar piece have gotten away from me again?"

"Are you *listenin'* to me, Ada? Here I am, stretched out on my back like a split fish laid out t' dry. Don't it occur to you to wonder *why?*"

The girl continued to count the pieces. "Did you fall?" she asked absently.

"Fall? No, no, o' course not. Why should ye conclude that I fell? I lay down here on the floor t' read my paper in comfort."

Ada gave a little giggle. But then her brows knit, and her eyes clouded over. "Oh, dear. You *did* fall. It was my fault, I suppose, or you wouldn't be so testy. You're not hurt, are you?"

"No, I ain't hurt, but it's no thanks to you that my leg ain't broken."

Ada got to her feet and looked down at her uncle in dismay. "What did I do this time?" she asked shamefacedly.

"Ye dropped one o' yer deuced pattern-papers, that's what ye did. I slipped on it. Blast it, girl, why can't ye keep yer mind on what ye do? If you weren't so scatterbrained, you could keep those papers safe where they belong."

"I'm sorry, uncle. Here, let me help you up."

"Don't touch me!" Jasper lifted himself up on his unjarred elbow and attempted to wave her off. "With yer help I shall only find myself on the floor again. Go back to yer business and let me get on wi' mine."

Ada ignored the order and helped the bony old gentleman to his feet, brushing off his trouser leg while Jasper rubbed his bruised elbow and gave his niece a final glare. Then he hobbled off with an exaggerated limp to the high-backed wing chair near the window while Ada returned to her labors.

Jasper, as soon as the pain receded, felt a nip of guilt for his earlier petulance. It wasn't Ada's fault that he'd fallen. She couldn't help it that she was so disorganized. The poor girl had always been dreamy and absentminded. Ever since her childhood he'd tried to teach her to behave in a purposeful way, but her mind seemed always to be somewhere in the clouds. He'd long since given up any hope that she would change.

Not that he didn't love the girl. The truth was—though he was not the sort to say these things aloud—he positively doted on her. She was like a daughter to him. After all, he'd raised her from the time she was five years old, after her parents (his brother and sister-in-law) had perished in the sinking of the merchant ship *Phallandre,* and he'd grown more attached to her than he would have thought possible. There was a certain charm in her dreaminess. Most of the time, this was enough to insure his love. But sometimes (he really hated to admit it) that very quality of otherworldliness could drive him to drink.

He lowered his newspaper and looked over the top of it to the table where she sat. Her hands had fallen still, and a piece of cut fabric dangled forgotten from her fingers. She was staring out the window, her mouth curved up in a little smile. Whatever was she thinking of, he wondered, when she stared out like that upon the snowy landscape she was obviously not seeing? The answer would always be a mystery to him, as well as a source of irritation. Yet he had to admit that there was something very lovely in the expression of her face in repose. There was a serenity in the smoothness of her forehead, the curve of her cheek, the silky neatness of her drawn-back brown hair, the upward curve of her lip, the unreadable pale-blue depth of her eyes. Those Italian masters who used to paint the oval-faced, sloe-eyed madonnas, they would have loved to recreate her ethereal loveliness on canvas.

The trouble was, he realized, that the world was too much for Ada. She had no interest in the minutiae of everyday life. The energies of her mind were expended on a dream world of her own, so that everything in the real world became an annoyance or a difficulty for her. Papers had a way of losing themselves out of her possession, carpets would lump up under her feet and trip her, facts would get twisted in her memory, buttons at the back of her dress would come undone—and all with irritating frequency. Jasper sighed with rueful dismay. Ada could have dealt a great deal better with life if things were simpler: if people always spoke in soft voices, if agreements were reached easily and without rancor, if houses could be run without servants, if buttons could remain permanently attached to clothing, if dress patterns could be designed with fewer than three pieces. *Oh, well,* he thought, returning his eyes to the report of the previous day's doings on the 'Change, *I've done all I can to improve the girl. What can't be cured must be endured.*

He had become completely absorbed in the financial news when the butler appeared in the doorway. Since neither Sir Jasper nor his niece bothered to look up at his entrance, Cotrell, the butler, had to clear his throat twice. "Lady Haydon t' see you, sir," he announced. "And she has Miss Cornelia with her."

Jasper groaned. Lady Dorothea Haydon, his overbearing sister, lived nearby and called often, but whenever she did, she always managed to cut up his peace. And her daughter Cornelia, in spite of being what the locals called a Diamond of the First Water, was as arrogant as her mother and made an equally irritating guest. "Why don't *you* see 'em, Ada?" he suggested, lifting up his newspaper again as if to use it as a barrier between him and his social obligations. "You don't need me. Give 'em some tea and get rid of 'em."

"What did you say, uncle?" Ada murmured absently.

"Damnation, girl, ain't you been listenin'? Don't you see Cotrell standin' in the doorway? Ain't you heard a word o' what's been exchanged between us?"

Ada's eyes focused on her uncle's face. "Oh! I'm sorry. I was thinking of the rose garden."

"The rose garden?" Jasper eyed his niece in disbelief. "The *rose garden?* It's under a foot o' snow! Why should ye be thinkin' of it *now?*"

"I was only wondering how it would look if we planted some of the new hybrid roses I've been reading about. I've always loved the rich crimson of our Chinas, of course, and they make a lovely sea of color in June, but..." She paused and gazed out of the window at the field of white below, the dreamy look in her eyes telling her uncle that she was seeing those blooming roses as clearly as if they were real. "... but wouldn't you enjoy seeing a bit of varied color in the garden for a change? Not a great deal of color—I wouldn't wish for too much excitement for the eyes, would you?—but only a touch of pink here and there. I've heard of an exciting new variety called Hume's Blush, a tea-scented China, which might be very lovely along the border, and perhaps a dozen Parson Pinks to edge the walks—"

"Ada, this is the outside of enough! Yer drivin' me to distraction, babblin' away about roses! Don't ye see Cotrell standin' there in the doorway waitin' for an answer?"

Ada blinked up at Cotrell in surprise. "Oh, I'm sorry, Cotrell. What is it you wish of me?"

The butler's lips twitched in amusement. Miss Ada's absentmindedness provided him with one of his few sources of entertainment. "Lady Dorothea and Miss Cornelia, Miss Ada. They're waiting in the sitting room."

"Oh." Ada glanced at her uncle uneasily. "And you want *me* to see them, Uncle Jasper?"

"Yes, I want you to see 'em! What have I been *sayin'* these past five minutes?"

"Very well, Uncle, if you wish me to," Ada murmured, putting down the piece of fabric that she'd absently held on to all this time, "but Aunt Dorothea will not be pleased at having no one to talk to but me."

The butler cleared his throat again. "Her ladyship asked fer *you,* Sir Jasper. Fer you most partic'lar."

"Oh, she did, did she? Deuced maggoty female! Does she think I've nothin' better to do than to spend my afternoons dancin' attendance on her? Be a good girl, Ada, and see if you can fob her off."

But Ada was gazing out the window again.

"Blast it, girl, has yer mind wandered off *again?*" her uncle barked.

She looked round with a start. "What?"

"I asked you to rid us of yer aunt and yer cousin. Will ye do it or no?"

Ada's clear eyes clouded again. "I can try, of course, but you know how Aunt Dorothea . . . and Cornelia, too . . . always manage to overwhelm me."

Jasper grunted. It was quite true. Sweet-natured, dreamy Ada was no match for either her cousin or her aunt. Sooner or later, he supposed, he would have to go to the library to rescue his niece from their clutches, so he might just as well get up now. He threw his newspaper to the floor in surrender to the inevitable. "Very well, then," he said, dismissing the butler with a wave and getting up with a sigh, "let's go."

But Ada seemed to shrink in her chair. "I needn't go, need I? Since you've decided to see them after all?"

Her uncle ceased his stride to the door and turned to her,

his brows knit. "I don't understand ye, girl. Why do ye always try t' avoid company? Cornelia's yer cousin . . . a female just yer age. One would think ye'd *enjoy* havin' a bit of a gossip with her."

"We've nothing to gossip about, Uncle."

"Hummph! Most women manage to find *somethin'* t' gossip about. Why are ye always different?"

"I don't know."

He peered at the girl intently. "Why did ye say, a bit ago, that she always overwhelms ye?"

Ada's eyes fell. "I don't know why I said that. I was just being . . . fanciful."

"No, I don't think ye were." He pulled up a chair, placed it in front of hers and sat down upon it, keeping his eyes fixed on her face. "I want the truth, Ada. Is that blasted, peacocky female unkind to ye?"

"No, no. I don't want you to think— It's all in my mind, really, Uncle."

"What's in your mind?" He leaned forward and took her hands, his face showing nothing but loving concern. "Speak up, Ada. Dash it, girl, I *ought* to know."

Ada sighed. "I don't know if I can explain, Uncle Jasper. Cornelia and I are on good terms, I assure you. It's just that she . . . she takes such pleasure in . . . in winning over me."

He didn't understand. "Winning?"

"Yes. She's quite *accustomed* to winning, you know."

"No, I don't know. Winning what?"

"Everything."

He put a nervous hand to his forehead. "Forgive me, my love, fer bein' a dense old man, but I don't follow ye. What do ye mean by everything? Can ye be specific?"

Ada shrugged. "Playing the pianoforte. Stitching. Engaging in conversational badinage. Everything from playing shuttle-cock to . . . to acquiring dance partners."

Jasper raised his brows in surprise. "But winnin' implies . . . a *competition*. Are all those things *battles* between ye?"

She dropped her eyes to her clenched hands. "It often seems so to me."

"And yer cousin *wins* these . . . these skirmishes? Always?"

Ada noted the tone of chagrin in his voice and hastened to

reassure him. "I don't mind it, uncle, really I don't. You mustn't take this seriously. I'm quite accustomed to it. I don't know why I even mentioned it."

"I'm *glad* ye mentioned it. I had no notion that ye found it so difficult to be in her company."

"I don't, usually. It's just that I'm a bit blue-deviled today. When I'm in low tide, I am not soothed by the fact that she so complacently takes for granted her superiority over me."

Her uncle frowned. "Lords it over ye, does she?"

"Yes, a bit. So please, Uncle Jasper, may I take my tea up in my room... just for today? Cornelia and Aunt Dorothea came to see *you*, after all..."

"No, I won't have it!" Jasper burst out, jumping to his feet. "I won't *have* that toplofty female lordin' it over ye! Dash it all, Ada, yer every bit as good as yer cousin. Why do ye permit her to win all the time?"

"It doesn't matter to me, Uncle, truly. Cornelia *likes* to win. It's important to her. And I don't mind it, not usually. Only today I'd sooner be... elsewhere."

Jasper's eyes narrowed angrily. "That's the trouble with ye, my girl. Y're *always* elsewhere. Even if y're *bodily* present, yer *mind* is elsewhere. Per'aps, if ye'd be *here* in yer mind, ye'd be able to stand up fer yerself."

Ada's eyes fell guiltily. "I'm sorry, Uncle."

"Sorry! Is that all ye can say?"

The poor girl could only bite her lip. "May I be excused?" she asked helplessly.

"No, ye may not! Ye'll go with me t' the drawin' room!" He put his hands roughly on her shoulders, turned her about and thrust her out of the room ahead of him, his anger churning inside his chest. It cut him to the heart to discover that his lovely niece thought so little of herself. He would have to do something about it. Dash it all, he thought glumly, females are a damned nuisance, even the best of them.

Ada paused at the drawing-room door and looked round at him, her eyes pleading. "Please, Uncle..."

"*No*, I said!" He glared at her as if, by the sheer force of his anger, he could make her strong. "If I can face them, so can you. So march! I won't permit ye t' be elsewhere today!"

Chapter Two

Lady Dorothea Haydon and her daughter had already en-sconced themselves in the drawing room and, making themselves quite at home, had rung for tea. Cornelia, elegantly tall, deep-bosomed and fair-haired, sat lounging gracefully upon the sofa, her left foot extended and her eyes fixed on the fashionable galoe shoe which peeped out from beneath her skirts. Her mother stood framed in the window, looking out upon the snowy landscape and tapping impatiently upon the palm of her left hand with a folded letter she held in her right.

Jasper clumped into the room, gave his sister a reluctant peck on the cheek, nodded to Cornelia curtly and threw himself upon an easy chair near the fire. "Well, Doro, what is it this time?" he demanded.

"Must you always greet me with such ill grace?" Dorothea Haydon asked in disgust. "And how many times have I asked you not to call me Doro? Really, Jasper, no one but you has used that name since I was a child. Even you must see how inappropriate it is for a woman of my years."

Jasper's eyes roamed over his sister with a gleam of amuse-ment. She was quite right. The name Doro poorly fit the woman she'd become. She had been a lively, tomboyish child, he remembered, but she'd turned into an overbearing dowager in recent years. Everything about her—her tightly curled grey hair, her ample bosom, her rigid carriage, the self-righteous set of her mouth, even her large feet—showed her to be a Woman of Authority. No wonder her husband had expired so early in their marriage. Living with Dorothea must have been a strain.

Lady Dorothea was taking no notice of her brother's rude stare. She was looking across the room at Ada, who stood hesitantly in the doorway. "Good heavens, girl, don't stand there like a ninnyhammer. Come in and give your aunt a kiss. There, that's better. Cornelia, move over and give your cousin some room on the loveseat beside you."

Ada did as she was bid and sat down beside Cornelia, stumbling only once in her passage across the room. Her aunt watched impatiently as she settled herself. Then, with an air of carefully controlled excitement, Dorothea looked down at Jasper and waved her letter. "Shall we wait for tea," she asked, "or would you like to hear my news at once?"

"Let's hear yer news," he responded with alacrity. "The sooner ye've announced it, the sooner I can get back t' my newspaper."

Lady Dorothea, accustomed to her brother's irascibility, took no umbrage. "Very well." Her eyes, gleaming with a mysterious inner triumph, flicked from her brother to the girls on the sofa and back again. "It's a letter from the Countess Mullineaux!"

"The Countess Mullineaux?" Jasper's look of impatient irritability faded. The Countess's name was well known to him. He had never met her, of course, since he never left his Gloucester estate to go to London, but he'd heard a great deal about her from both his sister and his now-deceased sister-in-law. The Countess and Ada's mother had been great friends in their youth, and the Countess had been named godmother to Ada at the infant's christening. (Dorothea had bragged for years that she'd made a third in the friendship, but Jasper suspected that the other two women had merely tolerated her.) Jasper had been regaled for years with accounts of the famous leader of London society. Lady Mullineaux was said to have everything—charm, generosity, wit, authority, taste, education and unquestioned importance in the world of the *haut ton*. Since Ada's mother's death, they had not heard much from the famous Countess, but Ada had not had a birthday on which the Countess had not sent a lavish remembrance. "Why on earth is she writing after all this time?" he asked with upraised brows.

"Listen to the letter, and you'll soon learn," his sister said with unaccustomed eagerness. "It's the most thrilling and unexpected pass." She unfolded the missive and started to read the contents aloud. *"My dear Doro,"* she began.

"Aha!" chortled Jasper on hearing the opprobrious appellation.

His sister glared at him but went on with her letter. *"You will no doubt be surprised to hear from me after all this time, but be assured that although I haven't written I have often thought of you. The memory of your dear, lost sister is always in my heart. She, as you know, was my dearest friend, and not a day has passed since she drowned at sea that I haven't missed her. It has occurred to me lately that I have also missed the pleasure of watching her daughter grow up, and yours as well.*

"Both girls must be of age by now. In thinking about them, I suddenly realized that neither of them has had a London season. Therefore, I wondered if one of the girls might like to spend the coming season with me. London will soon be bustling with the balls, the routs, the concerts, the plays and all the other 'divertissements' that mark a new season, and it would give me great joy to introduce a young woman to its pleasures.

"I wish I could invite both girls, but at my age the burden of escorting two lively young women about town might be too much for me. I leave it to you, dear Doro, and to Ada's guardian, to decide which of the girls would most benefit from the experience. Please discuss this with Sir Jasper, and let me know which of the two dear girls I can expect and the date of her arrival. I so look forward to having one of them with me. With my deepest affection, I remain yours, Celia Mullineaux."

Jasper's eyebrows rose in surprise. "Wants to take one of our girls to London, eh? Seems a queer start after all these years."

"Not so queer, if you know the whole," his sister responded, perching on the chair nearest to her brother and leaning forward conspiratorially. "It's that son of hers. Mabel Banning told me, when she visited last fall, that the fellow is a shocking rake. She said that his mother would love to see him tethered in respectable matrimonial harness, but he's resisted the lures of every matchmaking Mama in town, including his own, and remains in impregnable bachelorhood even though he's past thirty. Perhaps Lady Mullineaux hopes that—"

"That one of *our* girls will attract him? That's the most addled notion anyone's ever conceived, if you ask me."

Lady Haydon drew herself up in quick offense. "What's so addled about it? My Cornelia is quite capable of attracting the most *resistant* of gentlemen! Didn't she capture that guest of Lady Aldrich's at the assembly last winter? What *was* his name, my love? You know which one I mean . . . the elegant Corinthian with reddish hair whom every girl had set her cap for."

"Satterthwaite," Cornelia responded, leaning back against the pillows with a self-satisfied smile, "Sir Humphrey Satterthwaite."

Jasper frowned at mother and daughter in disgust. "I wasn't castin' any personal aspersions on anyone. Doesn't matter *who* the Countess will force on the fellow, the idea won't work."

"Why ever not?" his sister demanded.

"Because he won't favor *anyone* who's forcibly thrust under his nose. It's against human nature."

"That's ridiculous. A man would have a strange nature to reject a girl like my Cornelia merely because she is near at hand."

"Humph!" Jasper snorted scornfully. As far as he was concerned, Cornelia was a puffed-up fribble without character or substance, and he regarded any man who permitted himself to be attracted to her as beneath contempt. His sister was ridiculous to believe that a man as cosmopolitan as Mullineaux was reputed to be would cast a second glance at Cornelia, even if she *were* placed under his nose...

With a sudden gasp, he sat up in his chair, indignation dawning in his brain and spreading like a tidal wave through his chest. "Let me understand the implication of your remarks, ma'am. Are you sayin' that you mean to send *Cornelia* to London?"

"Of course that's what I'm saying. Did you think I would let such an opportunity go by? Lord Mullineaux, Celia's son, is London's most desirable eligible. Why, the income from his country estates alone must be upwards of ten thousand, and that says nothing of his worth on the 'Change."

"I don't give a rapper for Lord Mullineaux or his income. I'm concerned about your high-handed assumption that it's Cornelia who should go."

Lady Dorothea gaped at him. "But... what are you talking about? Surely you don't think that *Ada—?*"

"Of *course* I think it should be Ada!" her brother retorted furiously. "Why not?"

Dorothea drew herself up in surprised offense. "You can't be serious!"

"I'll lay *odds* he isn't serious," Cornelia remarked, smiling in languid superciliousness. "Uncle Jasper knows as well as anyone that Ada would find herself in an impossible muddle in London. Why, she's been known to get herself lost merely crossing through Bishop's Cleve."

"Just so," her mother agreed.

Sir Jasper jumped to his feet. "I'm *completely* serious!" he declared angrily. "Ada is in every way as deservin' as Cornelia to have a London season. More, if y' ask me. At least she has other things on her mind than matchmakin' and balls and fripperies. The Countess said herself that we should choose the girl who would benefit the most from the experience. Well, I say that Ada needs a bit of town-bronze more than your Cornelia does! Ain't that so, Ada?"

There was no answer. Three pair of eyes turned to the figure sitting quietly in a corner of the sofa. Ada's head was lowered, and she seemed to be studying the hands folded in her lap. "Heavens," muttered Lady Dorothea in disgust, "she hasn't been listening to a word we've said."

"Ada!" Jasper snapped angrily.

The girl's head came up abruptly, and her startled eyes flew from one face to another. "Is . . . s-something the matter?"

"Dash it all, girl," her uncle shouted, "we've been speakin' of matters that are of vital concern to ye. Can't you keep your mind from goin' *elsewhere* again?"

Ada's cheeks turned a deep pink. "I'm sorry, uncle. The letter from the countess set me to thoughts of . . . of my mother. It suddenly seemed that I could remember her face . . ."

Lady Dorothea snorted. "Not very likely. You were just a little bit of a creature when she was lost. But at least you were listening when I read Lady Mullineaux's proposal."

Ada's blush deepened. "No, I'm afraid I . . . I only heard the first few words . . ."

Both Dorothea and Jasper stared at her in disapproval, while Cornelia briefly (though scornfully) outlined the main points of the discussion. When she understood the thrust of the discussion she'd missed, poor Ada paled. The very *thought* of going to London to stay with a grand lady whom she'd never met and who would expect her to participate in all the doings of the social world terrified her. "But, uncle," she remonstrated, "you surely don't expect *me* to go to—?"

"Dash it, Ada, that's *exactly* what I expect!"

She fixed her pale eyes on his face in horror. "Even if I . . . I don't *wish* to?"

Jasper was nonplussed. "But *why* don't you wish it? *All* young girls want t' have come-outs and go t' balls and flirt with dandies and collect suitors and indulge in suchlike frolickin'!"

"I don't," Ada said quietly.

"Of course she doesn't," Lady Dorothea interjected. "The very idea of muddleheaded Ada living in a fashionable household among the *haute monde* is ludicrous."

Sir Jasper drew in a furious breath. "Damnation, Doro, get out o' my house!" he shouted, jumping to his feet. His sister had made him livid. He bounded across the few yards which separated them and confronted her, waving an accusing finger under her nose. "If you're goin' to call my Ada names, you can take yourself off right now! No, woman, don't open your mouth, 'cause I ain't goin' t' listen to another word. Take this flibbertigibbity daughter of yours and get out. Do you hear me, ma'am? *Out of my house!*"

"Please, uncle," Ada said softly, rising and putting a gentle hand on his arm, "Aunt Dorothea didn't say anything that wasn't true. I *am* muddleheaded, and I don't have any desire to spend the season in London, truly I don't. It wouldn't suit me at all."

"There, you see? The girl admits it. So it's all settled. Cornelia will go. I shall write to Celia tomor—"

"You will do *no such thing!*" Sir Jasper thundered, so ferociously that his sister instinctively raised her hands in self-protection.

"No need to shout," Cornelia said calmly, not the least disturbed by her uncle's tantrum. "If Ada doesn't wish to go, I don't see—"

"Never mind what Ada wishes," he barked. "Ada and I shall talk this over when we're calmer. Then, when I can bear the sight of you and yer mother again, we can all discuss this matter further. In the meantime, ye'll oblige me by sayin' good day. I've seen quite enough o' the pair of ye for the nonce."

"Really, Jasper, you can be the most *exasperating—!*" his sister declared. "We haven't yet had our *tea!*"

"You can take your damned tea at your *own* damned house," her brother snarled with what he considered perfectly appropriate hospitality. He propelled his sister and her daughter firmly to the door. "I bid ye a good afternoon." he muttered icily, and before they could utter another word, he shut the door on them.

Chapter Three

Ada, after the excitement and the rapidity of her pulse had
faded, was not unduly discomfited by the memory of the scene
in the drawing room. Such quarrels between her uncle and his
overweening sister were frequent and seemed not to affect the
habit of regular intercourse between the two parts of the family.
Nevertheless, she couldn't help feeling a twinge of alarm at
the prospect of a continuation of the discussion that had pre-
cipitated the argument. She wondered if her uncle would bring
up at the dinner table the subject that made her so uncomfortable: visiting the countess in London. But, no, she told herself,
he couldn't have been serious in what he'd said to his sister.
He knew better than anyone that she, Ada, was too featherbrained to cope with life in London. He hadn't meant what
he'd said, she was sure of that. He'd probably made that scene
in the drawing room this afternoon only to vent his spleen;
he'd merely been angry at his sister for paying him a visit and
insisting on seeing him when he wanted to read his *Times*.

He said nothing about the matter at dinner that night, so
Ada put the matter out of her mind. She told herself, in considerable relief, that he'd probably forgotten all about the subject.

But Uncle Jasper had done no such thing. He went to bed
that night with the matter of the London trip so much on his
mind that he could not fall asleep. The more he thought about
it, the more he realized that such an experience as a stay in
London with the worldly Countess Mullineaux would do his
foggy-headed niece a world of good. A few months in the
company of a sensible, practical, clever woman might be the
making of the girl. Cornelia, much as he hated to admit it, was
bound to make a successful match and live a comfortable life
even if she *never* went to London for a season. She was quite
beautiful, amazingly self-assured and could be very persuasive
about getting what she wanted. Ada, on the other hand, seemed
to be drifting through life with no focus, no goals and no

apparent concern for her future. If he did nothing about her, she might well end her days a lonely, eccentric, addled old maid. He made up his mind that he would present this assessment of the situation to his sister the very next day. When she understood the truth of his analysis, even *she* would agree that Ada was the logical choice to accept the Countess's invitation.

Much to his chagrin, however, the next day he learned from his valet (who was "stepping out" with Lady Dorothea's hairdresser) that her ladyship had *already* written to Countess Mullineaux accepting the invitation *in the name of her daughter!*

Nothing that his sister had done to him in the past decade so enraged him as that news. He was almost beside himself with fury. That Dorothea Haydon, his own sister, could have had so little feeling for the needs and concerns of poor Ada (who was *her* niece as well as his) made him wild. How *could* she have taken it upon herself to write that letter? Lady Mullineaux had *specifically* said that the decision was to be made *by both of them, together! How dared she make the decision alone?*

He stormed into the breakfast room where Ada was sitting on the window seat, innocently sipping her morning coffee. "Ada," he thundered, "get to yer feet at once!"

Ada gave a violent start. The coffee cup wobbled for a moment in its saucer and then tipped over, spilling the hot liquid all over the girl's skirt. "Uncle!" she cried, ignoring the spill and the precarious position of the cup in her alarm. "What's the matter?"

"Everything's the matter! Can I never say a word to ye without yer jumpin' out o' your skin? Get *up,* I say!"

Ada's hand began to tremble, sending the cup to the floor with a crash. She rose, shaking. She tried to read her uncle's face and mop her wet skirt (with a tiny, completely inadequate handkerchief) at the same time. "Have I . . . done something d-dreadful, uncle?" she asked timorously.

"Don't be a ninny! Why must ye always think ye've done somethin' dreadful? When have I ever accused ye o' doin' anythin' dreadful?"

"But you seem to be so . . . so angry . . ."

"Not at *you,* girl. At yer *aunt.*"

Ada let out her frozen breath in relief. Uncle Jasper was so often angry at Aunt Dorothea that his tantrums concerning her could no longer be considered a matter of importance. "Oh, is *that* all?" she murmured under her breath and knelt to pick up the pieces of the shattered cup.

But Jasper heard her. "No, it ain't all!" he snapped. "Get up, Miss Windmill-Head. Never mind the deuced cup."

"But what—?"

"We can't waste time jabberin'. Go upstairs and pack everything y' have that's suitable for London. Y're leavin' for the Countess's town house within the hour!"

Ada was stricken speechless. She could only gape at him.

"Are ye listenin' t' me, girl? Shake yerself awake, will ye? I intend fer the carriage t' depart *within the hour,* whether ye're ready or no."

"B-But . . . Uncle *Jasper!* You can't *mean* it!"

"Can't I? I'll show ye if I mean it or not." He stalked to the door. "Cotrell!" he shouted into the corridor. *"Cotrell,* ye looby! Tell Hines t' ready the carriage! He's t' start fer London in one hour!"

Ada, still trembling in shock, followed him across the room. "But uncle, this is *ridiculous.* I told you yesterday that I didn't wish . . . I thought the matter was concluded."

"Well, it *ain't* concluded. Not as far as *I'm* concerned."

"But it *is.* I heard from the housekeeper, who had it from Aunt Dorothea's cook, that Cornelia is already packing and is intending to leave within a very few days."

"Oh, she *is,* is she? Then that's too bad fer her, ain't it? Ye'll have almost a full day's head start."

"Head st-start?" the girl echoed in dismay.

"Yes. If you arrive at the Countess's door first, ye'll be welcomed with open arms. Then, when Cornelia arrives, she'll seem like an intruder." His face brightened. "Her ladyship'll very likely send her home in disgrace." He grinned wickedly at the prospect.

Ada blinked at her uncle in rebuke. "Surely you don't mean what you're saying, Uncle. You cannot wish to use Cornelia so unkindly."

"I'll take the greatest pleasure in it, I assure you. Now go upstairs and do as I've ordered. An' tell yer abigail t' pack as well."

"S-Selena? Why?"

"She'll go with ye, o'course. Ye don't wish t' arrive at yer godmother's door like a poor little waif, do ye? Ye'll make a proper entrance, with yer own maid and yer own coachman—

I'll have Hines wear his livery—and a mountain o' baggage. Pack everythin' ye own."

"Please, Uncle," Ada begged, her heart beginning to pound in real terror, "don't ask me to do this. I've no talent for living in society. And I couldn't steal this opportunity away from my cousin, when it is something she's wanted to do all her life."

"Don't be so blasted mealy-mouthed," her uncle growled. "She has no compunction about stealin' such an opportunity from *you.*"

Ada glanced up at him tearfully. "But—"

"But me no buts, girl. Ye'll do as I say, and at once! Do you hear me?"

Ada knew her uncle well enough to realize that there was no use debating the matter. Something had made him adamant. She gave him an obedient, though a tremblingly reluctant, curtsey and started to the door.

His eyes followed her, his face set sternly. "And if ye do *anythin'* t' foil my plans—if ye get lost, or fall ill on the way, or do anythin' else t' delay yer arrival so that Cornelia makes her appearance ahead o' you—ye can be sure that my wrath will be terrible!"

Ada turned round. She was quite upset by the sudden turn her life seemed to be taking, but she was too familiar with her uncle's essential soft-heartedness to be shaken by his ranting. "Come now, uncle, that's doing it a bit too brown," she said, offering him a shaky smile in the hope that it would calm him a little. "Your wrath will be terrible, indeed. If you want to play the ogre in a fairy story, find some little child to roar at, not me."

But he would not permit himself to be softened. "I ain't playactin', Ada. I mean every word. I'm warnin' ye, girl. If ye don't make it t' London on time, I'll make ye wish you'd never been born!"

And with those fearful words, he turned her about and pushed her toward the door.

Chapter Four

It wasn't Ada's fault that the carriage wheel cracked on a rut in the road. She hadn't even *wished* for such a delay in her race to London. Once her uncle had made clear that she had no choice, she'd resigned herself to the trip. She'd had every intention of obeying her uncle's orders to the letter. What else was there for her to do?

Ada had reasoned that Uncle Jasper had her best interests at heart; thus, if he thought a trip to London would do her good, she simply assumed he was in the right. In spite of her initial repugnance toward the whole idea, she told herself to make the best of the situation. She was not a rebellious sort. She'd never enjoyed arguments or confrontation but was comfortable only in an atmosphere of peace and serenity. If the only way to achieve that serenity was to succumb to her uncle's wishes, so be it.

By the time her baggage had been loaded into the coach, and she and her abigail had climbed aboard, her equanimity had been at least partially restored. Having accepted the trip as inevitable, she'd even managed to kiss her uncle goodbye with her usual affection.

During the first hour of the journey, her misgivings about living in London with a doyenne of society continued to trouble her mind, but soon she was distracted from her thoughts by a thick-sounding cough. Selena, her abigail, was sitting opposite her, and Ada noticed at once that the woman was looking distinctly unwell. Selena, a tall, gaunt, middle-aged fussbudget who'd cared for Ada since childhood, was normally sallow in complexion, but today her cheeks were flushed as if she'd rouged them, and her eyes were decidedly watery. "Are you not feeling quite the thing, Selena?" Ada asked in concern.

"I'd *better* be feelin' the thing," Selena answered, her voice unusually hoarse. "I promised Sir Jarsper I'd get ye t' Lunnon by dark, no matter whut. He wouldn' take kin'ly t' any delay, least of all me bein' sick."

Ada sighed worriedly. "Yes, I suppose he wouldn't. Here, stretch out on the seat and let me spread the laprobe over you. At least you can doze while we ride. Perhaps a few hours of sleep will help."

While Selena slept, Ada stared out of the window, letting her mind roam where it willed. She found herself dreaming of dancing at lavish balls, staring wide-eyed at glowing theater stages, dining at luxurious tables, shopping at fashionable salons where the *modistes* were as elegant as their patrons, and indulging in all the other voluptuous indulgences that a life in town suggested to the mind. In reality, she might find herself too shy to savor these pleasures, but in dreams she found them delicious. In her dreams she could be beautiful, charming, witty and self-assured—all the things that in reality she was not.

But dreams have a kind of reality of their own in the mind of the dreamer. If the dreamer concentrates on them, she lives as much in the world of her dreams as in the real. Ada knew that if, in London, she found herself in a modiste's salon in which the dressmaker treated her with disdain and dressed her in a dowdy gown of puce broadcloth, she had only to look in the mirror of her imagination and see herself, lovely and admired, clad in a flowing creation of pale blue lustring and silver lace. If she, in reality, found herself sitting in a corner of a crowded ballroom, neglected and alone, she'd have not the slightest difficulty imagining herself whirling about the dance floor on the arm of the handsomest bachelor of the assemblage, causing havoc in the hearts of all the watchers. Therefore, although the reality of this trip to London was undoubtedly frightening, in Ada's daydreams the journey was tremendously exciting.

So of course the accident on the roadway had nothing whatever to do with her. She hadn't expected, or even wished for, a delay en route. A broken wheel was the last thing in the world she wanted. But her uncle would never believe that. He would say she'd put the rut in the road on purpose!

Hines, the coachman, studied the wrecked wheel with a frown. "We'll 'ave t' find a wheelwright, Miss Ada. An' it's comin' on t' dark. I think we'll 'ave t' put up somewheres 'til mornin'."

Selena, having been rudely awakened by the shock to the carriage when the wheel cracked, moaned miserably. "Oh, no! We *can't!*" she muttered. "Sir Jarsper'll 'ave my *head!*"

Hines searched out a wheelwright at once, but by the time the fellow appeared on the scene, it had become too dark to effect the needed repairs. He promised to make the repairs at first light, but in the meantime there was no choice for the travelers but to spend the night at the nearest inn. Fortunately, Hines knew of an inn of respectable reputation that was not more than a mile down the road. The two women plodded disconsolately toward it, Hines following with the horses. By the time they reached it, the women were chilled through.

The Black Boar was a small, modest establishment with a thatched roof. It looked quite picturesque and welcoming to Ada's weary eyes. But the interior was disappointing. The walls were grimy with the effluvia of smoky chimneys, and the stale air smelled of malt and burned grease. "Humph!" Selena sneered at her first whiff. "I 'ope the bedrooms're better kept than this. Wouldn't surprise me t' find *bedbugs*."

Ada, trying to make the best of things, ignored Selena's mutterings. She arranged for rooms for her party and ordered Selena to take to her bedroom at once. "I'll manage to eat my dinner without you," she told the abigail reassuringly. "You're looking quite ill and shouldn't remain on your feet."

The abigail was too heavy-headed to object. While Hines went off to see to the horses and to take his dinner with the inn's stablemen, Selena took herself to bed. Ada, left alone, was brought into the inn's private parlor by the innkeeper's wife, who promised to bring her a good, hot dinner as soon as she could ready it.

Ada, weary and chilled to the bone, seated herself on the hearth before the room's huge fireplace and tried to warm herself. A snuffling sound caught her attention. She looked about and found that a shaggy, unkempt collie was sharing the hearth with her, looking up at her with dark, sad eyes. "What's the matter, old fellow?" Ada murmured, bending down to pat his head. "You look as if you have the weight of the world on your shoulders."

The dog whimpered and nuzzled her arm pathetically.

"Poor fellow. I don't suppose you've been groomed in weeks." She moved closer to the animal and smoothed his coat. There were a number of welts under the fur, and as her hand passed over them, the dog shuddered in pain. "Good heavens," she said in surprise, "what on earth is wrong here?"

She peered closely under the fur. The animal was covered

with scars and cuts on which the blood had dried. The wounds had obviously never been treated. The sight sickened her. The poor dog had been beaten, often and brutally, probably with a stick! She would have liked to take a stick to the person responsible for this cruelty. Something had to be done to help the animal, that much was plain. One couldn't permit such monstrous treatment of a poor dumb beast. She smoothed the collie's ears as she wondered what action to take.

The door opened at that moment, and a gentleman—a London gentleman, if one could judge by the number of the capes of his greatcoat and the elegance of his boots—entered the room. Not noticing Ada sitting on the hearth, he shut the door, tossed his hat and cane upon the table and strode across the room to the window where he stood frowning out at the winter landscape. Ada, watching him, decided that she liked his looks. He was dressed in the first style of elegance, but there was nothing of the dandy about him. His face was strong, and his eyes, though weary, seemed kind. He seemed to be the very sort who could assist her in discovering and berating the perpetrator of the crime against the collie. "Excuse me, sir. This sweet-natured dog is in pain," she announced without preamble. "Do you think we—?"

"What?" The man wheeled about, startled. "Oh, I beg your pardon. I was not aware that anyone was in the room. I was told this is the private parlor."

"So it is. But as I was saying, this poor animal—"

The gentleman held up a hand and shook his head. "Your pardon, ma'am, if I seem confused. You haven't introduced yourself, you see, and I don't believe we've met before. Are you employed here?"

"Oh, dear," Ada murmured, abashed. "I suppose I've made a *faux pas* speaking to you as I did. I *am* sorry. But circumstances made it necessary for me to omit the niceties. This poor creature—"

The gentleman let out a small, impatient breath. "If you might forget the collie for a moment, ma'am, I would appreciate an explanation of why I find you in my private parlor. *Are* you employed here?"

"No, I am merely waiting for my dinner. But in the matter of this dog—"

"Waiting for your dinner? Then *you've* engaged this room?" He glared at the door in annoyance. "Then why didn't the damned innkeeper—I beg your pardon, ma'am—why didn't the idiot tell me the room had been spoken for?"

"I engaged it through his wife," Ada explained. "Perhaps he didn't know the room had already been let."

"It seems a most inefficient way to run things," the gentleman said with a little gesture of apology, his eyes flitting over her in what seemed to be an attempt to determine if her need for the privacy of the parlor was greater than his. She suddenly felt ashamed of her rumpled travelling dress and the undoubted disorder of her hair, and her hand, without any conscious orders from her brain, flew to the back of her head and attempted to tuck in some trailing locks. But the gentleman had evidently already decided that she was a gentlewoman and was making her a bow. "Excuse me for having intruded on you," he was saying.

"Please don't go," Ada said quickly. "I'm rather glad you *did* intrude, sir, for I require your assistance. You see, I've been trying to tell you that this poor, abused animal seems to have been regularly beaten—"

But the gentleman was not listening. His attention had been caught by some commotion in the innyard outside the window. "Damnation!" he muttered under his breath. "How did he manage to trail me here?"

"I beg your pardon?" Ada asked, blinking. "I was speaking about—"

The gentleman, however, perturbed by what he'd seen outside, was unable to pay attention to her words. His brow furrowed, and his eyes flicked quickly round the room, coming to rest on Ada's face. He stared at her speculatively. "Excuse me again, ma'am," he said, glancing once more out the window and then starting across the room toward her, "but I'm about to make you a most shocking proposal. You will undoubtedly think me insane, but I beg you not to refuse me. I need your help in a matter of some urgency. Bear with me, and I promise I shall explain everything to your satisfaction afterwards."

"Yes, of course," Ada said, not understanding a word of the gentleman's speech but determined not to be distracted from her objective, "just as soon as we've done something about this dear, abused creature."

The gentleman shook his head impatiently. "You don't understand, ma'am. We have no time to—"

There were voices in the corridor outside the door. "Step

aside, man," someone growled. "I know he's in there!"

"Dash it all, it's too late," the gentleman hissed, pulling Ada rudely to her feet.

Ada gaped at him openmouthed. "What—?"

They could hear the rattle of the doorknob. "Forgive me," the man muttered, brazenly taking her into his arms, "and whatever happens, for God's sake, don't give me away!" Then, before Ada could utter another sound, he pressed his lips against her mouth in a strenuous—in fact, Ada thought, very immoderate—kiss.

She was dimly aware that the door had opened, and she felt, rather than saw, that more than one person had burst into the room. But the intruders evidently stopped in their tracks, for suddenly the room was completely silent. She supposed that they were staring at her. She should, she supposed, be feeling furious and utterly humiliated. But for the moment she wasn't feeling that way at all. Here she stood, being vehemently kissed by a stranger, and she was not at all upset. The stranger was evidently skillful at the art (for his hold on her waist was so comfortably firm, and the pressure of his lips on hers was so forceful and lusty that she was convinced he'd had a great deal of practice), and, truth to tell, she was enjoying the sensation immensely. She had never been kissed by a man before (for surely one couldn't count the pecks upon the cheek that her uncle had bestowed on her over the years), but she'd dreamed of it often. This experience was not entirely *un*like her dreams, but it was different enough to be fascinating. She had anticipated the emotional upheaval a kiss of this sort might wreak, but she hadn't expected the excitement generated by its sheer physicality. The closeness of their two chests, the way her arms almost involuntarily crept up round his neck, the turmoil of her pulse, the effervescence of her blood as it raced through her veins, the heated flush that swept up through her body and into her face—all this was a revelation to her.

Before she could make mental notes of all the various sensations, she felt his hold on her relax. He lifted his head. She opened her eyes and stared up at him. He was looking down at her in some surprise. For a moment their eyes held, as if both of them were attempting to remember where they were.

A snorting, bitter laugh from the direction of the doorway broke the mood. "Well, well, my lord, what have we here?

Are you trying to pretend you've snared *another* pigeon for your coop?"

The gentleman turned toward the door with a very convincing look of surprise. "Alcorn! What are you doing here?"

A pale, narrow-shouldered, grey-haired man stood in the doorway, a large wooden box tucked under one arm. His lips were pressed together so tightly they seemed edged in white, and he was tense with suppressed rage. Behind him, the innkeeper and a number of persons from the taproom were gathered in the corridor watching the proceedings with fascination. Ada felt herself blush. The humiliation, which had thus far not had an effect, suddenly swept over her.

The man named Alcorn took a step forward, a sneer disfiguring his lined face. "You know very well what I'm doing here. I *found* my wife, my lord, and sent her home."

"Did you indeed?" The gentleman moved in front of Ada as if trying to shield her. "And what has that very interesting statement to do with me?"

Ada wished she could leave the room. This was a private conversation that had nothing to do with her. But she had another matter on her mind. She tapped the gentleman on the arm. "Please, sir, the collie must be—"

The gentleman made a slight motion with his hand to indicate to her that she shouldn't speak, but he kept his eyes fixed on the other man. "Well, Alcorn? What has that to do with me?" he repeated.

Alcorn laughed mirthlessly. "Don't take me for a fool, my lord. I know my wife was running off with you."

"So that's what this is all about, is it?" the gentleman asked with icy scorn. "You *are* a fool, Alcorn, if you believe that."

"We'll see who's the fool." Alcorn's voice shook with anger. He walked into the room and set the wooden box carefully on the table. "I've brought pistols."

There was a murmur from the onlookers. The gentleman snorted. "If you're going to talk fustian, Alcorn, at least don't do it publicly. Close the deuced door!"

Alcorn did so, slamming it loudly in the faces of the onlookers. While he was thus engaged, Ada tapped the other gentleman's shoulder again. "That poor animal is still—"

But Alcorn turned from the door and spoke up belligerently to his adversary. "Very well, we're private now. So you may as well admit, my lord, that you've been involved with my wife for some time and were going off with her to Wales."

"I admit nothing of the sort."

"Do you *deny* that you set off for Wales today in her company?"

"I set off for Wales today, yes. But if you weren't so completely blinded by your outrage, you would see that my companion is not your wife."

"Ah, yes. That lady you're so carefully shielding. Who is she, my lord? Why haven't you seen fit to introduce us?"

"I don't think it's any of your business who she is. And since she *is* a lady, I think you can understand why, under the circumstances, I would rather not reveal her name."

Alcorn walked to the side to get a better view of the young woman partially hidden by his lordship's body. "She *is* a pretty little chit. Are you trying to tell me that *she's* the one you're taking to Wales?"

"No, I'm trying *not* to tell you. Good God, man, have you no discretion? Can't you see that you're embarrassing the young lady?"

The man called Alcorn stared at his lordship suspiciously for a moment and then dropped into a chair at the table. "I don't know *what* to make of this," he muttered, passing a shaking hand over his brow. "There have been *on-dits* about you and Julia circulating about town for months. I haven't heard a word about your having a *new* connection—"

"That only proves how little one should rely upon *on-dits,*" the other responded drily.

Alcorn was nonplussed. He obviously desired fervently to believe what his lordship was telling him; his eagerness to believe in his wife's innocence showed quite plainly in his face. But he didn't wish to play the gull. To counteract his gullibility, he clung to his suspicions tightly. "Dash it all," he growled, "I don't know what to believe. That embrace I observed when I burst in seemed convincingly ardent, but . . ."

"Take your buts and go home," the gentleman said in disgust. "You're decidedly in the way here, I can tell you."

"Perhaps," Alcorn said, still unsure. "Perhaps. But I wish you'd let the young lady speak for herself. You've done your best to keep her from involvement in this conversation."

"Wouldn't you, if you were in my place?"

"I suppose so. Dash it all, I realize that this entire encounter is decidedly awkward. But, my lord, I promise you that you can count on my holding my tongue about all of this . . . if your companion can convince me of the truth of your claims. So speak up, ma'am. Is it true that his lordship is . . . er . . . escorting you to Wales?"

The gentleman who'd kissed Ada so brazenly turned to her, his eyes beseeching her to support him in his lies. "Go on, my dear. Tell Lord Alcorn what he wants to know."

Ada looked from one to the other. "No," she said.

"No?" Alcorn rose slowly from his chair, his face whitening and his hand reaching for the pistol case. "Are you implying that you're *not* his . . . his . . . that is, that you're not going to Wales with his lordship?"

"I am not implying anything at all." With an air of impatience she brushed by her "protector" and strode to the door. "What I've been trying to say for the past quarter hour is that there is a poor, bruised, maltreated collie lying on the hearth whimpering in agony. And until one of you takes care of his needs and sees to it that his master is sharply reprimanded, I don't intend to say anything more to either one of you. Good evening, gentlemen."

Chapter Five

Ada paced about the slant-roofed bedroom. She was uncertain about what to do next. Could she leave her room without feeling embarrassed? What would happen if she came face-to-face with the gentleman who'd kissed her? It would be dreadful to have to endure such an encounter—she didn't think she'd be able to look into his face. She'd handled the situation very badly. She should have been more ladylike, she thought. She should have fainted in his arms when he embraced her so shamelessly; or she should have slapped his face in outrage. At the very least, she should have screamed for help. Instead she'd endured the offense with apparent equanimity, as if she were quite accustomed to having strange gentlemen snatch her up and kiss her.

So, of course, she would have to remain closeted in this tiny room. But it felt like imprisonment. She was very hungry, and she could not have her dinner without going downstairs. Furthermore, she had a deep and shameful desire to take one more peep at the gentleman's face. The episode in the downstairs parlor had been so confusing that she was left without a clear memory of his appearance. All she could bring to mind were fleeting impressions . . . a deep, authoritative voice . . . a pair of dark, unreadable eyes . . . broad shoulder swathed in exquisitely-cut blue superfine . . . thick, unruly hair. These details were not sufficient to bring his face clearly to mind. And she wished very much to be able to recreate it; that face would add a touch of excitement to her daydreams.

But she hadn't the courage to go downstairs. If she did encounter that impetuous gentleman again, she would not know how to behave. How *did* one behave after an incident such as that? Should she raise her nose and pass him by, haughty and disdainful? Should she stop, gasp and sink down in a swoon? Should she call for someone to challenge him to a duel to avenge her honor? None of these responses seemed appropriate to her nature. What, she asked herself, would Cousin Cornelia do in such circumstances? Take her riding whip to him, no doubt. Well, Ada was not the sort to engage in such rodomontades. In her imagination she might concoct a dramatic encounter, but not in real life.

A knock at the door caused her to stop her pacing abruptly. She froze in her place. Who could be—?

"It's Griff," the familiar, authoritative voice said loudly. Then he added, much more softly, "Please open the door."

Feeling her blood begin to race through her veins, she unlocked the door and opened it a crack. "Y-Yes?"

The gentleman who'd kissed her stood just outside, still wearing his greatcoat and carrying his cane and beaver in his hand. "Alcorn's watching us from down below," he said in a whisper. "You've gone so far already. Do you think you can go just a bit further and let me in?"

"Let you in?" she echoed dimly. She hadn't anticipated anything like this and was utterly unprepared with a response. "I . . . I couldn't do that, sir. It would be considered . . . er . . ."

"Indiscreet?"

"Oh, yes. Indiscreet at the very least."

"But it would be a rather splendid indiscretion, my dear. It might very well save lives."

"Save lives?" She gaped at him quite stupidly. She didn't really follow what he was saying. Only two thoughts flitted across her mind: one was that she ought to slam the door in his face, and the other was that she could never bring herself to do it.

His eyes—the same kind-but-weary eyes that had made her believe, at her very first glimpse of him, that he would help her rescue the collie—gleamed with sudden, amused understanding. "You're afraid I'm going to kiss you again, is that it? Have no fear, ma'am. I promise I shall behave like a perfect gentleman. I only want Alcorn to be convinced that you and I are lovers. Once he sees that you've admitted me to your bedroom, he'll have no more doubt. He'll return to his wife, and all will be well."

As if mesmerized, Ada widened the door-opening and stepped aside. The gentleman came in and closed the door quickly behind him. After placing his hat and cane carefully upon a chest of drawers, he turned to face her. "Thank you, my dear," he said, taking her hand and lifting it to his lips. "I'm more grateful to you than I can say."

Ada trembled inwardly at her own temerity. She had admitted a strange man into her bedroom and permitted him to kiss her hand. Such behavior was undoubtedly a symptom of a hitherto unrecognized depravity of character. She should really give herself a severe scolding. She would surely do so . . . but not tonight. Tonight she would live through this exciting adventure. There was plenty of time for self-recrimination tomorrow.

She gently withdrew her hand from his grasp and glanced up at him. "I don't quite understand why you find it necessary to engage in this deception, sir, but before you explain it to me, I would like to know if you've done anything about the collie."

His eyebrows rose in amusement. "What an unusually single-minded young woman you are, ma'am, if I may be permitted to say so. You seem to have thought of nothing but that collie since we met. But you may now safely put the matter out of that tenacious mind of yours. I've taken care of it."

"Have you really? You reprimanded the innkeeper? That was good of you. I hope your reprimand was severe enough to keep the fellow from renewing his behavior after we leave this place."

"You need have no worry on that score. I removed the animal from his control."

"Did you? But how—?"

"I merely purchased the collie outright."

"*Purchased* him?" Ada's cheeks colored guiltily. "Oh, but I never meant you to go so far!"

"It was not so very far to go, ma'am. Not compared to the distance you've gone for me. I intend to present him to you as a token of my gratitude."

She stared up at him, her eyes widening. "Present him . . . to *me?*"

"Yes." His brow furrowed in confusion. "You do *like* the dog, don't you? I thought—"

"Oh, yes! He's a dear, sweet animal and has been *so* much abused. But I can't take him! I can't arrive at . . . at my destination with a large, shaggy collie in tow. It wouldn't be at all the thing to do." She looked up at her visitor worriedly. "What on earth shall I *do* with him?"

But he was not listening. He was staring down at her with the strangest expression on his face. "Has anyone ever told you that you have the most remarkable eyes?"

"What?"

"Truly, they're quite remarkable. They're so clear and pale that they seem...unfocused. As if you're perpetually looking beyond the present scene and seeing something else entirely."

She felt her cheeks grow hot. His expression and the tone of his voice were enigmatic; she couldn't tell if he admired what he'd described or merely found her freakish. She turned away in embarrassment. "We were talking about the collie, sir," she reminded him.

He gave a little snort of laughter. "You *are* single-minded, aren't you? But you needn't concern yourself about the dog. If you can't accept him, I'll take him with me to Wales. My caretakers have a number of dogs. They won't object to taking on another."

"Oh, sir," she said, overwhelmed, "that is truly kind of you." She turned back to him and offered him the first real smile he'd seen on her face. "Now it's *my* turn to be grateful."

"Not at all. My providing for the dog is not an act in the slightest way equal to your kindness in admitting me into your bedroom. As I said, your conduct has been quite splendid."

"My 'indiscretion,' you mean. I believe that was the word you used."

"Your indiscretion, then. But you *have* been splendid, you know. You've prevented the shedding of blood tonight."

She stared at him in disbelief. "You can't be serious."

"I'm completely serious. Alcorn had every intention of forcing a duel upon me."

"I'm quite certain that the gentleman downstairs—*Lord* Alcorn, is it?—did not really intend to use those pistols."

"Oh, but he *did,* I assure you. He came all the way from London with just that purpose in mind."

"Good heavens! He must be *demented.*"

"Not at all. Any man would be inclined to reach for his pistols when he suspects he's been cuckolded."

"But surely he's demented if he believes that *you*—"

The gentleman tried to hide his amusement at her naivete. "It is good of you to assume that I'm innocent, ma'am. Would you still have agreed to help me if I were guilty?"

"Surely you aren't guilty, sir! I can't believe—"

"But I am, my dear. Quite guilty. If I were innocent, I would think myself cowardly to use a ruse like this to avoid a duel. If I were innocent, I would face Alcorn across twenty paces of open space and put a bullet in one of his arms without a qualm, just to teach him a lesson for being a fool. But since I am guilty . . ." He paused, sighed and walked to the window. "Since I am guilty, I cannot add to my sins by shedding his blood. I have done him enough harm by wounding his honor."

"How strange," Ada murmured, half to herself. "I took you for a proper, kindly gentleman, and now I find that you're . . ."

"Cowardly?" he offered dryly.

"No, no, of course not."

"Degenerate, then?"

"I was going to say a . . . a rake."

"But ma'am, my shocking treatment of you down in the parlor must surely have given you a clue to the depravity of my character," he said, turning from the window and cocking an eyebrow at her with a mischievous charm.

"No. I was too . . . surprised to make any analysis."

"Too surprised, and too preoccupied with the plight of the collie, I'd say. I think I was very fortunate that you are so single-minded. I might otherwise have found myself deep in the suds."

"Oh, I don't know," Ada said, considering the matter seriously. "Perhaps I'm the degenerate sort of female who *likes* rakes."

He shook his head. "No, I don't think so." He strode back across the room and lifted her chin in his hand. "There is nothing at all degenerate in those pale eyes of yours. And a young woman who defends abused animals with such steadfast energy can only be pure of heart."

Ada knew that he was gently teasing her and that he didn't take any of this conversation seriously. But she found the implications of these casual remarks arresting. He had touched on a question she herself had been mulling over in the back of her mind . . . the unexpected possibility of her own degeneracy. She had very much enjoyed his kiss . . . the kiss of a stranger and a rake. Didn't that mean that there was some part of her that was degenerate? "I think that character can not be so easily categorized," she said thoughtfully. "If I were so pure of heart, I would not have permitted you to enter my bedroom. And if you were as degenerate as you say, I would not feel so safe as I do, standing here unprotected while you hold my chin in your fingers like a cup."

The gentleman studied her face with fascination. "Are you saying, ma'am, that I am less degenerate than circumstances indicate and that you are more so?"

"Yes, exactly."

He laughed. "A bit of the angel in me and the devil in you, eh? Not very likely in either case, I fear. I cannot imagine even a *touch* of the devil in you, my dear, and as for me, I wasn't commended for my good behavior even as a boy." He held her chin cupped in his hand and, for a long moment, peered down at her. Her skin, which he judged was usually pale and translucent, was now charmingly rosy from her blushing discomfort at being so impudently studied. Her hair, pulled back from her face in a severe knot, looked so soft and silky that he itched to smooth back the strands that had burst from their fastenings. Her lips were deliciously full and red, and he would have thought them her most fetching feature had it not been for her large, amazingly-light eyes. Those eyes made her seem to be a creature not of this earth. Surely only angels in heaven could have eyes of such ethereal clarity! Imagine her trying to pretend she had a touch of the devil. There could not be even the *slightest* touch of evil behind those eyes. Feeling all at once a sharp twinge of guilt, he dropped his hold on her. "Well, whatever the truth, we shall not have time to debate it tonight. I've given my word to act the gentleman, and no gentleman worthy of the name would compromise a lady—especially one who's given him such unselfish assistance—by dawdling too long in her bedroom. I must leave you, ma'am."

He gave her a quick bow and went to the door. As he put his hand on the knob, however, he paused. "I wonder if Alcorn is still waiting. If only I could open the door a crack to take a look. But if I open the door and he's down there, I'll give the whole game away." He stared at the door speculatively for a moment and then shook his head. "No, no, he won't still be there. He couldn't be! Even a cawker like Alcorn wouldn't be so idiotic as to stand guard all night, would he? What do you think, ma'am?"

There was no answer. The gentleman turned about and discovered that Ada was sitting on the bed lost in thought. Puzzled, he crossed the room and knelt beside her. "Ma'am?"

She blinked and smiled at him absently. "Yes?"

"I asked what you think."

"I think it very unlikely that your behavior was reprehensible all the time. I'm sure that there were many occasions in your boyhood when you were good or kind or generous. Even now, although it is undoubtedly reprehensible to have cuckolded poor Lord Alcorn, you are doing all you can to keep from dueling with him . . . which anyone would agree is a very commendable act."

He studied her face in amazement. "But I wasn't asking you to defend my character, ma'am. We had ceased our conversation on that subject some time since. Where have you been these past few minutes?"

"Oh!" Ada's cheeks reddened at once. "I . . . I must have been . . . woolgathering."

"Woolgathering? Good God, woman, how can you be woolgathering when a strange man is in your bedroom, unable to think of a way to get out, and thus giving every indication that he will cause the ruination of your reputation?"

She twisted her fingers together in humiliation. "I'm sorry. I don't know what makes me so . . . so bubbleheaded. It's a very disturbing weakness of mine."

"Do you mean that you do this sort of thing often? Wander away mentally?"

"I'm afraid so. My uncle says my mind is *always* elsewhere."

"I suppose that shouldn't surprise me. That's what I was trying to describe in your eyes." With a shake of his head (a gesture which Ada interpreted as an indication that he was dismissing from his mind any attraction that he might earlier have felt toward her), he stood erect and looked at the door. "This is all very interesting, ma'am, but we haven't time to discuss it further. We must somehow manage to solve the *present* dilemma."

"Dilemma?"

"Yes. We have a dilemma. If I go out the door, I may come face to face with Lord Alcorn and thus give the game away. If I remain, I may ruin your reputation."

"I don't think my reputation will be ruined if you remain. You could roll up in your greatcoat on the floor near the fire and get some sleep," she suggested shyly.

"That, my dear girl," he said, touched by her innocence, "is a most generous offer. Much more generous than I deserve. If I were a true degenerate, I would certainly accept it." He smiled down at her with a warmth that stirred her pulse. "You must be closer to the truth of my character than I suspected, because I find that I *can't* accept. I will not premit the inn-keeper, the servants, or anyone but Alcorn to question your reputation, as they might do if I were discovered in this room in the morning."

"Then, what—"

His brow furrowed in concentration. After a moment, he strode back to the window, threw open the casement and looked out. "My bedroom is right next door," he said. "If I can climb across on that ledge—"

She came up beside him and looked for herself. "But it's so *narrow!* You can't possibly—"

"Yes, I can. If you give me a supporting hand while I lower myself to the ledge, I'll make it."

Without waiting for a reply, he sat down on the sill and swung his legs over it. With one hand gripping her arm and the other pressing against the wall, he turned his body so that he faced the wall and slid down to the narrow ledge below the window. The ledge, barely as wide as his boot, ran along the entire width of the building. Once his feet touched it, he re-leased his hold on her. "Thank you, my dear, for what you've done for me this night," he said as he began to edge slowly away from her.

"Never mind that," she whispered breathlessly. "Just don't fall."

He was half-way between her window and his. "Damna-tion," he swore suddenly. "I forgot my hat and cane!"

"Does that matter? I can give them to you in the morning."

"What if someone came into your room before you managed it? What if a housemaid or the innkeeper's wife discovered them? In such a case, this quixotic escape would have been made in vain."

"You do seem to think of all the possibilities," she mur-mured. "You must have had a great deal of experience in such subterfuge."

He was inching his way back toward her. "A very great deal," he responded crisply. Glancing up at her, he caught the measuring look in her eyes. "Aha. There you are. You see it now, don't you? I'm not so angelic as you thought, am I?"

"Perhaps n-not."

He looked away. "Be a good girl and get my things, will you?"

"You can't possibly hang on while holding something in your hand," she objected.

"Oh, ye of little faith. Just get them, please."

She did as she was bid. With heart beating in fear, she leaned from the window and handed him his hat. He clapped it on his head and resumed his sideward movement. When he'd almost reached his destination, he stretched out his hand toward her. "Now the cane," he instructed.

She held it by its bottom tip and reached out. He grasped the silver head, edged closer to his window and used the tip to pry open the casement above him. It took a great deal of dangerous maneuvering before the window gave way and this caused Ada a great deal of heart-stopping consternation as she watched him teetering on the ledge. When the casement finally budged, he tossed the cane inside. He then removed the hat, sent it following the cane and centered himself below the sill. Grasping the sill with both hands, he was about to heave himself up when he suddenly paused and began inching back in her direction.

"What are you doing?" she gasped. "Are you *mad*, moving back and forth along that . . . that precipice?"

"It's not as dangerous as all that. Even if I fell, the damage would not be great. We're only a story off the ground."

"But why are you doing it? What's wrong now?"

He didn't respond until he was just below her window. "You may have noticed that I haven't asked your name."

"Good God! Is *that* why you came back? To ask my *name?*"

"No, because I could more easily have asked the innkeeper in the morning. But I suddenly wondered if *you* would wonder why I hadn't."

"Why, no," she said in surprise, "I hadn't thought of that at all."

He made a rueful face. "I should have known. Your mind was probably elsewhere. But I think it only right to tell you that I don't intend to ask for your name after all."

"No? Why not?"

"Because if I knew your name, I should find myself tempted to call on you, and I don't think it would be wise to do so."

"Oh?" She was shocked at the sharp pang of disappointment which constricted her chest.

"We shouldn't suit at all, you see. Despite your kind denials, I have too much of the devil in me for such an innocent as you. And I haven't enough patience to deal with . . ." He hesitated while he tried to search for the right word.

"Bubbleheads?" she ventured bleakly.

"I don't believe you to be a bubblehead."

"Woolgatherers, then."

"Let us say 'dreamers.' Men of my ilk have been known to wreak havoc in the lives of innocent young dreamers, you know. So I think it better that I don't learn your name."

"You must please yourself on that score, sir," she answered quietly. "It would not be proper for me to offer my name to a stranger in any case."

"Then there's nothing left but to exchange goodnights," he said and began to inch back.

Once under his window, he grasped the sill, heaved himself up and threw himself inside, top over tail.

Ada, having seen him safe, was about to withdraw when his head and shoulders reappeared. "Goodnight, ma'am," he whispered. "I will always be grateful to you."

"Goodnight," she replied and withdrew her head. She was struck with a feeling of deep depression that the night's adventure was at an end. *What on earth is the matter with me?* she asked herself, on the verge of tears.

"Ma'am?" His hissing whisper came wafting through the night air into her still-open casement.

She took a deep breath, swallowed the tears that had lumped in her throat and leaned out again. "Yes?"

"You *do* have the most *remarkable* eyes," he said.

Chapter Six

The inn was very quiet when Ada and the still-feverish Selena sat down to breakfast. There was no sign of the gentleman who had visited her room the night before, or of Lord Alcorn either. Ada wondered if either of them were still in the hostelry. It would have brightened her mood considerably to learn that the gentleman whose face had invaded her dreams all night had not yet left, but she was too proud to ask. All through breakfast she looked up at every sound, hoping to see him standing in the doorway. She imagined him smiling at her, saying he'd changed his mind, that he'd learned her name from the innkeeper and that he hoped she would permit him to escort her to London. "Escort me to London?" she'd ask with a flirtatious laugh. "Whatever for?"

"So that I learn where to come calling, of course," he'd respond.

But the only man who loomed up in the doorway was Hines, who announced that the wheelwright had made the repairs and that the carriage was ready to leave. Ada's dream evaporated in the bustle of departure. Selena, conscious of the hours of delay, hurried her charge into the carriage without giving the girl a moment for a backward look. By the time Ada was settled into her seat in the coach and had caught her breath, the scene of her previous night's adventure was left far behind.

"Oh, Miss Ada," the abigail wailed through the first hour of the ride, "we'll be too late. I know we'll be too late."

"Stop worrying, Selena," Ada ordered at last. "We shall not be late, I promise you."

"'Ow kin ye be sure o' that, Miss Ada? Miss Cornelia may 'ave passed us in the night!"

"I'm certain she did no such thing. You know Miss Cornelia. It will take her a week to pack her clothing."

It was this offhand remark that silenced the abigail. Anyone who was acquainted with Cornelia knew that the girl never traveled anywhere without a mountain of trunks and bandboxes.

Surely she would not have set out from Bishop's Cleve for London without her entire wardrobe, a wardrobe so extensive that it *would* require a week to pack it. Even Ada was soothed by the certainty that Cornelia was still at home, safely readying her clothing.

Selena's cough sounded worse by the time they arrived in London. She fell into a severe paroxism of gasps just as Hines was maneuvering the coach up the curved driveway of the Countess Mullineaux's town house. Ada was so concerned with soothing her stricken abigail that she failed to notice the number of carriages which lined the driveway. But when they drew up before the imposing domicile, Ada couldn't help but take note of the dignity of the building's facade. It was three stories high, its height emphasized by the tall windows which were now all brilliantly lit. Most impressive of all was the stone pediment over the wide double door. It was decorated with sculpted flags and fluting, and at the center it bore a graven coat of arms. While Ada gaped at the edifice through the coach window, the abigail sniffed pathetically into her handkerchief and spoke yearningly of her own bed in her own room in the Surringham house at Bishop's Cleve. Ada, who was convinced she'd never in her life seen a more magnificent mansion, could scarcely believe her ears. "Don't you think you'll be comfortable here in the Countess's staff quarters?" she asked her abigail.

"There ain't no place like 'ome," Selena wheezed, "'specially when yer ailin'."

"Then, Selena, why don't you go home with Hines."

"Go 'ome? T' Bishop's Cleve? Oh, Miss Ada, I *couldn't,* could I? Sir Jarsper wouldn' take it kin'ly if I deserted ye."

"You wouldn't be deserting me, my dear. Even Uncle Jasper wouldn't accuse you of that. You helped get me here safely, after all. Of course, I do believe he wanted you with me to impress the countess, but even if I had *ten* abigails in tow I wouldn't impress the countess." She sighed. "I'm just not impressive. *Cornelia* is the impressive one." In her mind's eye, Ada could imagine how Cornelia would make her arrival. She would have a coachman, an abigail and two liveried footmen. One of the footmen would lower the steps of the carriage while the other knocked at the door. Cornelia would alight with the dignity of a Royal Queen, her abigail fluttering behind her, holding aloft an umbrella to protect her charge from either sun or rain and clutching in her other hand a little case containing

Cornelia's jewelry. The Countess Mullineaux, her butler and
all the household staff who would hurry to the door at the sight
of Cornelia's retinue would be bound to be impressed.

Selena did not follow all of what her mistress was mur-
muring, but she was quite used to Ada's way of thinking. The
abigail understood that Sir Jasper's primary purpose in sending
her on this trip was to make certain that his niece arrived at
her destination safely and on time. That she had done. As for
the rest, perhaps what the girl said was right—Miss Ada was
Miss Ada, and she wasn't likely to stir up much attention
whether she had an abigail beside her or not. In that case, why
shouldn't she go home? She'd be no good to anyone, sick as
she was. "Are ye sure, Miss Ada?"

"Sure?"

The abigail frowned in annoyance. Miss Ada was off in the
clouds again. "Are ye sure I should go 'ome? Ye'd not mind
doin' without me?"

Ada shook herself into the present with an effort. "I shall
miss you, of course, Selena. But I'm certain that her ladyship
will be able to provide me with an abigail. So, please, go home
and get yourself well again."

Hines, having unloaded the portmanteau and the two bandboxes (which held every item of clothing, every pair of shoes,
every comb and brush which Ada possessed) and placed them
on the doorstep, turned to Ada for further instructions. "Go
along, Hines," Ada ordered. "It's time you started for home."

"We'd better wait until ye've gone inside," Hines suggested,
looking at the huge oak doors dubiously.

"Why should you wait? Even if her ladyship is not at home,
there are surely enough servants on hand to take care of me.
Go along now. You must take poor Selena home. She needs
to be put to bed as soon as possible."

Ada waved goodbye until the carriage trundled out of the
curved driveway and was lost to sight. Then she took a deep
breath to build up her courage and knocked at the door.

After a long wait the door was opened by a trim but elderly
woman wearing a black bombazine dress with a ring of keys
hanging from the belt and a frilled white mobcap. Ada was
surprised. This was evidently the housekeeper. Why, she wondered, was the housekeeper answering the door? Where was
the butler?

The housekeeper studied her coldly, her eyes sweeping over

Ada's form from her bonnet to her laced half-boots. "What are you doing *here?*" she asked.

The question was so rude and unexpected that Ada was at a loss. "I . . . I'm Ada Sur—"

"I know who you are, girl! You've been expected since noon. But you should have come to the back."

"The b-back?"

"Yes, you fool girl, the *back!* You shouldn't've expected to be admitted here. Especially tonight, when her ladyship's entertainin' forty for dinner. How would you feel if one of the guests, like the Duchess of York herself, should see you comin' in the front door?" She looked round over her shoulder to make sure nobody was about. "Well, you may as well come in, now you're here. You'll have to carry your things yourself; none of the footmen can be spared tonight."

Ada was so startled by this unexpected welcome that she was bereft of speech. She picked up her portmanteau and one of the bandboxes, but she had difficulty getting hold of the second bandbox. The housekeeper watched her for a moment in annoyance, but then she relented and picked it up herself. With a finger pressed cautiously against her lips, she led the way on tiptoe across the polished marble floor of the magnificent entry hall.

Ada, wearily hauling her baggage, could hear the sounds of merriment from somewhere down the hall. She followed the housekeeper to the stairway. She would not have believed that anything could surprise her after the peculiar greeting she'd just received, but when the elderly woman led her not *up* the stairs but right *past* them, she was more surprised than before. Where was this creature leading her? she wondered. If the idea were not so preposterous, she would have believed she was being taken to the servants' quarters.

The elderly woman led her down a rear hallway to the back of the house. Surely this *was* the servants' quarters! Ada couldn't understand what was happening. If Lady Mullineaux was indeed occupied with a dinner party for forty guests, Ada didn't expect her to leave her guests and greet her with an eager embrace and tears of affection. But she certainly had a right to expect more warmth than *this!*

They came to the back stairs, where the housekeeper put down the bandbox she carried. "I suppose you haven't had supper," she said sourly. "Well, leave your things here and come down to the servants' hall. We can probably find somethin' for you without disturbin' Monsieur Albert and the staff."

"Monsieur Albert?"

"Our cook. But be sure to stay out of everyone's way. When we have a dinner party of *this* size, everyone on the kitchen staff becomes jittery."

"I . . . I'm not very h-hungry," Ada stammered. "I don't wish to be in anyone's way. If you could just show me to my room . . ."

Something in the quiver of Ada's voice caught the housekeeper's notice and softened her irritated spirits. She turned and peered into Ada's face. "Oh, dear," she muttered, suddenly friendly, "I've upset you, haven't I? I'm sorry I was so pettish. I expected you earlier, y'see. I said to Eva—she's her ladyship's dresser, y'know—I said to her when you failed to appear by four, 'She'll come in the midst of the dinner,' I said, and that's just what you did. And you can see that this is the worst possible time to show your face . . ."

"Yes," Ada managed, wondering what sort of household she'd fallen into, "I am sorry . . ."

"But you needn't look as if you'd stabbed your own mother, girl," the housekeeper said, suddenly smiling. "We'll get through the evening right enough." She put out her hand. "I'm Mrs. Mudge. You'll like me better once you get to know me. Come downstairs. We can't let you go to bed hungry, now, can we?"

The stairway led to a pleasant, square room fitted with a huge table surrounded by at least twenty chairs. "Here's where we eat," the housekeeper said. "Sit down, and I'll see what I can find for you."

She went out through a swinging door through which Ada got a glimpse of the kitchen. It was evidently a beehive of activity. Through the door came a flood of sounds—a babble of voices shouting orders both in English and French, the scuffle of feet on a wooden floor, the clatter of dishes and pans. But what interested Ada more were the smells . . . the tantalizing aroma of roasting meats and baking pastries. Ada hadn't realized how very hungry she was.

In a few minutes Mrs. Mudge returned, followed by a young maidservant with a ruddy complexion, swathed in a long apron that almost covered her clothes and a white kerchief that almost covered her hair. The maid carried a tray laden with dishes.

"This is Clara," Mrs. Mudge told Ada. "We've brought you

a bowl of soup, a bit off the end of the roast, a hot muffin, some sprouts and, of course, a pot of tea. Set the tray down here, Clara. Serve the soup, if you please, and pour me a cup of tea. They can spare you in the kitchen for a while, now that the second course's been served."

The housekeeper laid out two table settings and took a seat beside Ada, while the maid Clara set down the tray and ladled out some soup from a tureen into a bowl. She placed the bowl in front of Ada and smiled shyly at her. "It's the same soup they served upstairs," she confided in a friendly way, "so ye're bound t' like it."

"Thank you," Ada said and picked up her spoon.

Clara eyed Ada with interest as she served the tea to the housekeeper. "So yer the one who's come t' assist Mr. Finchley-Jones," she said admiringly. "I wish I had the schoolin' t' do bookwork."

Ada blinked at her. "Assist Mr. Finchley-Jones?"

"Of course," Mrs. Mudge said impatiently. "Didn't the librarian's society tell you his name when they hired you? He's a famous scholar, Mr. Finchley-Jones is. Lord Mullineaux interviewed him hisself before he engaged him."

Ada wondered briefly if she'd been daydreaming and had missed some important part of this conversation. "Lord Mullineaux?" she asked faintly.

"Her ladyship's son. He's very proud of his library, you know, and he wanted it—what did his lordship call it? Catalogued? Yes, catalogued by the best librarian in England. If his lordship engaged Mr. Finchley-Jones, you can be certain he's the best. You're a lucky girl to work for him."

Ada stared at the housekeeper as a sudden insight broke through the clouds in her mind. This entire episode, from the first moment Mrs. Mudge had opened the door, had been a *mistake*. A silly, almost farcical comedy of mistaken identity! The housekeeper had mistaken her for someone else . . . someone who was to assist this Mr. Finchley-Jones. "I think, Mrs. Mudge, that you've mistaken my identity," she began. "I'm not—"

The door to the kitchen swung open at that moment, and another aproned housemaid burst in. "Mrs. Mudge, Mrs. Mudge," she shouted breathlessly, "they're callin' fer you upstairs."

Mrs. Mudge jumped to her feet, her keys jangling. "Upstairs? Whatever for? What's gone wrong?"

"It's that protegee of 'er ladyship's. One of the footmen spilled the poivrade sauce, and a bit of it spotted 'er gown. They say she's raisin' a terrible fuss. 'Er ladyship wants ye t' take the girl upstairs and see if ye can get rid of the stain."

"There, you see?" the housekeeper flung back over her shoulder to Ada as she ran for the stairs. "I told you how it would be. Whenever there's a dinner party for so many, things are bound to be at sixes and sevens!"

Ada gazed after the housekeeper until she disappeared up the stairs. Her head was spinning with a new possibility. Upstairs, at a dinner party for forty, a "protégée" of the Countess Mullineaux was "raisin' a fuss." Could this "protégée" be—?

"Is somethin' wrong wi' the soup?" Clara was asking in friendly concern.

"N-No," Ada muttered. "Nothing."

"Then why ain't ye eatin' it? Ye ain't upset by Mrs. Mudge's scold, are ye? Ye mustn't take no notice of 'er. She's a good sort when you get to know 'er."

Ada nodded and tried to sip some of the soup. "I wonder, Clara . . . is this protégée of her ladyship called Cornelia?"

"Yes, indeed, that's 'er name. But how did ye know?"

Ada stirred her soup. "Er . . . ah . . . Mrs. Mudge must have told me."

She bent over her soup, her mind in a turmoil. It was clear that she'd arrived too late after all. Cornelia was already installed upstairs, having dinner with the Duchess of York and the other thirty-odd guests of the Countess Mullineaux. Cornelia had won again. Ada would have to make her way back to Bishop's Cleve and admit her failure. And Uncle Jasper had said that his wrath would be terrible. *I'll make ye wish ye'd never been born*—wasn't that what he'd threatened? He'd always been a kind, even soft-hearted guardian, but when he'd sent her on this journey he'd sounded angrier than ever before. For the first time in her life she was afraid to face him.

And even if she could work up the courage to face her uncle, how was she to get to Bishop's Cleve? She'd sent her carriage home without a thought for the future. She had no transportation, no pocket money, no resources of any kind. She could, she supposed, make her identity known to Countess Mullineaux and rely on her ladyship to provide the wherewithal for her return, but the prospect of such a solution was appalling. It would be mortifying to have to reveal the truth—that her uncle had forced her to engage in this humiliating race, that she'd floundered on the way, and that she needed assistance to return home. The very *thought* of telling this tale to the worldly countess made Ada feel ill.

But was else was she to do? To return home without letting the countess know of her existence would require some money. Could she possibly sell her belongings to someone in exchange for passage on the stage? But to whom could she go? Where? She was a stranger in London. She didn't even know where the stagecoach terminal was located. If only—

"Miss? *Miss?*" The maid Clara was bending over her, looking at her strangely.

Oh, dash it all, Ada thought in self-reproach, *I've done it again. I've been woolgathering!* She looked up at the maid in embarrassment. "I'm sorry, Clara. Were you asking something of me?"

"I was only askin' what ye meant when ye said a moment ago that there was some mistake concernin' yer identity. Ain't ye the one they've engaged t' assist in the liberry?"

Ada blinked at the maid, her pulse suddenly arrested. *Why not?* she asked herself. Why not stay and assist this Mr. Finchley-Jones? It would be better than admitting the truth to the Countess and being shipped home in disgrace to face Uncle Jasper's wrath. She could remain for a while safely hidden in the library and the servants' quarters, areas of the house where Cornelia was quite unlikely to appear. Why not?

It was a wonderful idea. She could stay right here, unnoticed among the household staff, until she'd saved enough money to return to Bishop's Cleve on her own. And while she stayed hidden, Uncle Jasper would believe that she had done his bidding and was having a grand time in London. He wasn't likely to discover that Cornelia had beaten her in the race, for he had made it clear that he and Lady Dorothea were no longer on speaking terms. Sooner or later, of course, he would discover the truth, but with any luck at all she should be safe for at least a fortnight. In that time she would surely be able to concoct a story to tell her uncle that would ease his wrath and make her return to her old life possible. And meanwhile, it would be very interesting to see if she could manage to live on her own resources and even earn a wage. If the experiment proved successful, she might be able to believe that she was not such a bubblehead after all.

The maid Clara had cocked her head and was frowning down at her. "Miss? Did ye hear me? 'As Mrs. Mudge made some mistake 'ere?"

She looked up at the curious maid and smiled. "No, Clara, there's no mistake. I'm Mr. Finchley-Jones's new assistant."

Chapter Seven

By the time Mrs. Mudge returned to the servants' dining hall, Ada had thought through the problem of taking on a new identity. It was all worked out in her mind. If the real assistant to Mr. Finchley-Jones had been due to arrive at noon, something serious must have prevented her from appearing. It was extremely unlikely that she would make an appearance at this late hour. Chances were good that she would not arrive at all. And since she was obviously unknown to Mrs. Mudge, she was probably unknown to Mr. Finchley-Jones as well. Therefore, Ada convinced herself, it was quite safe to continue to play the role of the librarian's assistant for the time being.

Mrs. Mudge returned to the servants' dining hall in a cheerful mood, having successfully cleaned the stains from the gown of her ladyship's new charge. "It's a most modish gown, I'd say, considerin' it ain't London made," the housekeeper revealed to Clara and Ada confidentially, seating herself beside Ada with a fresh cup of tea. "Saxe blue jaconet with satin panels. I managed to clean it with just a rub of lime soap and a wipe with a damp cloth, so the young lady didn't have to leave the party for more than a few minutes. She was very nice and proper. I don't know why Anna said she'd raised a fuss. Miss Haydon—that's her name, Miss Cornelia Haydon—was most pleasant to me . . . even offered me a vail, which of course I told her that as I am the housekeeper and not a common housemaid, I do not deign to accept."

"They should've sent fer me," muttered Clara under her breath. "I'd've taken it right enough."

"Now that's enough of that sort of talk," Mrs. Mudge admonished sharply. "You don't want to set a poor example for Miss—" She looked at Ada with a sudden blink. "What's your name, girl? I've forgotten—"

Ada had told herself she'd thought of everything, but here in the first moments of her deception she was already stumped. "My n-name?"

"I know I should remember. Mr. Finchley-Jones showed me the letter the society sent about you . . ."

"It's Ada. Ada S-S-Surrey."

"Surrey? That's strange." The housekeeper stared at her with knit brows. "I would swear the letter said somethin' like Latcham . . . or Letcham . . ."

"Good gracious, Mrs. Mudge," Clara interjected, "the girl knows 'er own name, don't she?"

Mrs. Mudge shrugged. "I'm gettin' old, I suppose. Don't remember things as I used to. Well, Ada, I suppose you'll be wishin' to see your room and take to your bed. Follow me. I'll show you where you'll be stayin'."

Mrs. Mudge maintained a lively monologue as she led Ada up the stairs to her room, enlarging on her impressions of Miss Haydon, her ladyship's new house guest. "A bit spoilt, I think one might say, and too mindful of her clothes and her looks, but she's a real beauty. I can see that her ladyship's pleased with the girl. This Cornelia Haydon'll suit her ladyship's purposes very well."

"Her ladyship's purposes?"

The housekeeper nodded conspiratorially. "It wouldn't do for you to bibble-babble this about, Ada, but her ladyship'd like nothin' better than to see this girl catch her son's interest. Her son is Lord Mullineaux that I've told you of. He's slipped out of more marriage traps than an eel out of nets. Never knew a gentleman so wary of gettin' hisself leg-shackled." She'd been walking ahead of Ada on the stairs, but at this point she waited for Ada to come up beside her and whispered the rest of her tale into her ear. "It's said he only interests hisself in ladies that are already wed, so that he'll be perfectly safe from matrimony. Got hisself into any number of scrapes because of his habits, I can tell you. Not that I wish you to think ill of him. Lord Mullineaux is as fine a gentleman as ever walked. Kind and generous and as devoted to his mother as anyone would wish. Once he settles down, he'll be a most ideal gentleman. It's better for a man to sow his wild oats before he's wed than after. No man makes a better husband than a reformed rake, as I've heard her ladyship say on more than one occasion. I ain't inclined to disagree with her, are you?"

"I don't know much about rakes, I'm afraid," Ada answered. But as she settled herself into the little room to which the housekeeper had brought her, she couldn't help wishing that she'd been given the opportunity to try to reform a certain rake of her own acquaintance.

It was a wish that permeated her dreams all night. In one dream she was standing at an altar in a dimly lit church beside the gentleman of the inn. It was obviously a wedding ceremony in which she was the bride, but while the groom held fast to her hand, his attention was fixed on a lady standing at his other side. "Do you know," he said to the other lady, "you have the most remarkable eyes?"

In another dream, she found herself on a strange country road. Near by, a farmer was walking down a furrow which had been newly turned. "What are you doing?" she called to him from the roadway.

"Can't you see? I'm sowing seeds."

She was startled at the familiar sound of his voice, for she was sure she'd never been in this neighborhood before and could never have seen this man. "What sort of seeds?" she asked.

"Oats," the farmer answered. "Wild oats."

"What good are wild oats?" she persisted.

"Don't you know anything, girl?" the man scoffed, crossing the field in long strides, coming up to her and cupping her chin in his hand. "If a man sows wild oats early, he's all the better for it later."

But when she looked into his strangely familiar eyes, she saw reflected in them a laughing devil, and she woke up trembling.

She resolved, as she dressed herself at daybreak for her forthcoming meeting with the awesome Mr. Finchley-Jones, that she would make every effort to put the memory of the gentleman-of-the-inn out of her mind. Thinking of him would be to no purpose, for neither of them knew the other's name and were thus unlikely ever to meet again. Remembering him in daydreams or night dreams would only distract her and make her all the more bubbleheaded. If she was to succeed in her new life with her new identity, she would need all her wits about her.

Mr. Finchley-Jones was not present in the servants' dining hall for breakfast. Clara explained to Ada that the librarian did not reside in the household but came only for the day. Mr. Finchley-Jones held a special status in the Mullineaux household. Since he was a scholar, he was considered above the servants and did not take meals with them. But he was not socially equal to her ladyship or Lord Mullineaux (though Clara revealed that his lordship had once actually sat down to lunch with his librarian while they discussed the plans for the library) and was therefore served his luncheon on a tray in the library. *Poor Mr. Finchley-Jones,* Ada thought. *Neither fish nor fowl.*

Before Mrs. Mudge bustled off to supervise the reordering of the household after the festivities of the night before, she informed Ada that the librarian always appeared in the library on the stroke of seven. "You may as well wait for him there. Since it ain't yet time, you'll have a few minutes to look round."

The library was located in a huge, high-ceilinged corner room at the back of the house. It had evidently been in disuse for some time. The windows were grimy with dust, allowing only a pale gleam of sunlight to filter through. Several beautiful leather chairs had been pushed out of the way into a corner, and a sofa against the wall had been shrouded in a Holland dustcover. That left only one piece of furniture—a long library table—in the center of the room. It was completely covered with piles of books of assorted sizes, with additional piles surrounding it on the floor. Ada had never seen so many books in her life.

Even though the atmosphere was one of disarray, one couldn't help admiring the magnificent carved oak bookshelves. They climbed up three of the walls from floor to ceiling, even over the doors and windows. Only the area over the fireplace had been kept free of shelves, probably to provide space for the huge painting which had been hung there. The painting, completely encased in a Holland cover, hovered over the room like an angular, misshapen ghost. Ada made a mental note to peep under the sheet after she'd finished her examination of the room.

The bookshelves themselves had been partially denuded of books. Those that had been removed were lying in uneven piles on the floor along the walls, while those volumes that still remained on the shelves lay this way and that in the dust, adding to the room's dismaying air of disorder and desolation. Only one place in the room stood out in unexpected, pristine neatness—a large-topped desk with a chair behind it, placed between two of the windows opposite the entrance door. Completely free of dust or chaos, the desk was as discordantly out of place as an alabaster chess piece might be if it were found in a mud puddle. The desk's wood shone, its brass fittings glowed, the leather insert on its top gleamed with polish. A serviceable but remarkably clean inkstand had been placed precisely at the center point of the rear surface, with a pen tray in front of it. Three thick notebooks lay at the exact center of the leather insert, and at their right and left were two identically high piles of notes, each one held in place by a brass paperweight in the shape of a globe.

The symmetry of the placement of the items on the desk fascinated Ada. What sort of man, she wondered, would take the time to divide his papers into two such precisely even piles? And weight them down with matching globes? But on closer examination, she was amused to discover that although both globes were indeed alike in having been engraved with maps, the map on the right-hand globe was celestial while the one on the left was terrestrial.

She was still holding the celestial globe in her hand when she heard the door open. "Don't ever," came a shrill outcry from the doorway, *"ever* touch anything on my desk!"

"Oh!" she gasped, dropping the brass ball in alarm, "I . . . I beg your pardon."

A tall, thin figure in a black coat bounded across the room and snatched up the paperweight from the floor. The man (for despite the frightened beating of her heart, Ada could now see that the black-clad apparition was indeed a man) lifted to his nose a lorgnette which hung from a black cord about his neck, clipped the nosepiece to the bridge of his nose and peered through the glasses at the little globe. Now that the first shock of his arrival had worn off, Ada saw that he looked less tall and much less ferocious than her first glimpse of him and his first shriek had led her to believe. He was a man not much above average height, but his long, thin legs and arms made him seem taller. Everything about him was thin and bony. The skin on his face stretched over high, sharp cheekbones and a sharp nose. Even his hair was thin and long, and he'd combed it to the side from a parting on the right side of his head to cover a place on his pate where he'd gone bald. He appeared to be a man in his middle years, but the intensity of his scholarly grey eyes made her realize that he was younger than he first seemed.

After examining all of the globe's surface, Mr. Finchley-

Jones breathed a sigh of relief and replaced it carefully on the desk. "There," he said more calmly, "that's better. No harm done. Although I must say, Madam, it's no thanks to you." He stared at her through the glasses. "Who are you? You can't be Miss Latcham."

"N-No, I'm... I'm not Miss Latcham."

"That's what I *said*. I dislike useless repetition. You didn't need to offer me such obvious information. I deduced it for myself at once."

"D-Deduced it?"

"I was given to understand that Miss Latcham had been employed by Lord Lesterbrook's librarian for twenty years. You can not have been employed by *anyone* for twenty years. I would venture to guess..." He pointed at her with a long, bony finger as if making an accusation. "... that you have not been *alive* for twenty years!"

"I am... p-past twenty-two."

"Then I am in the wrong, but not by much. However, since you are twenty-two and not forty-two, I am *not* in the wrong in my deduction that you are not Miss Latcham. Where, may I ask, is she?"

Ada, having decided that Mr. Finchley-Jones's bluster was not any more threatening than her uncle's, recovered her composure during this exchange and made up her mind to continue with her pretended identity to the end. "I... we... don't know where Miss Latcham has disappeared. The... er... the society sent me in her place."

"Did they indeed? And who are *you* to take her place? A little slip of a girl like you. What do you know of bibliography? I'd warrant you've never been inside a library in the entire twenty-two years of your existence."

"Then, sir, you'd be in the wrong again," Ada said bravely, putting up her chin. "I was told, Mr. Finchley-Jones, that you have an excellent reputation in scholarly circles. But jumping to conclusions seems to me not at all the mark of a scholar. One would think that a man with a scholarly mind would seek adequate information before making judgments."

"Hmmmph." Mr. Finchley-Jones peered at her through the lorgnette for a moment or two longer. Then he removed the spectacles from his nose and turned away from her. He crossed the room to a small door in the corner behind the leather chairs and disappeared inside what appeared to be a closet or retiring room. When he emerged a moment later, he was in his shirt-sleeves and waistcoat and was pulling on the second of a pair of black sleeve protectors. "You are familiar with libraries, you say?" he asked, seating himself at his desk.

"Oh, yes. We have a reasonably good one in my uncle's..." She caught herself up short. "I mean, before I was...er...orphaned..." Her voice trailed off helplessly.

"Ah, I see. It is as I suspected. You are well-born but impoverished, is that not the case?"

"Well, I..."

"So you are forced to find some way to support yourself. You must not believe that I am unsympathetic to your plight, madam, but I should have thought you more suited to a post as a governess. The art of bibliography cannot be practiced by the untrained. I warned the society of that. I had hoped to find a young scholar...a man...but Miss Latcham's experience was admirably extensive. I am sorry. You won't do. You should go to one of those agencies that find governesses for good families and ask them to find you a post as a governess."

"But I...I don't wish—"

"One shouldn't expect to be granted all one's wishes, child. If you are not suited to this work, there is nothing to be done."

"But...how do you know so quickly that I'm not suit-ed—?"

He stopped her with a glare. "I think I have enough information to make a judgment. There was a library in your an-cestral home, yes, but you are not, I hope, going to claim to have done extensive *reading,* are you? I would venture to guess that you've never *heard* of, say, Erasmus."

"I am sorry to say that you're in the wrong a third time," Ada responded, stung. She had taken on a new identity and was beginning to live the part. Poor, without resources and having nowhere to turn, the newly created Ada Surrey had to fight for her existence. "I am reasonably well-read, I think," she told him proudly. "I've read the classics, though not in Greek, a good deal of history and a bit of philosophy. I admit, however, that I am more partial to poetry and the works of Shakespeare than I am to Erasmus or Aquinas or Hume."

"Hmm." Mr. Finchley-Jones raised his eyebrows in sur-prise. He put on his spectacles and stared at her again. Then he shook his head in disbelief. "I must say, you don't *appear* to be the sort who reads. You seem to me to be the sort who writes romantic verses and capitalizes every noun in them. Who loves to put curlicues on her *T*'s and *Y*'s and little circles instead of dots on her *i*'s. I despise females who put circles on their *i*'s."

"I am guilty of having written romantic verse from time to time," Ada said, suppressing an urge to smile. "But I write a very neat hand. Would you like me to demonstrate?"

"Naturally I shall wish to examine your writing. It is the most important function you will be performing . . . *if* I should decide that you are suited to this post. However, we are still a long way from making such a decision, Miss . . . Miss . . ."

"Surrey. Ada Surrey."

"I admit, Miss Surrey, you seem to have more qualifications than I at first credited, but a bibliographer's assistant needs more than a good general education and a fine hand. To build a fine library, one is required to have a depth of knowledge in a wide variety of academic disciplines, a mind capable of classifying that knowledge, a sense of organization—"

"I should be surprised if you found *anyone* to fill all those requirements," Ada murmured dryly under her breath.

"I do not mean to imply that a mere assistant needs the qualifications of a fully trained bibliographer," the librarian pointed out coldly. "After all, the assistant can rely on the guidance of her employer—"

"Yes, that is what I meant," Ada assured him.

Mr. Finchley-Jones rose from his chair and came around the desk toward her. Taking off his lorgnette and using it to gesture, he proceeded to lecture the girl on the subject closest to his heart, the importance of a well-catalogued library. "It is necessary for you to understand, young woman, that there is more to setting up a fine library than listing and shelving the books. Books contain knowledge, but the knowledge in them is useless unless it can be *found*. A library has value for its books alone, but if those books are well indexed, the library becomes even more valuable. The more complete the index, the more valuable the books and the more efficiently the reader can retrieve the knowledge within them. I regret to have to admit that many collectors with whom I've come into contact still believe that a list of authors, inscribed alphabetically in a notebook, is enough of a catalogue for a private library. Why, I have even come upon some who believed that a mere *accession* list is enough! But fortunately Lord Mullineaux is not of that ilk. He has the true bibliophile's perspicacity to understand that books should be catalogued in many ways: according to subject, author, publication date, acquisition date . . ."

Ada had been nodding her agreement throughout most of this monologue, but as the bibliographer began to expound on the methods of cataloguing that he intended to pursue, she found her mind wandering. She wondered what sort of man this Lord Mullineaux was. She had not heard of many noblemen who took such interest in their books. This household into which fate had brought her was certainly a strange one.

As Mr. Finchley-Jones prosed on about the complications of bibliographical notation in a private collection, Ada's eyes wandered about the room. She began to realize that there was some sort of order in the piles of books on the floor; some of the piles had slips of paper of varying colors sticking out of them, some seemed to be grouped by similarity of size, and those on the table were distinguished by the elegance of their bindings. The librarian had evidently done a great deal of work already. She looked carefully around the room, trying to ascertain how many volumes the library contained.

Her eyes, rising from the contemplation of the piles of books on the floor to those on the shelves, fell upon the painting hanging over the fireplace. The Holland cover had slipped since she'd first looked at it, and the painting was now partially revealed. It was a portrait of a seated woman, with a gentleman standing behind her, his hand on her shoulder. There was something about the man's face that made her chest constrict.

". . . which is no small task in a library of this size," Mr. Finchley-Jones was saying. "I don't suppose you could even *guess* its size, could you, Miss Surrey?"

"Good God!" Ada murmured, her eyes fixed on the portrait.

"You find it an overwhelming question, do you?" the librarian said with a superior smile. "With the room in this condition I don't blame you. But why don't you hazard a guess?"

But the girl remained staring at the portrait with such concentration that she didn't even hear the question.

"Miss Surrey?" Mr. Finchley-Jones took a step toward her. "Miss Surrey! Haven't you been attending?"

His sharpness of tone caught her ear but could not deflect her mind. "Good God," she repeated, "who *is* that?"

Mr. Finchley-Jones frowned at her. "Who is who?"

"The man in the portrait."

"The late Lord Mullineaux, of course. With the Countess. But what has that to do with the subject of our—"

"The Countess? The *present* Countess?"

"Yes. That is she. Although I must say, Miss Surrey, I would have expected that a young woman in search of a position of employment would try to keep her mind on the subject at hand—"

"Then are you saying that the man in the portrait is the father of this Lord Mullineaux of whom you've been speaking?" Ada persisted.

"I was certainly *not* saying it, although it is quite true that you are looking at a portrait of Lord Mullineaux's parents. What I *was* saying was on the subject of the size of the library!"

Ada had torn her eyes from the portrait and turned for a moment to Mr. Finchley-Jones, but she didn't really see him. Instead, she was seeing the face of the gentleman from the inn, a face almost exactly like the one in the portrait. "Do you think, Mr. Finchley-Jones, that your Lord Mullineaux resembles this portrait of his father?" she asked, her heart pounding.

"I think, Miss Surrey, that it is none of your business. What *is* your business is to convince me that you would make a suitable assistant. I will tell you frankly that, with this tendency of yours to easy distraction, you are not succeeding in impressing me."

If she heard his reproof, she gave no sign. She was again staring fixedly at the painting. "He *does* resemble his father, doesn't he?"

"Very closely, if I'm any judge," the librarian said grudgingly. "Now may we return to the subject at hand?"

She was remembering the moment when the man with the face like the one in the portrait pounded on her bedroom door at the inn. He'd spoken a name, but she couldn't recall it. Not that it mattered. She didn't need to match the name. The man who'd kissed her at the inn was the same man who owned this library, who was the son of the Countess (her mother's best friend and her own godmother), and whom Cornelia (now lying abed upstairs in a luxurious guest bedroom) was here to snare. There wasn't any point even to *dream* of him any more. "What is his given name?" she asked anyway, unable to tear her eyes from the painting.

The librarian was glowering at her. "You are a most addlepated female. I don't see how you can pretend to believe that such conduct is suitable for a bibliographer's assistant. His lordship's given name is, I believe, Ivor."

"No," Ada murmured, shaking her head. "That wasn't it."

"Well, I *have* heard the Countess call him—"

"Don't tell me," Ada said, the sound of his lordship's voice ringing so clearly in her ears that it was more reality than memory. She turned away from the portrait with a sigh. *"Griff.* The Countess calls him Griff."

Chapter Eight

Despite his description of Ada as an addlepated female, Mr. Finchley-Jones agreed to employ her. The reasons he gave her for his decision were quite logical: first, he said, her handwriting proved to be neat and free from the feminine flourishes he so despised; second, she was indeed well-read, especially for a female of her years; and third, she seemed genuinely interested in bibliography and very willing to learn.

Deep in his heart he knew that the logical reasons he'd given the girl had nothing to do with his decision. He'd intended from the first to employ her. He'd intended to hire her even if she'd never heard of Erasmus. Or even if she always put circles on her *i*'s. She was young and very pretty, and she brought a radiance into the dingy room that had never been there before. His life's work was important to him, and his bibliographical pursuits were, he was convinced, making a real contribution to society, but he couldn't deny that his days had always been drab. Why shouldn't he permit a little brightness to enter into his life?

His outward attitude, however, showed nothing of this. He remained cold, critical and forbidding. He put her to work at once copying the publishing information from the title pages of a pile of scientific books into one of his pristine notebooks. But he helped clear a portion of the library table for her to work on and dusted off one of the leather chairs for her. And during the morning he couldn't keep himself from looking up frequently from his work and letting his eyes feast on her bent head. It was the most pleasant workday morning he'd ever spent.

When Clara brought his lunch on a tray, he excused his new assistant (so that she could take her luncheon downstairs) most reluctantly. He would have liked her to join him for luncheon, but it was not appropriate for a lowly female copyist to take her meals with a scholar-bibliographer of his importance. Clara's shrewd eyes did not miss the look on his face as he watched his assistant leave the room. "He likes ye, Ada," she giggled as the two made their way down the back stairs. "I think y' made yerself a conquest."

Ada grinned back. "Don't be silly. He thinks I'm an addlepate."

"That may be," the maid laughed, "but that never stopped a man from admirin' the addlepate's pretty mouth or tiny waist."

Ada didn't debate the point. She liked Clara and enjoyed the girl's teasing. Clara had paid her a visit in her bedroom the night before, just to get acquainted and make her feel welcome. None of the other maids had done so. It had been fun sitting on the edge of the bed with Clara, listening to the maid's description of the downstairs life, of the quirks of the various members of the staff, of the view of their employers that the servants held. Clara was a cheerful, honest, shrewd young woman who viewed her world with a lusty optimism. Ada felt that, in this life of deception she'd embarked upon, she would need a friend like Clara. The outspoken, straightforward maid would not only be a good companion but a good advisor.

The budding friendship between Ada and the housemaid turned out to be more beneficial than Ada dreamed. One night, two days after her arrival, when all the staff had retired for the night, Clara tapped at the door of Ada's tiny bedroom. When Ada opened the door, Clara refused to come in. She stood glowering in the doorway in her nightdress and worn swansdown robe. Ada could see her pursed mouth in the light of the candle the girl carried. "Clara?" she asked. "Is something amiss?"

"Sssh," Clara whispered, "someone'll 'ear." She raised the candle so that she could see Ada's face more clearly. "Who are ye, Ada?"

"What? I don't think I understand what—"

"I asked who are ye? I mean, *really.*"

Ada felt her heart sinking. The past two days had been so pleasant and uneventful that she'd begun to feel safe. "Wh-Who *am* I?" she echoed, trying to hide her alarm.

Clara looked nervously up and down the narrow corridor to make certain no one else was about. "I know ye ain't Mr. Finchley-Jones's real assistant," she hissed, "so don't playact wi' me."

"What makes you say that?"

"The real one came t' the back door this noon. Miss Latcham." With another quick glance down the hall, she stepped over the threshold and closed the door quietly. "Lucky there was no one about t' answer the door but me."

"Oh, dear!" Ada dropped her eyes from her friend's face. "What did you say to her, Clara?"

"Ye don't need t' worry. I didn't give ye away. I told 'er that 'is lordship changed 'is mind about organizin' the liberry. I said that Mr. Finchley-Jones ain't no longer employed 'ere."

Ada bit her nether lip guiltily. "She . . . she must have been very upset."

"No, she wasn't. She said she'd only come t' explain t' Mr. Finchley-Jones why she 'adn't kept 'er appointment. Seems 'er sister's took ill, and she 'as to go t' Manchester t' care fer 'er, so she couldn't take the post."

"Well, that's a relief," Ada sighed. "I wouldn't have wished to deprive a worthy woman of her employment."

Clara frowned at her suspiciously. "That's very well an' good, Ada, but it don't explain 'ow you come t' be in Miss Latcham's place."

Ada shook her head unhappily and sank down upon her bed. "I can't explain it to you right now, Clara. All I can say is that I'm very grateful to you for helping me . . . and for keeping my secret."

"Ye kin *keep* yer gratitude!" Clara declared in her forthright way. "I ain't goin' t' keep yer secret unless I'm sure y' ain't up to somethin' havey-cavey. Y' ain't plannin' on robbin' 'er ladyship, are ye? Or doin' somethin' t' hurt the family?"

"No, of course not. You can't really believe that."

"I don't know what t' believe."

"Just believe that a mistake was made and I . . . I took advantage of it, that's all."

"A mistake? Ah, yes, I remember somethin' about a mistake when ye first came 'ere. You said somethin' to Mrs. Mudge about mistaken identity." She set her candle on the nighttable, sat down beside Ada and peered at her closely. "Ye never came 'ere to work in the liberry at all, did ye? Ye didn't even know anythin' about it."

Ada lowered her head. "That's right. I didn't."

"Then why *did* ye come, Ada? I suspicioned from the first y' ain't the sort fer domestic service. If ye came t' the wrong door, why didn't ye say so and leave?"

"It wasn't the wrong door."

"It wasn't?" The housemaid shook her head in confusion. "Then ye must've come t' see 'er ladyship. Well, why didn't ye do it?"

"I discovered that I was too late."

"Too late to see her ladyship? Because of the dinner party, you mean?"

"Too late to see her at all. Please don't ask me anything more, Clara. I can only tell you that my coming here was a mistake, but I didn't realize it until too late. I had neither the money nor the means to go back home, so when I realized I could find employment here, I took the chance. Some day I promise to tell you all. But meanwhile, if I swear that I mean no harm to anyone, will you remain my friend?"

"There was never no question that I'd stay yer friend," Clara said, letting go of her suspicions and permitting herself to smile. "I just wanted to know that bein' yer friend wouldn't bring me t' the gibbet." She picked up the candle and went to the door. "If we *do* end up on the gibbet, Ada," she whispered as she let herself out, "I 'ope ye'll tell me *then* what it was all about. Goodnight, m'dear."

Mr. Finchley-Jones was not entirely happy with his new assistant. She was certainly delightful to look upon and intelligent enough when she attended to his instructions. But she had an infuriating way of taking mental absences at unexpected moments. He would look up from his work and see her staring out ahead of her, her pen poised in her hand unmoving. Sometimes a simple clearing of his throat would rouse her, and she would immediately resume work, but at other times he might cough like a consumptive for five minutes without shaking her from her reverie.

Another case in point was the girl's dismaying habit of staring at the portrait. He'd made no objection to her removing the dust cover from the painting, but sometimes, when he caught her staring at it, he wished he'd not given his permission for the cover to be removed. It was done now, and he was not the sort to go back on his word—he disliked to appear indecisive—but if he'd known that she would spend long moments gazing at it, he would have ordered that the cover be kept in place. One time he'd even asked her what she found so fascinating about it. "Everything," she'd murmured. "The late Lord Mullineaux looks so assured . . . as if he understood completely what sort of man he'd made of himself and was satisfied with the result."

"Ha!" he'd responded gruffly. "That's a very fanciful interpretation. I'm told the fellow was a gambler and a notorious rake."

But Ada didn't even seem to hear him. "And her ladyship is fascinating as well. She was beautiful, wasn't she?"

"She is still beautiful. You will see that for yourself one day, for she sometimes comes to visit here to see how the work is progressing."

Ada still seemed not to hear. "But there is something about her . . . a self-consciousness, I think . . . as if she always feels the world's eyes on her. An *awareness* of her beauty that weakens her character."

"You can see all that in the painting?" he'd asked, being himself drawn into a fascinated contemplation of the portrait. But at that point she'd become aware of his presence and blushingly returned to her work.

Another problem—and this was the most serious source of his discomfiture concerning her—was her inability to keep track of the papers, lists and notes that passed through her hands. It wasn't that she lacked neatness or the ability to grasp the intricacies of the cataloguing system. No, the problem was her forgetfulness. She simply could not keep track of papers. Slips of notepaper, information cards, sheets of records somehow managed to hide themselves away from her. Long hours would then have to be spent tracking them down. One accession slip was found in a copy of *The Shepheardes Calender* (which she'd begun to read in fascination until his cough roused her) where she'd evidently placed it to use as a bookmark. An important acquisition list was found (after three hours of desperate searching) folded into a wad and wedged under the leg of her chair. "The chair was a bit wobbly," she explained sheepishly when he finally discovered it and waved it angrily under her nose.

It was when Ada was engaged in one of these humiliating searches that her ladyship, the Countess Mullineaux herself, paid her first visit to the library. In fact, Ada was on her knees at the time, searching for the second volume of a three-volume set of Grotius' *Rights of War and Peace* among the piles of books on the floor. It was Mr. Finchley-Jones, of course, who'd discovered that the volume was missing. He'd made a great outcry about it, pointing out in a tone of pained impatience that the set was very valuable and that the loss of one volume would make the other two worthless. Ada assured him that she would find it. She remembered quite clearly that she'd had it in her hand the day before when she was doing her assigned task of listing all the works in the collection on the history of jurisprudence. "I'm certain," she explained to her apoplectic employer, "that it is only temporarily mislaid." What she failed to explain was that she'd mislaid the volume when she'd come upon an ancient and very shabby book called *The Songes and Sonnettes,* poetry of Wyatt, Surrey and others, collected by a printer called Tottel. It contained so many wonderful lyric poems (many of which she'd never seen before) that she'd carried it with her to read over luncheon and then up to her bedroom to read by candlelight before retiring. Somehow, while she'd been distracted by *The Songes and Sonnettes,* the Grotius volume had disappeared.

The Countess didn't even notice the young woman kneeling on the floor in the corner. "Mr. Finchley-Jones," she clarioned from the doorway, "I have news for you from my son." She sailed into the room in a flurry of gauze ruffles (trimming a green silk morning robe that looked shockingly out of place in this room of dusty books), an open letter in her hand. "He writes from Wales that he's crated and sent you no fewer than three thousand volumes from his grandfather's collection, in addition to some interesting manuscripts and plates."

"Three thousand!" the librarian exclaimed, overwhelmed. He jumped to his feet. "Your ladyship! That is most exciting news. I had no *idea* he would be able to accomplish so much so soon."

"My son is indefatigable when he's embarked on a project that interests him. He asks me to tell you that he himself is on his way home and will give you the details of his selections in person. I think we may expect him home by tomorrow evening at the—Good God! Who is *that?*"

Ada scrambled to her feet, her heart thudding in her chest. Here was the Countess Mullineaux herself—her deceased mother's best friend, her own godmother, the mother of the gentleman she could not erase from her mind—and Ada had been discovered on her hands and knees in the dust! She brushed nervously at her skirt with one hand and pushed back her hair from her forehead with the other (leaving a wide streak of dirt across her forehead as she did so) and dropped an awkward curtsey. "Your l-ladyship," she stammered.

The Countess gaped at her. "You can't be Mr. Finchley-Jones's assistant, can you? I was under the impression she was a woman well into middle age."

"That was Miss Latcham," Mr. Finchley-Jones explained hastily. "Miss Latcham seems mysteriously to have vanished. This is Miss Ada Surrey who was sent in her place."

"Oh, I see." The Countess graciously held out her hand. "How do you do, Miss Surrey? I must say that your employer seems to be misusing you."

"But . . . you don't look *at all* the same," Ada murmured, staring at the Countess with a sudden, intense concentration.

"I beg your pardon?" the Countess asked, nonplussed.

"I don't think the artist's view of you was sound. You are much more lovely than—"

Her ladyship turned to the librarian in surprise. "What is this young woman babbling about, Mr. Finchley-Jones?"

"Miss Surrey, *please!*" the librarian hissed. "Forgive her, your ladyship. It's your portrait. She is quite fascinated with it."

"Oh, I *see.*" She turned to Ada with a smile. "Are you saying, Miss Surrey, that the artist didn't do me justice? That is a very kind of you, considering that he painted it twenty-five years ago. Good God! A quarter of a century! I hadn't realized . . ." She turned to study the painting herself. "Heavens, was I ever that young? What is it you see, young woman, that you think the artist missed?"

Ada, waking up to the fact that she'd permitted herself to be distracted from reality by her first glimpse of the Countess's face, reddened in embarrassment. "The eyes, I . . . I think. He missed the . . . the sweetness in them."

Lady Mullineaux studied the young woman with interest. "I must say, Mr. Finchley-Jones, you've found yourself a most unusual assistant."

"Yes, so it seems," Mr. Finchley-Jones agreed ruefully.

"But as I was saying before we were diverted into contemplating my portrait, you seem to be using the girl ill. Do you always require that your assistants crawl about in the dirt as Miss Surrey was doing when I came in?"

The librarian winced in chagrin. "I don't . . . that is, it isn't a requirement, exactly . . ."

"It's my fault entirely," Ada put in quickly. "I mislaid a book, and I've been searching—"

"But, my dear child, that is no excuse for him to expect you to crawl about like that. Surely, Mr. Finchley-Jones, you could have done the searching *for* her."

"Yes, but I . . . I . . ."

"What he means, my lady," Ada explained, "is that he cannot *always* be crawling about for me."

"Always?" Her ladyship's eyebrows rose curiously.

Ada twisted her fingers together behind her back and lowered her head miserably. "I'm always misplacing things, you see."

"Really?" The countess looked from the librarian to the girl and back again, her lips twitching in amusement. "That seems an odd quality for a bibliographer's assistant."

"It is an unfortunate trait, to be sure, your ladyship," Mr. Finchley-Jones said in hasty defense, "but I assure you that in every other way Miss Surrey is quite admirable. She is remarkably well-read for someone of her years, she has an excellent understanding of my goals for cataloguing Lord Mullineaux's collection, and she is a superior scribe."

The countess held up her hands. "You don't have to defend her to me, Mr. Finchley-Jones," she said, casting Ada a warm smile, "especially after she has been kind enough to describe me as having sweetness about the eyes. I certainly did not mean to imply that there was any question in my mind about the suitability of this young lady for the post. Even if there were such a question in my mind, my son would surely object to my interfering in your selection of an assistant. So, please, my dear girl . . ." She crossed the room and took Ada's hand. "What did you say your given name was?"

"Ada, your l-ladyship."

"Ada. It is a lovely name, I have a goddaughter by that name, you know. Please, Ada, you needn't look so frightened. I have no intention of sacking you, even if you *do* have a tendency to mislay things."

With that, the Countess waved her letter in a farewell gesture to Mr. Finchley-Jones and wafted to the door. "But in future, if there is any crawling about on the floor to be done, call one of the footmen to do it. Good day to you both."

Chapter Nine

The news of Lord Mullineaux's imminent return spread with amazing speed through the household, causing waves of excited activity below stairs. This unusual stir surprised Ada greatly. Since the house was already very efficiently run, she didn't know why his lordship's arrival should cause such a flurry. Clara explained that Lord Mullineaux was so popular with the household staff that they went to great lengths to welcome him on his return from a journey. Everyone from Mrs. Mudge (who saw to it that there were fresh flowers in his bedroom no matter what the season) to the cook (who prepared all his favorite delicacies for his homecoming dinner) made special efforts to please him.

Ada could only gape in wonder at the stir. Everyone seemed to know that Lord Mullineaux was a rake, yet this fact seemed not to affect the feelings of the members of the household in the least. Everyone, from the Countess to the youngest of the scullery maids, spoke of him with respect and affection. All of them were quite willing to excuse his excesses, as she had done that night at the inn.

Ada *herself* anticipated his lordship's arrival with severe inner quaking. Uppermost in her mind was the fear that he would come into the library and recognize her. What a humiliating moment that would be! It would be horrible for them both, *she* because she would have to lie about her identity and maintain her pretense of being a lowly servant in his household, and *he* because he would find someone in his own employ who knew firsthand about his rakish tendencies. It was all well and good for his lordship to accept being surrounded by a staff who knew all his secrets (and who were so devoted to him that they forgave him his trespasses), but to harbor in his own household someone who *had actually been involved with him in one of his exploits* might be beyond what one could expect of him.

And there was something else that caused Ada to quake at the prospect of Lord Mullineaux's arrival. It was the problem of Cornelia. What if Cornelia should discover her presence in the house? Ada had been dreading that possibility since her arrival, but that it might happen in front of Lord Mullineaux was an unbearable prospect. She seriously considered running away before his lordship set foot on the premises, but she was in no better position *now* to make her way back to Gloucester than she'd been on her arrival. Wages, she'd learned from Clara, were dispensed monthly. She had occupied her post for less than a fortnight. (She had never asked Mr. Finchley-Jones what her wages would be, but she'd convinced herself that the money would be sufficient for passage on the stage to Gloucester.) She had yet another fortnight to wait for her pay, and that meant that immediate flight would not be possible.

Her only consolation was the fact that she'd been able to avoid being discovered by Cornelia thus far. With any luck, she should be able to avoid a confrontation for a while longer. All she could do was hope that she could stay out of Cornelia's way for the short time that still remained.

But Cornelia's presence in the house presented still another problem for Ada. If the Countess truly intended to throw Cornelia at her son, Ada didn't wish to be a witness to the affair. It was painful enough to know that her dreams of attaching the appealing "Griff" Mullineaux to herself were quite hopeless; she certainly didn't wish to exacerbate that pain by watching Cornelia attach him. Ada had, over the years, become quite accustomed to Cornelia's taking precedence over her in all sorts of competitions both major and minor, and she'd believed that she'd trained herself to rise above petty jealousy at Cornelia's successes. But her character was not strong enough to rise above jealousy in *this* particular case. Ada had to admit to herself that she hoped with all her heart that, this time, Cornelia would fall on her face.

At the very moment that Ada was thinking these thoughts, her cousin Cornelia was discussing Lord Mullineaux's arrival with his mother. "I hope his lordship will not dislike finding a stranger in his home," she remarked as the two sat over breakfast making plans for the afternoon. Both ladies, still casually bedecked in their morning robes, were sipping their coffees while her ladyship went through the pile of invitations, bills and messages that the butler had placed at her elbow. "After all, he doesn't even know of my existence, I imagine."

"My dear child," the Countess said, glancing over at her

guest with a small frown, "I am mistress of this house. My son would be the first to assure you that, while he may be nominally the head of it, the ruling hand is mine."

Cornelia ran her fingers through her thick, still-undressed hair with languid grace. "I didn't mean to imply," she laughed, "that he would throw me out in the cold. I only meant that he might not be pleased to find it necessary to make polite conversation with a stranger after returning from a long and tiring journey."

The Countess did not answer even with a smile but merely turned her eyes back to her letters. She knew what Cornelia expected to hear in reply: *Oh, la, girl, my son will be so taken with you at first glance he'll be grateful to me forever that I arranged for you to be with us,* or words to that effect. Well, Lady Mullineaux had no intention of uttering them to feed the girl's vanity. In the fortnight that Cornelia Haydon had been with her, the Countess had had ample time to recognize the signs of vanity in her guest and to have had her fill of the girl. In fact, she was regretting that she'd ever invited her. When she'd sent the letter to Cornelia's mother in Gloucester, she had hoped that the woman would have the generosity to send Ada Surringham down. Ada was her goddaughter, after all, and had not had a mother to nurture her since she was a babe. But Dorothea had sent her own daughter, with the message that Ada herself had declined the invitation. It was too bad. Lady Mullineaux would have liked to get to know the daughter of her dear, lost friend.

Of course, she'd had a more pressing—and more selfish— purpose in mind when she'd sent the invitation. She'd hoped to find someone suitable for Griff. When she'd first glimpsed Cornelia, she'd been overjoyed. The girl seemed to embody everything the Countess had had in mind for her son. The tall, willowy, almond-eyed Cornelia was undeniably a beauty. On the three occasions since her arrival that Lady Mullineaux took her into society, the girl had been instantly surrounded by admiring men. Even Griff, she was sure, would not be immune to such spectacular looks. And the girl had other qualities to recommend her: she was of impeccable lineage, she was properly reared, she could play the pianoforte with considerable ability, and she could converse with some wit and without the simpering, giggling inanities which afflicted the conversation of so many of the females on the current Marriage Mart. But even with all these assets, Cornelia failed to win her affection. After the girl had been with her for only two days, Lady Mullineaux discovered that she'd changed her mind—she didn't wish Griff to be attracted to Cornelia after all!

It was not merely that Cornelia was vain. Lady Mullineaux could forgive that in a young beauty. She'd suffered from vanity herself in her youth. She knew how hard it was for a youthful beauty to keep from being vain; she remembered very well how it was when every man who looked at her (and it didn't matter what his age; he could be seventeen or seventy) ogled or petted her, played the poseur, flirted, flattered and behaved foolishly. How could an innocent young girl *keep* from having her head turned by such obvious admiration from the men? She remembered that she herself had been odiously conceited in her youth. It was only when she matured, after having benefited from the wise counsel of her good friend and the challenge of life with a demanding husband, that she'd realized how ephemeral and insubstantial was reliance upon a pretty face.

Yes, she could forgive Cornelia's vanity if she could see a sign that the girl's character showed promise of improvement in maturity. But the Countess could find no such sign. Instead, she discovered something else about Cornelia she could not like. It was hard to put a finger on, but there was something so . . . so complacent, so self-satisfied about the girl that at times the Countess would have liked to wring her neck. It was as if it had never occurred to the girl to doubt herself. She simply floated through life assuming that every choice she made was in the best of taste, that every remark she made was unquestionably clever, and that everything she did was right. What made these assumptions especially irritating was that Cornelia was, except for her looks, not at all above the ordinary.

But the Countess had invited her and was now trapped. She had promised to keep the girl for the season. There was no way to prevent Griff from crossing her path. What an irony! Before Cornelia had arrived, the Countess had occupied herself with plans to trap Griff into paying her heed and escorting her about town. But now that she wanted her son to ignore her guest entirely, he would undoubtedly be attracted to the girl. Why shouldn't he be? He'd been attracted to the wrong sort of female for years.

"Shall we dine at home tonight, if Lord Mullineaux arrives in time?" Cornelia asked suddenly, putting down her coffee cup.

"Yes, I expect so. I told Dolly Harrington that we were unlikely to attend her ball tonight." She looked across at Cornelia with a gleam as a hopeful idea struck her. "Why do you ask, Cornelia? Do you prefer to attend the ball tonight?" She smiled at her guest archly. "Did you perhaps plan an *assignation* at the Harringtons', my dear? If so, I have no objection to your going off to the ball without me. I'm certain that Mrs. Delafield will be willing to act as your chaperone in my place."

"Go off without you?" Cornelia dismissed the idea with a languorous wave of her hand. "I wouldn't dream of it. Besides, I wouldn't miss his lordship's homecoming for anything in the world. I think I shall wear my new green jaconet for the occasion. It is cut in the latest mode, yet it is perfectly appropriate for an intimate dinner. Didn't you say the other day that his lordship has a weakness for green?"

Lord Mullineaux arrived in plenty of time for dinner. His mother greeted him with her usual affectionate cheerfulness, hiding the fact that she felt a great deal of inner trepidation. She couldn't shake off a sense that she'd brought on a catastrophe by trying to interfere in his life. When Cornelia rustled in to the drawing room in her clinging green gown (with the décolletage cut so daringly low that the Countess felt her eyebrows climb in spite of herself), she introduced her son to her guest. Cornelia was a breathtaking sight; her green gown clung to her tall, shapely form as if it had been damped, her gold curls fell in charming disarray from a jeweled fastening at the top of her head, and her almond eyes glowed. *Good God*, the Countess thought, *my goose is cooked!*

But if Griff was taken with the girl, his mother saw no sign of it. Throughout the dinner he appeared to be preoccupied with other matters, and he gave the girl no more than the minimal attention that good manners required. Cornelia tried in vain to capture his attention by making flirtatious remarks, obvious sallies that grew more challenging and less subtle as the dinner progressed. "I've heard much about your prowess with the ladies, your lordship," she ventured with desperate coquetry at the meal's conclusion, smiling at him enticingly over her wineglass. "One common *on-dit* has it that you are able to win the most icy heart by a mere smile or an easy witticism.''

"Is that what you've heard?" Griff answered indulgently. "Surely you don't credit such nonsense as that."

"I did credit it until now." She leaned back in her chair with an air of saucy disdain. "But now that I've seen your smile and heard you speak, I find that thus far you haven't been able to crack *my* icy heart."

"Then that, Miss Haydon," Griff responded with the pleasant patience one might show to a cocky child, "should be a lesson to you on the nature of *on-dits*. They are always exaggerated and should never be believed."

Her ladyship smiled to herself as they rose from the table. She should have known better than to worry about Griff. If he was to be captured, it would take more than a pretty face and a modish green gown to bait the trap.

Chapter Ten

One of Mullineaux's acquaintances had recognized his returning carriage and had immediately reported to his cronies at White's that Griff had returned from rustication. Thus it was that, early the next morning, Aubrey Tait burst into his lordship's bedroom. "Why didn't you tell me you were back?" he demanded of the sleeping figure on the bed.

Griff's valet tried valiantly to pull Aubrey from the room. "His lordship told me to wake him at eleven, Mr. Tait. *Eleven!* It is now barely ten. Wouldn't you care to wait in the breakfast room for a while? Symonds will be happy to serve you some breakfast."

"Go away, Crowley, go away. I have important matters to discuss with his lordship. Come on, Griff, wake up!"

Griff stirred, blinked up at the friend bending over him and groaned. The valet, hovering guiltily in the background, threw Griff a gesture of helplessness. Griff sat up, stretched and fixed a baleful eye on his friend. "Confound it, Aubrey, have you no feelings?"

"I *asked* Mr. Tait to wait in the breakfast room," Crowley said, throwing the intruder a look of reproach.

"It's all right, Crowley. Open the drapes, and take yourself off. We'll let the impatient Mr. Tait help me to dress in your place."

"Who," Aubrey demanded as soon as the valet had left the room, "was the magnificent creature who passed me in the outer doorway?"

"What magnificent creature?" Griff asked, yawning as he threw his legs over the side of the bed and headed for the washstand.

"Don't play games with me, Griff. You must know her. She seems to be living here." He followed his friend across the room. "I assume you know whom you have residing on your premises."

Griff lowered his face into the bowl his valet had thoughtfully filled before departing and came up sputtering. "You must mean Miss Haydon," he said, vigorously towelling. "She's a guest of my mother's. From Gloucester."

"A relation of yours?" Aubrey queried interestedly.

"No, I don't believe so. I think she's the daughter of a childhood friend of Mama's. Why are you so interested?"

"Who *wouldn't* be interested? Have you taken a good look at her? She's a regular out-and-outer!"

"Is that why you roused me, you bobbing-block? I ought to draw your cork."

Aubrey was gazing out ahead of him pensively. "I don't suppose it would do me any good to ask the Countess to introduce me. She probably invited her here in order to catch *your* eye."

"Oh, I don't think so. If an introduction means so much to you, go ahead and ask for it. Tell Mama you have my blessing."

"Thanks, old man, I will."

"Just hand me a shirt from that drawer before you go, will you?"

"I'll hand you a shirt, but I'm not going just yet. I haven't told you why I came."

Griff paused in the act of buttoning his smalls. "Was it not to worm an introduction to Miss Haydon?"

"No, for I didn't know of her existence 'til I saw her gliding out the door. She was wearing the most fetching bonnet, Griff... with a rose hanging over the side and brushing her cheek. I was shaken, I can tell you. Of course, she didn't even throw a glance at me. I suppose I shan't ever manage to win her attention, shall I? She stands at least a hand's breadth taller than I."

"Don't worry, old fellow. I'll have Mama whisper in her ear that you're as rich as Croesus, and you'll appear a foot taller the next time she sees you."

"Don't tease, Griff. I wouldn't mind if you *did* tell her that I'm well to pass. It's the height of vulgarity, I know, but if it would help to make her notice me..."

"Why don't you wait until you're introduced before you fall into despond? Who knows? Perhaps she'll adore your apple cheeks at first sight. In the meantime, see if you can find my boots, will you? If you're supposed to be taking Crowley's place, you're doing a paltry job of it."

As Griff drew on his boots, Aubrey forced his mind to return to the matter that had brought him. "I think you came back too soon," he said, sitting down beside his friend on the bed. "The Alcorn matter is still not settled, you know."

"Don't be a nodcock, Aubrey. I took care of that before I reached Wales."

"Took care of it?" Aubrey asked, confused. "What do you mean?"

"I mean that after you and I parted company in Oxfordshire, I went to a country inn called the Black Boar. It was a quiet place, quite out of the way, but Alcorn managed to find me. I thought for a while that a duel would be inevitable. But through the most fortunate circumstance, I managed to convince him that I was making off to Wales with someone else entirely."

"With someone else? You don't mean it! Are you implying that he believed there was *another* lady—?"

"Yes. Just so."

"I don't believe it! Even Alcorn wouldn't swallow such a fantastic tale!"

"But he did. And so would you, Aubrey, if I'd introduced you to the lady herself."

"You *introduced* him? To a living, breathing lady?"

Griff grinned at his friend's dumbfounded expression. "Yes, you mooncalf, she was very much alive. And, I might add, a very taking little creature in every way."

"Griff, you *Trojan!* Where did you find her? Did you dress up a tavern wench to play the role?"

"Not at all. I found a genuine lady. She had soft hands, a voice like music and the most unforgettable eyes. Alcorn was completely taken aback when he laid eyes on her."

Aubrey chortled and shook his head with admiration. "Dash it, I'd have given a monkey to see his face." But his elation quickly faded and his expression became dubious. "But, Griff," he added worriedly, "that may have been the case at the time, but the effect must have worn off afterwards. He's been heard to make threatening remarks about you at the club. I heard him do so myself, just the day before yesterday. And when the rumor spread that you were on your way home, they say he packed Julia off, kicking and screaming, to his mother in East Anglia."

"The man's a fool. If he were less severe with her, she might feel less inclined to flout him."

"Yes, but this talk don't signify where you're concerned. What will you do if Alcorn comes looking for you *again* with his pistol case under his arm?"

Griff peered into his shaving mirror and rubbed at his stubbled chin. "I can tell you what I *won't* do, Aubrey. I won't run off a second time. If the man is bound to have his duel, there can be nothing for it but to let him have his way. Shall I shave now or take you down to breakfast first?"

"Let's take breakfast. Perhaps the divine Miss Haydon will return, and you can make me known to her." He helped Griff into a dressing gown and the two headed for the door. "Are you really as indifferent to your mother's breathtaking guest as you pretend, old man?"

Griff shook his head. "It's no pretense. Something's happened to me, Aubrey, and I don't know what to make of it. I have no interest in my mother's guest, undeniably lovely as she is, or in any other female who's crossed my path lately. Except for..."

Aubrey cocked an interested eyebrow. "Except for whom?"

"The girl at the inn." He paused with his hand on the doorknob, his brows knit and his eyes puzzled. "Ever since the night at the Black Boar Inn, I haven't been able to get that young lady out of my mind."

Aubrey, just stepping over the threshold, stopped in his tracks. "What young lady?"

"The one I told you of. The one who pretended to be running off with me."

Aubrey gaped at his friend for a long moment, and then his face took on the closest approximation of a leer that his apple cheeks could manage. "Aha!" he chortled. "Don't tell me that Griff Mullineaux, who's never let a female get the best of him, has finally succumbed to a weakness of the heart!"

"I wouldn't go so far as that," Griff objected, urging his friend to the stairs. "You needn't fly into alt over this, you know. Besides," he added ruefully, "nothing can come of it."

"Come now, you don't expect me to swallow such fustian. Are you trying to make me believe that this creature from the inn—a girl who appeared out of nowhere—has spurned your advances?"

"No, that wasn't it. I didn't *make* any advances. I didn't even ask her name."

Aubrey, clumping down the stairs ahead of him, turned

round in surprise. "You clunch! Why didn't you?"

"I don't know." He lowered his head as the memories of the night in the inn assaulted his mind. "I was afraid she was a bit . . . maggoty."

"Maggoty? She was *maggoty?* Good God! I thought you disliked those muddleheaded sorts."

"I do. But she was only *slightly* maggoty. Just whimsical, you know, with her head a bit in the clouds. Very charming, all the same. I'm quite sorry, now, that I didn't get her name. If I had guessed that she would linger in my memory like this . . ."

Aubrey couldn't believe what he was hearing. He considered the matter for a while and then shook his head. "Do you know what I think? I think your journey has put you out of frame." He turned and proceeded down the stairs. "Once you've resumed your normal activities, you'll realize this is some sort of temporary aberration. A fortnight from now, or sooner, I'll remind you that you claimed to have lost your heart to a maggoty female, and you'll laugh me out of the house. Ivor Griffith, the Viscount Mullineaux, with a maggoty female! That's a tale beyond belief! If you ask me, it's a good thing you *didn't* get her name."

"Easy for you to say," Griff muttered under his breath as he followed his friend down the stairs. "You didn't see her eyes."

Chapter Eleven

Aubrey lingered on the premises until after two, but when the beautiful Miss Haydon had still not returned from her shopping trip at that late hour, he gave up the vigil and departed. Griff, taking advantage of his temporary solitude, started toward the library to see Mr. Finchley-Jones. He had intended to make the interview with the librarian his first order of business for the day, but he'd had to wait until Aubrey took his leave. Neither Aubrey nor any of his friends knew much about his bibliographical activities. He'd always been interested in books, but it was not an interest shared by his London circle. His friends were members of the Corinthian set, most of whom admired—and even envied—his reputation as a sportsman and a Lothario, but few of whom would be pleased to learn about this freakishly bookish aspect of his nature. They would think it inconsistent with his character, and they would find it as pathetic and inexplicable as his falling in love with a maggoty female.

The only person who was aware of this passionate interest in books was his mother. The Countess, although not a very great reader herself, had been educated by her husband to appreciate the value to the nation of increasing the number and quality of private libraries. When her son showed, at quite an early age, an interest in continuing the work of his father and grandfather, she encouraged him. Almost from the first it was clear to her that her son had greater intellectual gifts than his forebears and would make of the library a noteworthy achievement. It made her proud to realize that her son, who in other ways was as profligate, spoiled, self-indulgent and rakish as the other men of his class, had this one overriding interest to make his life less superficial and more purposeful than that of most of his contemporaries.

On his way down to see his bibliographer, Griff passed the sitting room where his mother sat at her desk writing letters. "Are you very busy, Mama?" he asked, pausing in the doorway.

She turned. "Only writing invitations for the ball I'm giving for Miss Haydon next week. They can wait, if you have something to speak to me about."

"A ball for Miss Haydon? I didn't know you were planning such elaborate festivities in her honor."

The Countess sighed. "I'm afraid I must. I promised her mother that I would introduce her into society. A ball is *de rigueur*."

"I see. Then I won't keep you, since you're so busy. I only wanted to ask if you'd care to come down to the library with me. I thought you might be interested to hear Finchley-Jones's report of his progress and my report on what I found in Wales."

She put down her pen at once. "Of course I'm interested, dearest. But why go down into the dust of the library? Have Mr. Finchley-Jones join us here."

While waiting for Mr. Finchley-Jones to arrive, Griff described to his mother with enthusiasm some of his discoveries in his grandfather's collection. "I didn't dream of the riches I'd find. There was a great deal of duplication, of course, but more than three thousand volumes were worthy of shipment. I'm deucedly impatient for the crates to arrive so that I can show you what I found. There's a hand-lettered Chaucer, an edition of Montaigne I didn't know existed, a tall Elzevir with the widest possible margins and several other volumes of considerable interest."

"Was there anything the equal of your Tottel's?" his mother asked, smiling at his un-Corinthian excitement.

"I doubt that I shall ever equal *that* find, Mama. A first-edition Tottel's is a jewel. A rarity of that kind is not to be found every day. Nevertheless, the Wales library held a number of gems. Grandfather may not have realized himself how many treasures he'd garnered over the years. When his books are added to mine, and all properly catalogued and indexed, you may find yourself putting up with a good many visiting scholars. How will you feel when one of your tonnish friends comes face-to-face with a shabby, bespectacled scholar in the hallway?"

"I shan't mind, my love. Not a bit. In fact, I shall make it clear to all and sundry that having scholars about the house is quite the thing. Lady Heathley has her orphanage, Tricia Farrington has her Bibles-for-the-Heathen, and I shall have my scholars."

Mr. Finchley-Jones arrived carrying several of his notebooks under his arm. As was his wont in time of stress, he chewed nervously on his underlip. Knowing full well that his lordship would not be pleased, he reported on the progress he'd made in the weeks of his lordship's absence. He was quite right. Lord Mullineaux's face fell in disappointment. "I should have thought you'd be much further along by this time," he said. "You did engage an assistant, did you not? I seem to remember your showing me a letter about a woman who had been of help to Lord Lesterbrook's librarian."

"Yes, my lord. A Miss Latcham. But she disappeared. The Bibliographical Society sent along a Miss Surrey in her place, and I engaged her. She has not the experience that Miss Latcham had, but she is quick to learn."

"Not quick enough, I daresay. Most of these entries seem to be in *your* hand. What has this Miss Surrey been *doing* for a fortnight?"

Mr. Finchley-Jones shifted uncomfortably from one foot to the other, bit his nether lip again and dropped his eyes to his shoes. "She has been . . . er . . . concentrating on jurisprudence. She has much to recommend her, my lord, but she has a tendency, sometimes, toward . . . er . . . abstraction . . ."

"Abstraction?"

"Yes, my lord. Her mind, though decidedly a good one, does sometimes . . . wander."

"Good God!" Griff muttered in disgust. "Just what we need . . . an assistant with a wandering mind. Get rid of her, Finchley-Jones, and find yourself someone capable."

"Get *rid* of her?" the librarian echoed miserably. "But I—"

"Really, Griff," his mother interjected, "aren't you being hasty? You haven't yet set eyes on Miss Surrey."

"I don't *need* to set eyes on her. You know, Mama, how I dislike these dithering females with pencils stuck in their hair and spectacles on their noses, shuffling through their stacks of tiny notes and muttering in their rusty sopranos, 'Now *where* did I put that acquisition slip? I had it *right here* in my *hand* not a *moment* ago . . .' Have I characterized your Miss Surrey rightly, Finchley-Jones?"

Mr. Finchley-Jones nodded miserably. "In some ways, I suppose . . ."

"That's quite unfair," the Countess said firmly, recollecting

that the sweet child in the library had given her a charming
compliment. She would not permit so lovely a girl to be sum-
marily dismissed, not if she could help it. "Miss Surrey did
not seem to me to be *at all* like that. She wasn't a *bit* dithering!"

"Oh?" Mullineaux turned to his mother with brows upraised.
"You've met her, then? You found her to be efficient?"

"I'm not qualified to comment on her efficiency, although
I recall that Mr. Finchley-Jones spoke highly of her abilities.
I *can* say, however, that I liked her a great deal. Haven't you
told me more than once that men in responsible positions, like
Symonds and Finchley-Jones (and even Mrs. Mudge for that
matter), should be permitted to select their own staffs?"

"Yes, of course I said that. But in this case, with the disappointing results of the last fortnight's efforts here in front of
me—" He looked over at his librarian with knit brows. "I say,
Finchley-Jones, do you *object* to sacking the woman?"

"Well, to be honest, your lordship, I . . . I would prefer to
try her for . . . for a while longer."

"Would you indeed? It sounds to me as if you're being
rather too softhearted."

"I think, Griff," her ladyship persisted, "that you should at
least *see* Miss Surrey for yourself before you sack her. Perhaps
when you meet her, you'll understand Mr. Finchley-Jones's
reluctance to let her go."

Griff shrugged his acceptance of the suggestion and went
to the bell-pull. The butler presented himself almost immediately. "Go down to the library, Symonds, and tell Miss Surrey
we'd like to see her here at once."

While they waited, Griff sat down and told Finchley-Jones
about some of the treasures he'd discovered in Wales. The
librarian beamed in pleasure. "An early Montaigne!" he exclaimed. "I can hardly wait to see it."

Griff nodded in agreement. "I think we may find it a true
rarity. Not like my Tottel, of course, but—"

"Tottel? What Tottel?"

"Good heavens, fellow, haven't you seen my Tottel? It's
the star of my collection."

The librarian paled. "You have a Tottel's *Miscellany?* Not
the 1557 edition, surely."

"The very one. It has *The Songes and Sonnettes* as its title.
Do you mean you haven't come across it?"

"No. I probably wouldn't have believed my eyes if I had.

You should have mentioned—"

"Dash it all, how can I have overlooked mentioning it? But, man, how can you have missed seeing it for yourself? It was on the shelf with the sixteenth century poets."

"Then I know just where to find it," the librarian said in relief. "I shall seek it out as soon as I return and lock it in my desk. A volume like that should not be kept out in the open."

"Nonsense, Mr. Finchley-Jones," the Countess said. "There is no need to keep valuables under lock and key in this house. The household staff is completely trust—"

At that moment, however, the butler returned. "I'm sorry, my lord," he said, looking unusually distressed, "but Miss Surrey refuses to come."

Everyone gaped. "What's that?" his lordship barked. *"Refuses?"*

"She was very apologetic, of course, my lord. Most upset. But she is quite covered with dust, you see, the library's condition being what it is, and she insists that it would not be proper to enter your lordship's presence in all her dirt. She asks that you excuse her for today, and she hopes you will find it convenient to interview her at some other time."

"Oh, she does, does she?" Griff jumped to his feet in a fury. "I've never heard of such temerity! I'm sorry to override your wishes, Finchley-Jones, but this is the outside of enough. Like it or not, Mama, that woman is getting the sack, and *right now!*" With that, he strode angrily out the door.

"Griff, wait!" his mother begged, rising from her place and running after him.

But Lord Mullineaux paid no heed. He marched angrily down the stairs, his mother scurrying behind, trying vainly to catch up with him, and the librarian, his face a study in distress, at her heels.

His lordship burst into the library without a pause in his stride. "See here, Miss Surrey—!"

She was standing on tiptoe on the top step of a small library ladder, reaching for a book which lay neglected on a high shelf. At the sound of his voice, she wheeled precariously about on her perch gasping in alarm, the book clutched in one hand and the other flying to her mouth as if to catch the gasp before it flew into the air.

Griff froze to the spot. The girl on the ladder was dishevelled from top to toe. Strands of hair, loosened from their clasp, fell over her forehead and across her cheeks. The overskirt of her dress had been pinned up for protection against the dirt, but the underskirt and bodice were grimy, as were her hands and face. The trembling hand that covered her mouth would have served, in ordinary circumstances, as an effective mask. But the pale eyes that stared at him, horror-stricken, from her dust-streaked face could not be masked. They were instantly recognizable. "Oh, my God!" he muttered, feeling quite certain that he'd wandered into some sort of crazy dream. "It's *you!*"

His mother and Mr. Finchley-Jones burst into the room behind him. "Miss Surrey!" the librarian choked out. "What on earth—?"

Ada held the book out toward him. "It's the...the m-missing volume of the Grotius," she stammered. "I... f-found it."

Chapter Twelve

Lord Mullineaux, his eyes fixed on Ada, dismissed everyone else from the room and shut the huge library doors with a bang. "Come down from there," he ordered sharply.

Ada climbed down unsteadily. "M-May I be excused, your l-lordship?" she asked from the bottom of the ladder.

"No, you may not. There are a few questions I'd like answered first."

"I have no d-doubt there are. But I . . . I'm so v-very dusty . . ."

"Yes, so I see. Nevertheless, the dust will not keep you from telling me how you found me. Go on, my girl. Speak up!"

"Found you? I don't know what you mean."

He glared at her from under lowered brows. "It's the eyes, I think. Those blasted eyes. They seem so pure . . . so clear and innocent. They make it difficult for me—for *anyone*, I imagine—to suspect you of having sinister motives."

"S-Sinister motives?"

"Yes, ma'am. Sinister motives. What motives could you have other than sinister ones? Why else would you have gone to the trouble of tracking me down?"

Her light eyes widened in her streaked face. "Is that what you think? That I tracked you down?"

"Are you trying to pretend you *didn't*? That my finding the girl from the Black Boar Inn standing on a ladder in my library is sheer *coincidence?*"

"But that's . . . that's *exactly* what it is, my lord."

"Do you take me for a fool, Miss Surrey? My meeting you at the Black Boar could, I suppose, have been an accident, but all the rest? Miss Latcham's peculiar disappearance? Your timely appearance in her place? My turning out to be your employer? All of this is *coincidence?*"

She twisted her fingers together miserably. "I know it s-sounds unbelievable. I was very shocked, myself, when I saw the p-portrait."

"Portrait?"

"Yes. That one there. That's how I first learned your identity, you see. Your resemblance to your father is very marked."

"Let me make certain I understand what you're saying." He circled about her, eyeing her suspiciously as he spoke. "You applied for a post as a librarian's assistant at the establishment of a Lord Mullineaux, a gentleman quite unknown to you? And it was a complete surprise to you to find that he was, in fact, the same person you met at the Black Boar?"

"Yes. S-Something like that."

"Ha!" he snorted. "A likely story." It was too foolish a story for anyone with sense to swallow. Despite the innocence of her eyes, he couldn't swallow it. The girl was lying. Did she think she could make him accept her claim to be a household servant, even one of education like a librarian's assistant? She was quite obviously a girl of breeding. There were too many discrepancies, coincidences, unlikelihoods for her story to be accepted.

He was surprised at the powerful surge of fury smiting his chest. How dared the little minx look up at him with that expression of pained purity? He would get the truth out of her if he had to wring her neck! With a sudden turn, he grasped her waist with both his hands and lifted her up from the floor so that they were face to face. "I want the truth, girl. The *truth*. What is the motive for your establishing yourself in this house? Blackmail?"

She heard the words he spoke, but they didn't seem to have meaning. It was the anger in his voice that had significance to her. The words he said were only sounds that reverberated in her head, but the fury behind them struck her like little darts that pierced her with stabs of pain. It seemed to her that, for reasons that were completely beyond her, he hated her now. The cruel pressure of his hands grasping her waist was the physical sign of that hate. What had she done to inspire it? "Please, my lord," she managed to utter through a throat that burned, "put me d-down."

"*Tell* me! Was it a bit of blackmail you had in mind?"

"I . . . I don't even know wh-what that is."

"Don't you?" He stared at her for a moment in disbelief. She had to be lying, but he found it hard to remain unmoved by the guilelessness of her expression. She was so very innocent of face. Streaked as it was by grime, her face nevertheless seemed ethereally lovely. Her lips, trembling in agitation, were appealingly rosy and full, giving a touch of earthiness to her otherwise unworldly pallor. Her shiny brown hair, framing her face with soft tendrils of unruly curls, seemed completely in keeping with her air of artlessness. But more than anything else, her unbelievably soulful eyes, swimming in unshed tears, gazed down into his with a directness and sincerity that were almost impossible to doubt. In spite of himself, he felt his rage recede. Soon, unable to bear the look in those pained eyes, he set her down. "I thought the word was familiar to everyone," he said, turning away. "It's of Scottish origin, I believe. It refers to a letter sent by a miscreant for the purpose of extorting money from the recipient. It says, in effect, 'If you pay me the specified sum, I will not report to the world at large the heinous secret you are hiding.'"

Ada, with a sudden flash of horrified comprehension, gasped. "Are you s-suggesting, my lord, that I am here to present *you* with such a letter?"

"Are you not?"

That he could believe her capable of such a vile scheme was, to her, a final cruelty. She put a trembling hand to her mouth to keep from crying out.

He wheeled about to face her again. "Well, ma'am?"

"How can you *th-think* such a thing?" she asked, appalled. "Even if I had the sort of mind that could conceive of such a plan, what heinous secret of yours could I threaten to report?"

"Are you *joking*, ma'am? The facts you learned about my relations with Lady Alcorn would keep tongues wagging for a year!"

She looked up at him blankly. "Facts about Lady Alcorn?"

There was something so disarmingly sincere about the blankness in her eyes that he was taken aback. *But no*, he thought, *it must be a performance. A very skilled performance.* A person practicing blackmail must of necessity be adept at dissembling. He wouldn't permit himself to be disarmed. "Come now, Miss Surrey, you can't have forgotten the Alcorn business! You heard Lord Alcorn make accusations against me with your own ears."

"Oh, that." Ada sighed and brushed her still-shaking hand across her forehead in her attempt to concentrate. "Yes, of course. The Alcorn business. I'd forgotten for a moment."

"You'd *forgotten?*" He almost wanted to laugh. Such

featherheadedness was too ridiculously innocent to be feigned. She *couldn't* be pretending! Not even an actress as gifted as a Mrs. Siddons could enact sheer innocence so convincingly. He felt a surge of relief dissipating his hot anger like a sudden rain in a desert. But with the relief was an irritated impatience at her muddleheadedness. "Good God, woman," he exclaimed, shaking his head at her in wonder, "what did you think we'd been speaking of all this time?"

Her eyes welled up with tears. "I d-don't know *what* we're s-speaking of," she muttered miserably, dropping her face in her hands. "When you c-came in s-so furiously, I th-thought you were d-dissatisfied with my *l-library* work."

"I don't give a ha'penny's damn for your library work!" He pulled her hands from her face and peered down at her. Her dirty cheeks were pathetically streaked with tears. Her flooded eyes, so pale they were almost translucent, were completely unguarded and artless. Her hands trembled in his; he felt as if he'd taken hold of a pair of terrified birds. Suddenly, all he wanted to do was take her in his arms and comfort her. "Confound it, girl, when you look up at me like that I'm incapable of judgment. If you told me you were the *Queen Mother* I'd probably believe you." He lifted one hand to her cheek and absently wiped away a teardrop with his fingers. "Very well. Tell me what you want me to believe, and I shall believe it. Your name is Ada Surrey, you came here as an assistant to the librarian, and you had no idea that the man at the Black Boar would turn out to be your employer. Is that how this all came to pass?"

A look of startled guilt flashed into her eyes before she lowered them from his face. He didn't hate her, after all. He was so . . . so kind . . . so lovable . . . so forgiving. She couldn't bear to have to lie to him, even a little. But she couldn't bring herself to admit to him the whole, silly truth. "Until I saw that painting, my lord, I had no idea who you were or that you lived in this house," she said quietly.

"Hmmm." He cocked his head, studying her speculatively. "Why do I feel, all at once, that you've given me an evasive answer? Have you something else to tell me, ma'am?"

"No, my lord. Nothing."

"Are you certain? You needn't be afraid, you know. Whatever I suspected when I first saw you perched on that ladder— all my mistrust, all my fury—is quite gone. You've completely won me over. So if there is anything at all you wish to confess..."

She merely shook her lowered head.

"Dash it all," he muttered, taking an impatient turn away from her, "why should I even bother to pursue this matter? I ought simply to sack you."

"Yes, I suppose you ought."

He came back to her and lifted her chin. "But I can't, you see."

She blinked up at him. "You can't?"

"Of course not. After what you've done for me—"

"What I've done for you?" she echoed bewilderedly.

He threw up his hands. "Hang it all, woman, you *are* a bubblehead sometimes! Are you forgetting the incident of the inn *again?* Well, it may flit like a breeze through the filigree of that peculiar mind of *yours,* but *I* can't forget it quite so easily."

"Oh, the Black Boar incident again," she said with a dismissive motion of her hand. "I wish you *would* forget it. The episode reflects no credit on either one of us."

"Why so? It reflects no credit on me, certainly, but your action was positively noble."

"Perhaps. But my unc—but some might see it as positively foolhardy. Or bubbleheaded at the very least. After all, if you were a different sort of man, I might have found myself in dire straits."

But he paid no attention to her compliment to him. He was caught by her strange little stumble. "Were you going to say your uncle?" he inquired, brows knit. "Why did you stop yourself?"

She shook her head. "It was not important."

"There's a great deal you're not telling me, isn't there?" he asked with a helpless sigh, fighting the urge to shake the truth out of her. He could no longer believe her a fortune-hunter, but there was something she was holding back. He wished he could make her trust him. But continued urging was beneath him. "Never mind," he said. "I shan't press you. I shall merely take your word that this second encounter between us is merely a wild coincidence...a gigantic joke. What now, ma'am? Where shall we go from here?"

"I don't know, my lord." She recognized the sigh of acceptance in his tone. He believed her. She could sense that he had ceased his questioning and that this agonizing interview was coming to an end. She had gotten through it without inciting the wrath of the gods. The world had not trembled on its foundations nor had the walls come tumbling down about her head. She took a deep breath of relief before going on. "If you are not going to sack me, then I assume we shall go on as before."

"As before? You are amazing, do you know that, Miss Surrey? Quite amazing. Do you mean that you wish to continue to labor in the dust of the library, to continue your existence as a mere servant in this house?"

"Yes, that is what I wish."

"Even though you know and I know that this sort of labor is not what you were bred for?"

She did not take his bait. "I enjoy my work very much, my lord," was all she would say.

"What of me, ma'am? What do you expect of *me* while you continue in my employ?"

"I don't know what you mean," she said in surprise. "I don't expect anything of you."

"Don't you? You merely expect me to ignore your existence, is that it?"

"Well, I don't see what else . . ."

"No, of course you don't. You, with that cloudy brain of yours, have no recollection of the reason why, from the time of our first meeting, I didn't want to know your name. Do you recall it, ma'am? Do you remember my giving you my reason?"

Her pulse, which had calmed down considerably, began to race again. "Yes, I . . . I do recall it. You said you . . . you didn't wish to c-call on me."

"I said I didn't wish to be *tempted* to call on you. I hope you perceive ma'am, that the difference between those two statements is considerable."

There was a difference. He was implying that she'd made a mark on him. A flush of real pleasure surged up inside her, but she didn't permit herself to encourage the feeling. "I do perceive it, my lord, but since I am only a servant here, there *is* no possibility of your c-calling on me."

"Do you think I'm not aware of that? How do you suppose that makes me feel?"

She threw him a quick, enigmatic glance. "I don't know."

"Do you think it will be easy for me to ignore your existence?

Just try to imagine it, my dear." He walked to one of the windows and stared unseeing through the dusty pane. "I, who wished to avoid even knowing who you are, shall now not only know your name and where you can be found at any time of the day or night, but I shall be constantly aware that I need only to trot down to the library or pull the bell cord to indulge myself in the pleasure of gazing at those eyes of yours."

She felt herself flush again. *"Will* you indulge yourself so, my lord?" she heard herself ask.

He gave a mirthless laugh. "I shall certainly fight against the urge, my dear. It would not be considered seemly behavior for the head of the household. But as I said, it won't be easy."

There was a protracted silence in the room as she stood unmoving, watching him fixedly as the setting sun silhouetted his form in the window. *And how easy do you think it will be for me?* she asked herself in sudden bitterness. *Do you think I shall take pleasure in observing Cornelia's attempts to win your affections? Or in hearing tongues wagging about your renewed liaison with the Alcorn woman, which is what the gossips below stairs are already predicting? Or, if other prognosticators are in the right, learning that you're embarked on a new affair with another lady of easy virtue?* The prospect of living as a servant in this house, even for a fortnight, was fraught with danger for her emotions. But even if she could manage to make an escape, she wouldn't do it. This was where she had to stay... where she *wanted* to stay. As long as the fates permitted it, she would remain, at whatever cost, as close to this man as could be.

At last she forced herself to speak. "I don't know what you wish me to say, your lordship. If my presence here makes you uncomfortable, then I suppose you must... send me away."

"I've already told you I cannot." He took a deep breath before turning round to face her again. "Very well, Miss Surrey, we shall do as you suggest. We shall all go on exactly as we should have done if I'd never laid eyes on you. You will continue, in your abstracted way, to assist Mr. Finchley-Jones here in the library, and I—"

"And you will continue, in your rakish way, to have affairs and avoid duels and live as you please," she said in rejoinder, astounding herself as well as his lordship by this bitter outburst. "So you needn't sound so sorry for yourself," she added lamely.

His lordship's laugh was both surprised and rueful. *"Touché,*

Miss Surrey! A palpable hit. I didn't expect a riposte of such cutting accuracy from—"

"From a bubblehead?"

"I was going to say, from someone who not so long ago tried to point out that I must be in possession of some angelic qualities. I regret that you no longer believe those qualities exist in me."

"I *do* believe they exist, my lord. You would not have permitted me to remain in your employ if they didn't. Please forgive me for my outburst. I didn't mean to . . . I had no right to disparage your way of life."

"You had every right, having been witness to one of my life's more reprehensible displays."

"I thought we'd agreed to forget that incident," she reminded him.

"Very well, Miss Surrey. The subject is dropped. From this moment on, we go on as if our shared past had never happened. For the moment at least, you have won. But I'm well aware that there is something you haven't told me. I warn you, ma'am, that whatever it is, I shall discover it. I intend to get to the bottom of the mystery of Ada Surrey." With that he turned back to his contemplation of the window pane. "You may go, Miss Surrey. I have kept you from your ablutions long enough."

"Thank you, my lord."

He turned round in time to see her drop a very proper curtsey and start for the door. "I hope, my dear, that you have no apprehension concerning my treatment of you," he said as she put her hand on the knob. "There is enough of the angelic in me to behave like a gentleman toward the females employed under this roof. Whatever else the gossips say about me, I'm certain they don't say that I've ever fondled an abigail or ordered a housemaid to share my bed."

"You didn't need to tell me that. You proved to me you were a gentleman that night at the inn."

"Yes, so I did. But I don't want you to think it wasn't bothersome, even then."

"*Was* it bothersome?"

"More so than I care to admit. However, I managed to act the gentleman with you then, and I shall certainly do so now."

"Yes, my lord. I was certain that you would."

When the huge double doors had closed behind her, he remained staring at them with a self-mocking smile. Yes, he would act the gentleman with her. There was no question in his mind about that. But it would be a great deal harder than it was the last time.

Chapter Thirteen

Sir Jasper had had two letters from his niece, one each week since her departure, but he had not found them satisfactory. She'd written in detail about the house, the servants, the meals and even the library, but she'd said not a word about her own state of mind. Jasper was not the sort to read between the lines; what was said outwardly was what he believed, but he was beginning to wonder if, in this case, his niece was hiding something from him. Was the girl unhappy in London?

When the butler delivered the third such missive into his hand, he hoped that this letter would tell him a bit more than the others. With a look of undisguised eagerness (for there was no one to see him, and thus there was no need to act the curmudgeon), he ensconced himself comfortably in the large easy chair in his study and broke the seal. His eyes flew over the page eagerly, but soon his eager expression changed to a frown. Ada was as uncommunicative in this letter as she'd been in the others.

He groaned aloud in irritation. If the girl was having an exciting time in the world's greatest city, there was no sign of it in these letters. The tone was cheerful enough, but the matter of the letter was the same as before: she liked Lady Mullineaux, who was kind and beautiful; the house was large by London standards and decorated in the first style of elegance; the meals were superb; the library was remarkable. Any other sort of detail—what she was doing for amusement, for example— was sadly lacking. "The library is remarkable." What sort of comment was that? He didn't force her out of the house for the purpose of examining the Mullineaux *library!* Where were the comments about balls, dances, theaters, suitors, callers, and all the other pleasantries Lady Mullineaux's letter had led him to expect?

He pulled himself out of the chair and went angrily to his desk. He would write and give her a piece of his mind. If she was enjoying herself, he wanted to know about it. And if she was not, he wanted her home at once. He prepared the nib of his pen, pulled out a sheet of paper and was about to write the salutation when the butler knocked. "Lady Dorothea is calling," Cotrell, trying not to show his surprise, announced importantly.

"Doro? You don't mean it! She ain't showed her face at this door since Ada left. Is that dashed pattern-card of a daughter with her?"

"No, Sir Jasper. She's alone. The only thing she brought is a letter."

"A letter, eh? Per'aps she's heard from Ada, too." Jasper chortled gleefully. "She must be *livid*. Wager she *still* ain't recovered from the shock o' havin' our Ada beat her Cornelia to London."

"I don't know about that, sir. She appeared to be in good spirits."

"Don't be misled, Cotrell. I know my sister. She's probably puttin' a good face on it 'cause she wants a favor from me or some such thing. But inside, she's seethin'. I know she's seethin'. Else why ain't she come callin' since that day, eh?"

"I couldn't say, Sir Jasper. Are you going to see her?"

"'Course I'm goin' t' see her. Do ye think I'd *miss* the opportunity to laugh in her face? I've been waitin' fer this chance a long, long time. Is she in the drawin' room?" He started for the door. "I say, Cotrell," he added before departing, "don't bring us tea until I ring, do ye hear? I want to have plenty o' time t' enjoy my moment o' triumph!"

Dorothea gave an uneasy start the moment she heard Jasper cross the threshold of the drawing room. Her manner confused her brother; it was nervous, yes, but there was an air of excitement underneath. Could it be that the butler was right? Had Doro recovered from her disappointment so soon? If so, he would soon overset her good spirits. He intended to make the most of this rare opportunity to gloat. "Well, well," he said jovially from the doorway, "it's been some time. How do ye go on, Doro, my dear?"

"Jasper!" she gasped, obviously relieved at the warmth of her welcome. "I'm so happy you've recovered from your . . . er . . . pet."

"Are you referrin' to the little altercation the last time ye were here? I recovered from that the very next day, as well you know."

"How would I know that?" Dorothea said, her eyebrows rising. "I haven't heard a word from or about you since our last visit."

"Oh, is *that* how ye're goin' t' play the game? All innocence and good spirits, eh? All right, ma'am. Suits me." He perched on a chair, crossed his legs jauntily, folded his arms over his chest and grinned at her. "If you can be a good loser, I can be a good winner."

"I don't know what you're babbling about, Jasper. You sound as addled as Ada. But I don't wish to precipitate another quarrel, so I'll merely tell you why I'm here. I've had a letter—"

"Have ye indeed? A letter, eh?" He had to hold himself back from rubbing his hands in glee and chortling aloud. "I don't suppose it's necessary fer me t' guess from whom."

His sister smiled. "Of course you don't need to guess. Who else's letter would concern me? Well, she writes that Lady Mullineaux is giving a ball in her honor next week and that she would be happy if I attended. I've been thinking, Jasper, that I might indulge myself this once and go. It needn't disturb anything at Mullineaux House. I would stay with my friend Mabel Banning and remain for only a month—"

"Ball?" Sir Jasper's high spirits seemed suddenly to have exploded like an overblown balloon. Why had there been nothing in *his* letter on this subject? "Did you say *ball?*"

"Yes, a ball. Not a come-out, exactly, for the girl is twenty-two, after all, but a very special ball to introduce her to society."

Jasper's face fell. "A ball in her honor?"

"Yes, of course. Didn't you think the Countess would—?"

"She's invited you to her ball? *You?* Why did she not say a word to *me* about it?"

Dorothea blinked at him. "What a very strange thing to say, Jasper. Why should you expect her to write to *you?* After the way you treated her at your last meeting—"

"How do ye know *how* I treated her at our last meeting? Our last meeting, if ye must know, was perfectly amicable—"

"Amicable? Have you gone *mad?* You ordered us out of the house! Without even a drink of tea!"

"It's *you* who's gone mad. It's *you* and *Cornelia* I ordered out of the house. Not *Ada.*"

"Who's speaking of Ada?" Dorothea peered at him worriedly. "Are you sure you're quite well?"

Jasper jumped up from his chair impatiently. "I think it's you who's sick," he accused, pointing a wagging finger at her. "You! Touched in yer upper works, if ye ask me. Who else were we speakin' of if not Ada?"

"We were speaking of *Cornelia!*" his sister shouted, waving her letter as evidence. "Who *else* would be writing from London?"

"Ada, that's who!" His gesturing arm with its pointing finger froze in midair. "Are you sayin' that that letter is from *Cornelia?"*

"Yes, that's what I'm saying! Come and look at it yourself, and then we'll see who's touched in his upper works!"

"Let me see that! Good God, this *is* from London. What's Cornelia doin' in London?"

"You know perfectly well what she's doing in London. What do you think our last argument was all about? Didn't we sit here in this very room and discuss the Countess Mullineaux's invitation? Really, Jasper, I'm beginning to believe you are becoming senile."

"Senile, ma'am? *Senile?* When it was I who arranged for Ada to get to London and cut your daughter out?" He laughed triumphantly at the look of shock on his sister's face. "Yes, that was all *my* doin'! So whom are you callin' senile, eh?"

Lady Dorothea rose from her chair like one in a trance. "Isn't Ada *here?"* she asked, lifting a limp hand to her breast.

"Here? How can she be here? She's in London, just as I've been sayin'. In London, with the Countess."

"With the . . . the Countess *Mullineaux?* At Mullineaux House?"

Jasper rolled his eyes heavenward in exasperation. "Well, I couldn't have sent her t' Buckin'ham Palace, now, could I? The invitation didn't come from there."

"But . . . Cornelia never wrote a *word* about it!"

"Why should she? She probably doesn't know. If she's gone to London, too, it don't follow that they've run into each other. London's a gigantic place."

"But Jasper," Lady Dorothea mumbled, utterly confused, *"Cornelia* is at Mullineaux House."

Jasper frowned at her suspiciously. "Ridiculous. Ada certainly would have mentioned—"

Dorothea sank back into her chair. "I don't know what Ada may write in her letters, jingle-brain that she is, but Cornelia would certainly have said something." She picked up the letter that had fallen from her brother's hand. "Here. Just look at this. She mentions everyone she's come in contact with. Griff Mullineaux is back from Wales, she writes. And her ladyship went with her to call on a certain Mrs. Wingate. Lady Hereford and the Princess Lieven called one morning. She met my friend Mabel Banning at the Pantheon Bazaar. She had three callers herself . . . she names them all: a Mr. Spencer, Sir Nigel Lewis and someone she calls Monty Moncrief. Three-and-a-half closely written pages full of names, and not once is Ada even mentioned. Here, take it and see for yourself."

Jasper shook his head bewilderedly. "I had a letter from London today myself. There's nothin' in it about Cornelia's bein' there. I don't understand what this is all about."

"Nor do I. Did you say that you sent Ada to London the day after our last conversation?"

"Yes. The very next mornin'."

"That was the very day that Cornelia departed."

Jasper walked thoughtfully back to his chair and sat down abstractedly. For a moment he said nothing. Then he looked over at his sister, his brows knit. "I dislike to say this, Doro, but I think Cornelia's lyin' to ye. If she was stayin' with Ada at Mullineaux House, Ada would certainly have mentioned it *once* in the three letters—"

"I've had *four* from Cornelia," his sister retorted. "Perhaps it's *Ada* who's lying."

"Ada don't lie. You know that. Besides, I have proof! Ada's abigail—and ye know that Selena's a reliable woman if ever there was one—went to London with her. She then took ill and came home. But not before havin' delivered the girl right to the Countess's door. Told me so herself, with the coachman backin' the story in every detail."

Lady Dorothea shrugged helplessly. "I don't know what to make of this, Jasper. But Cornelia doesn't lie either. And I, too, have proof. Look at this, that Cornelia tucked into her letter."

"What is it?"

"It's a gilt-edged invitation to the ball. It's written in the Countess's own hand, and it has a few informal words of regards to me from the Countess herself, scrawled across the bottom. What do you make of that, eh? You cannot imagine it to be a forgery, can you? Even *you* cannot believe that

Cornelia would go as far as forgery!"

Jasper examined the card, nonplussed. Then he sagged against the back of his chair, his spirit gone. "Then what do ye make o' this, Doro? What's goin' on there at Mullineaux House that makes each one o' the girls invisible t' the other?"

"I don't have the slightest idea. But this, of course, makes me quite decided. I shall leave for London in two days' time and shall get to the bottom of this at once. You have my word, Jasper. I shall solve this riddle and get word to you in the first post."

He fixed a lugubrious eye on his sister and shook his head. "I ain't goin' to wait fer word from you, Doro. I'm goin' myself."

"Very well. Perhaps that *would* be best. We can go in my carriage. I'll stop for you at first light, the day after tomorrow. That would bring us to London by evening of—"

"Do you think I'd be able t' bear waitin' till the day after tomorrow? I wouldn't get a wink o' sleep or a minute o' peace in my mind!" He rose from his chair abruptly and strode toward the door. "I'm goin' right now . . . or at least as soon as Cotrell can call fer the carriage. Yer welcome t' come along, Doro, but I ain't goin' to stop along the way fer any trumpery reason whatsoever."

"But I can't come now! I haven't packed. And neither have you, Jasper. I know this whole situation is worrisome, but you can't run off to London without so much as a hairbrush or a change of clothes."

"Yes, I can. Cotrell can throw a few necessaries into a bag for me—and for you, too, if ye had a mind—and I can purchase whatever I need once I get there. But there's no need fer you t' hurry yerself. Take yer time an' pack yer fineries. When ye finally arrive, Doro, you can find me at Fenton's Hotel. Cotrell! *Cotrell,* ye sluggard! Where are ye?" Without another glance in her direction, he hurried from the room.

She stared after him in a daze, a hand pressed upon her heaving bosom. Then, with a sudden shake of her body, like a dog shedding raindrops from its coat, she jumped to her feet. "I'm coming with you," she shouted excitedly. "Do you hear me, Jasper? Wait for me!"

Chapter Fourteen

"I don't know how I'll be able to face his lordship," Mr. Finchley-Jones muttered miserably as he climbed down from the library stepladder after his desperate examination of the last book on the last shelf in the room. "Such a loss will be impossible for him to bear."

"But it's only a book," Ada said, attempting to be soothing.

"Only a book! Only a *book!* I'll have you know, Miss Surrey, that the *Miscellany* is one of the most prized of rare books. Tottel printed only seven small editions of it between 1557 and 1574, each extant copy of which is precious, but the 1557 edition is the most prized of all. Most collectors only *dream* of finding it. But to have owned it and then *lost* it—" He shuddered at the horror of it. "It doesn't bear thinking of."

"Don't lose hope, Mr. Finchley-Jones," Ada said, turning back to the work at her table. "Books don't just disappear. The missing treasure will turn up, probably in the most unlikely place. I myself once left a book under the sprinkling can in the rose garden. I didn't find it again for months, for it was the last time I sprinkled the flowers that fall."

"Yes, I quite believe it of you," the librarian said reprovingly.

"So it will be this time," she said cheerfully, ignoring his little slur.

The librarian sighed hopelessly. "That's what I shall say to his lordship, of course. 'It's bound to turn up,' I'll say. But I don't really believe it. The Tottel's been stolen. A magnificent, 1557 Tottel—stolen! I can think of no other explanation."

"There *must* be another explanation," Ada insisted. "I know almost everyone on staff by this time, and no one of them seems to me to be dishonest. And furthermore, none of them seems remotely interested in books or the doings in this library. Whenever I speak of library matters at the table, they are all very quick to change the subject. There are not many people in the world, it seems, who have your fascination with books."

"But, my dear girl, it requires only *one* of them to be a thief. You admit you do not know them all. And even if you did, you cannot be certain that you've correctly judged all their characters. It is the nature of a thief to hide his true character. He could easily have fooled you as to his real nature. You, if I may say so, are not the sort to see the evil that lurks in people's hearts, being so very good yourself."

"Thank you, Mr. Finchley-Jones, for your kind opinion, but I am neither so good nor so gullible as you think me."

She returned to her task of listing, by author, the books on jurisprudence which had become her special responsibility, but she found it difficult to keep her mind on the work. She wondered if Finchley-Jones had been right about her judgment of people. She tried to bring, one by one, the faces of the household servants to her mind, to see if she could determine any signs of dishonesty or wickedness in any of them. But on examination each one she conjured up seemed to be open, honest and free of guile. Yet the book was gone. Could she swear that none of them was capable of stealing it? How could one really tell what was in the secret heart of another?

Mr. Finchley-Jones, meanwhile, was gazing at her bent head adoringly. The girl was quite the prettiest creature ever to have come his way. He never got his fill of staring at her. More than once he'd considered the prospect of asking for her hand. But as often as the thought had come to him, he'd as often thrust it aside. He was almost forty years old and had long ago decided that marriage was not for him. He was very precise in his habits and style of living and did not relish the prospect of making adjustments to suit a female. Women were, in general, a messy breed. They were given to emotional outbursts of tears, to leaving their pots of facial preparations uncovered on their dressing tables, to licking chicken grease from their fingers, to dusting only the tops of things, to manhandling a man's possessions, to all sorts of other, repulsive tricks of behavior. Not that he'd seen Ada indulge in many of these quirks, but he had seen her cry, and she was very forgetful and addled. He knew enough about women to surmise that even if some of them were charming in their youth, they invariably developed these repulsive traits in later years.

Still, Ada Surrey had something about her that was unique. She seemed very much a lady. Though merely a servant in this household, she had an air of gentility that was unmistakable. For her he might forgive an open jar on the dressing table. To have her with him always, to be able to gaze at those wonderful eyes and shiny hair at any time of day or night, might be joy enough to make her absentmindedness and other feminine weaknesses bearable. Perhaps he should reconsider his stand on the subject of wedlock. For a girl like Ada, a change of heart might be in order.

"Have you ever thought, Miss Surrey, that taking care of a husband, a home and children might be more suited to you than library work?" he asked suddenly.

Ada was conjuring up the face of Symonds, the butler, in her mind. Could Symonds, she was asking herself, be capable of deceit? "Yes, Mr. Finchley-Jones," she murmured absently.

"I am glad to hear you say that," he said, taking a deep breath and beginning to pace about the room. "I believe that I can offer you the sort of life you would wish for, and, undoubtedly, better than a young woman in your circumstances could have expected. I am not without resources. An uncle of mine left me a legacy which is sizeable enough to have permitted me to follow my chosen profession without undue concern with remuneration. Fortunately, however, my employers thus far have been quite generous, and I've been able to live within my means, without touching my inheritance. With (if I do say so myself) shrewd investment of that inheritance, my income is now more than seven hundred per annum. For the past few years I've made my home in rented rooms, but with my present income I could certainly afford a pleasant house in one of the recently settled sections north of the New Road. What do you think of that, Miss Surrey?"

"What, sir?" she asked, blinking up at him.

"Don't you think a house north of the New Road would suit a newly wedded couple?"

"Oh, yes, I expect so," she agreed, deciding in her mind that Symonds the butler was too loyal to the family to even *contemplate* doing them an injury.

"Good. I would have no objection to your employing a housemaid and cook, provided they were exceptionally neat and tidy in their personal habits. I'm sure that you will have surmised by this time—even though our acquaintance has not been long—that I am a man of precise habits. I cannot endure slovenliness of any sort, so any servant I decide to employ must be impeccable in conduct and appearance."

"Yes, of course," Ada said, thinking about the two footmen who assisted Symonds. They were the youngest of the six footmen on staff (being not much above nineteen years in age) and were given to making ribald remarks. But Ada could not imagine them being deceitful. She rather liked their lusty sense of fun. Ribald remarks were a sign of high spirits, nothing more. She doubted very much that they, singly or together, would choose to engage in anything dishonest.

"As I said, we have not known each other for very long—a little more than a fortnight only—but we've worked together for many hours each day. When one thinks about it, one might court a lady for a year, calling on her weekly, without spending as much time in her company as I have in yours. So I don't believe it to be hasty to come to a decision at this time. After all, it is already clear that we have similar likes. We both enjoy quiet contemplation, we both refrain from easy intercourse with strangers, we both prefer reading to other pastimes . . . isn't that so?"

"I beg your pardon?" She was now reviewing the upstairs maids in her mind. Clara was, of course, beyond reproach, and the talkative Sally, who was close to sixty years old and had been with the Mullineaux family for forty-five of those years, was not likely to turn dishonest at this stage of her life.

"Reading *is* your favorite pastime, is it not?" he repeated.

"Reading and gardening, I suppose," she answered, wondering briefly why he was asking so personal a question. But her mind returned at once to the problem at hand—the honesty of the staff. There was Mrs. Mudge, of course. Mrs. Mudge had a mercurial temper. Could she, in a moment of anger, bring herself to steal something from her beloved Lord Mullineaux? It was not at all likely.

"There is every reason to believe we would have a happy life," the librarian went on thoughtfully. "I may be called, from time to time, to travel to parts of Britain some distance from home, but I would not accept a commission that would keep me from home for great lengths of time. In any case, most of this nation's serious library work is taking place right here in London. You can expect me to return to hearth and home almost every evening at sunset. It is a pleasant prospect, is it not?—

you greeting me at the door, both of us sitting down to sup in our little dining room (which should face south, I think, for the best evening light), then settling down together in our own library (for I have not stinted in acquiring a considerable collection of my own) where we would spend the evening reading, sometimes even aloud, I on my easy chair and you on a hassock with your head resting on my knee? In fact, the prospect is more than pleasant. It is quite delightful, is it not?"

"Oh, yes," she muttered abstractedly. "Delightful." But her cogitations were becoming less than delightful. Whereas she couldn't choose a particular person on whom she might pin a suspicion, there were a number of members of the staff about whom it would be difficult to swear *with absolute certainty* that they would never do a dishonest act. The French cook, for example, kept to himself; everyone considered him a man of mystery. And Mrs. Mudge *was* temperamental. The young footmen *were* bawdy and high-spirited. And then there was Grisha, the stable man, who'd come from Russia; some of the staff whispered that he'd run away from his home in Murmansk because he'd murdered someone there. None of them had aroused her suspicions before, but perhaps that was because she was gullible. She still believed that none of them would steal anything in this house. But she couldn't be certain. She had to admit that perhaps Finchley-Jones was right after all.

"Then you agree with me, my dear?" he was asking.

She gave a reluctant shrug and smiled up at him ruefully. "Yes, I think, after all, that I do."

His face reddened in pleased surprise. "You *do?* Oh, my dear *girl—!*"

"Yes, I do. I've been thinking it over carefully these past few minutes, and I've come to the conclusion that there is much in what you say."

"Ada, my dear!" He crossed the room to her chair, his eyes misty. "I hope I may call you Ada from now on. You have made me the...the happiest of men!" He lifted her hand to his lips. "I'm quite overcome. Please...forgive me." And he ran off to the tiny closet room in which he always changed his clothes and shut the door.

She stared after him in astonishment. Had there been tears in his eyes? But why?. What could account for so peculiar a reaction to her simple statement that she agreed with his judgment that a theft of the *Miscellany* was a possibility? Her agreement seemed to have touched his emotions with unwarranted force. Good heavens, was it possible that even *Finchley-Jones* had deeper aspects to his nature than she'd supposed?

Chapter Fifteen

Clara was sitting on Ada's little bed, munching an apple, while Ada sat on the room's only chair, stitching a newly-washed-and-ironed white tucker on the blue bombazine dress that she would wear the next day. Clara had recently finished relating to Ada the day's gossip, mostly concerning Mrs. Mudge's speculation about the romantic prospects of her ladyship's houseguest. The housekeeper and the staff were impressed with the number of suitors who had called on Miss Haydon that day. "Three this afternoon alone," Clara reported, "an' she ain't yet 'ad 'er ball." She leaned back against the pillow and lifted her weary legs up on the coverlet with a sigh. "Once 'er ladyship shows 'er protegee to all the *ton,* there'll be no end t' the knockin' at the—" Her eye fell on a shadowy object in the corner. "What's that book doin' there on the floor?"

"What book?" Ada asked, not looking up from her sewing.

"That one there. In the corner."

Ada looked round. "Oh, yes. *The Songes and Sonnettes.* I'd forgotten all about it. I really must remember to return it to the library one of these days. I've been using it to prop up the mirror, which stands too low for me to see the top of my hair. I'm sure that Mr. Finchley-Jones would not approve of my using one of his books for that purpose."

"Ye could ask one o' the footmen to 'ang the mirror proper," Clara suggested. "That cheeky Lawrence'd do it if ye asked 'im." She grinned wickedly at her friend. "'E'd do anythin' ye asked ... gladly."

"Come now, Clara, are you implying that Lawrence is taken with me? He's a mere child!"

"Ye can't say 'child' about a chap that's almost nineteen. An' nineteen is about time fer a chap t' turn top over tail over a girl. Lawrence is top over tail about you, my girl, or I don't know my name is Clara."

"Your name is Clara, but that doesn't make you right. If you're to be believed, every man on staff is enamored of me."

"No, I didn't never say that. Howsomever, there's a *few* of 'em in that condition. 'Ave ye noticed that Mr. Finchley-Jones 'as been smellin' of April and May the past few days? I ain't never seen him like that afore. All smiles 'e is!"

"Smiles? That proves how little you know of him. The poor man's worried sick! He hasn't yet got up enough courage to tell his lordship that his library's greatest treasure has disappeared."

Clara shrugged. "It's true I don't know anything about that, but I do know that the man glows like a candle when 'e looks at ye." She took a final nibble of what was left of her apple, got to her feet and tossed the core into the grate of the tiny fireplace. "If ye've a mind, Ada," she teased, throwing her friend a leering look, "ye could worm an offer from that there gentleman."

"An *offer?*" Ada shook her head in amusement. "You can't mean it."

"Easy as pie. As my pa used to say, 'e's a pigeon ripe for the pluckin'. A girl could do worse, Ada." She threw herself back upon the bed and raised her legs again. "Mr. Finchley-Jones is a proper gen'leman."

"Yes, he is," Ada agreed, a mischievous twinkle lighting her eyes. "And so handsome, too."

Clara giggled. "Just so. If ye find scarecrows 'andsome."

"I think he's more like a crow than a scarecrow. But that is quite beside the point. I'm not good enough for Mr. Finchley-Jones. What ordinary woman is?" Ada held an imaginary lorgnette to her nose and looked at her friend with pursed lips. "Don't you realize, madam, that a wife for Mr. Finchley-Jones cannot be an ordinary female?" she asked in a good imitation of the librarian's nasal manner of speech. "She must be precise, meticulous, exact. In a word, faultless."

"Oh, quite right," Clara agreed with a snort. "She can't never touch 'is papers nor move 'is possessions even an inch from where 'e's placed 'em..."

Ada grinned. "Nor misplace so much as a comma when she copies his notes..."

"Nor leave out the thing connectin' 'is names. What do ye call it, Ada?"

"The hyphen." She burst into a laugh. "Can you imagine the poor girl who marries him, Clara? She'll have to go through life being Mrs. Finchley Hyphen Jones!"

Clara guffawed. "There must be *some* female we know who'd be good enough fer 'im," she said, putting her hands behind her head and grinning up at the ceiling speculatively. "Somewheres in this world there's someone who's the perfect match—" She suddenly gave a wicked little cackle as a ludicrous idea burst into her mind. "I know just the female who'd suit! *Miss Haydon!*"

Ada gaped at her for a moment and then choked. "Good heavens! *Cornelia?*" The thought was so funny that her needlework slipped from her lap unnoticed.

Clara hugged herself with delight at her puckish notion. "Wouldn' that be—what is it Mrs. Mudge is always sayin'?—deevine retribution? Instead of snatchin' up 'is lordship fer 'erself, it'd be *deevine retribution* fer Miss Haydon to be paired with Finchley-Jones."

"Why, Clara," Ada said reprovingly, trying not to laugh, "one would think you didn't wish Miss Haydon well. Don't you *like* her ladyship's beautiful houseguest?"

"Not much," Clara said frankly. "Thinks she comes out o' the top drawer, she does. Always talks t' me like I was an insect wi' a bad smell. Wrinkles 'er nose up, like this, when she speaks t' me." Clara gave a regretful sigh. "Acourse, she'd never look twice at Mr. Finchley-Jones. Not she. She'll 'ave more suitors than she'll know what t' do with when the ball is over."

"Yes, I'm sure she will," Ada murmured, picking up her sewing.

"Ye should see 'er ballgown, Ada! Green *peau de soie,* wi' seed pearls an' sparklers sewed all over the bosom. Fair took my breath away when I saw Mrs. Prentiss—the Countess's seamstress, y' know—fittin' it on 'er." Clara made a moue. "She'll 'ave the gentlemen buzzin' round 'er like bees."

"I suppose so." Ada poked her needle into the fabric viciously. "Lord Mullineaux, too, I'd wager."

"Wouldn't be a bit surprised," Clara agreed. "That's why I think it would be deevine retribution fer 'er to be paired wi' Finchley-Jones." She grinned again as the appealing vision reshaped itself in her mind. "Can't ye just *see* it, Ada? Just think o' their bedroom, fer instance, (if ye could imagine they're the sort t' share a bedroom). Can you picture it? 'Er gowns an' frills an' furbelows strewn all about 'er side o' their bedroom, lookin' like a mingle-mangle; while on 'is side everything neat as a pin."

Ada, unable to help herself, gurgled at the vision. "There she'd be, all dressed for a ball, while he'd insist that they stay home and *read* together!"

"Exac'ly! Wouldn't that be just like 'im? Wishin' t' stay at 'ome an' read?" Clara chuckled heartily. "And no novels, neither. Only very serious stuff."

"Of course. Frivolity is not to be permitted." A giggle, made up of pure delirium, bubbled out of Ada. "Can you envision my cousin Cornelia being forced to sit and listen to Finchley-Jones reading Grotius aloud? All three volumes of *The Rights of War and Peace?*"

Ada dissolved in laughter, but Clara stiffened. Ada had made a slip, and Clara did not miss it. She sat up straight and stared at her friend with knit brows. "I don't know who this Grotius is, acourse," she said carefully, "but I take it yer *cousin* wouldn't find 'im t' be entertainin'."

"Entertaining?" Ada wiped the tears of laughter from her cheeks. "She'd find him dull as dishwater after three pages, much less three vol—" Her smile suddenly faded. *"What* did you say?"

"I said, yer cousin Cornelia wouldn't much care fer this Grotius."

"Oh, dear," Ada winced, putting a hand to her mouth. "I seem to have spilt some beans."

"It's true, then?" Clara asked tightly. "Cornelia Haydon, 'er ladyship's guest, is yer *cousin?"*

"Yes, it's true."

"Might you be a well-born lady then?"

Ada glanced at her worriedly. "Would it trouble you if I were?"

Clara looked her up and down, her face wary. "I should 'ave knowed." She got up and edged toward the door, rubbing her hands on her apron nervously. "What's a fine lady like you doin' in the servants' quarters anyway? 'Tain't right nor fair."

"Clara! Wait a moment, please. Good heavens, you're behaving as if I'm here to spy on you."

"What *are* ye doin' 'ere, then?"

"Certainly not spying. I only . . . I needed to earn some money."

Clara snorted. "Ye should 'ave asked yer cousin t' give ye some. They're sayin' downstairs that 'er ballgown alone cost more'n three 'undred pounds. Surely she could 'ave spared you somethin', even if it meant she'd 'ave t' choose a gown fer the ball not quite so posh."

"I couldn't ask—"

"Y'know, Ada, or whatever yer name really is, it ain't easy fer me t' believe that it's *money* what brought ye here. Yer wages fer laborin' away in the liberry won't amount t' much. Not fer a lady's needs, anyway. Ye wouldn't earn three 'undred pounds if ye worked 'ere fer *six years!*"

"I know. But I couldn't ask Cornelia. It would be another defeat for me. Besides, she doesn't know I'm here, and I don't want to tell her. I was . . . it was I who was supposed to be Countess Mullineaux's guest, you see."

"What's that? *You? I* don't understand. If it was supposed to be you, why ain't ye—?"

"Please, Clara, sit down again. I'll try to explain it all to you. You promised to remain my friend, remember? Even to the gibbet, you said. Don't desert me now."

Clara, eyeing her suspiciously, allowed herself to be led back to the bed. "I'll stay fer a bit . . . but only if ye agree t' tell me the true tale. Though I don't know as I'll ever believe that a fine lady truly needs t' work below stairs."

The night was well advanced before Clara was satisfied that she'd heard the whole story, but by the time they embraced and bade each other goodnight they were fast friends again. The stiffness that Clara had felt when first realizing that Ada was far above her in station was soon eased by the sincerity of Ada's warm affection for her. But affection and a renewed friendship did not keep Clara from telling Ada that she was a fool. "Ye should've asked her ladyship fer help right away," she insisted. "She would've taken you in, and it would be *you* havin' a green *peau de soie* gown and bein' the center of eyes at a ball."

"No, Clara. I would be playing second fiddle to Cornelia again, and I have quite enough of that at home. Once I'd heard that Cornelia had arrived here before me, I knew I'd lost the game."

Clara frowned. "That's nonsense. Ye can't lose a game ye didn't even play!"

Ada blinked at her friend in surprise. Was Clara right? Had

she been cowardly in not entering the lists in the battle to conquer London? She considered the matter for a moment and then shook her head. "What sense was there in playing the game? With Cornelia so beautiful and clever, what chance had *I* to make a mark? It would have been difficult enough for me to make a satisfactory impression on the *ton* if I'd been here alone, but in competition with Cornelia it would have been impossible. I would only have made the Countess ashamed of me, bubblehead that I am."

Clara remained unconvinced, but she agreed that matters were now too far advanced to change. Familiar with Cornelia's character as she was, Clara could understand Ada's reluctance to ask Cornelia for any help. Cornelia would certainly laugh at her and hold her up to riducule before the family. It was bad enough that Ada was forced to endure Cornelia's annoying condescension at home in Bishop's Cleve; here in London the girl had a right to be free of it.

It was also clear to Clara that Ada did not wish to disappoint the Countess, who had been her mother's best friend and was her own godmother. If she'd been courageous enough to introduce herself to her ladyship from the first, matters might have turned out better than the timid girl expected, but Clara had to admit that it was too late to do so now.

With all the problems made plain, Clara finally understood why Ada needed her wages. She wanted to make her way home without seeking help from either the Countess or Cornelia. "Don't you see?" Ada explained. "The person called Ada Surrey, as soon as she's earned enough money to travel, will disappear. Ada Surringham will reappear in Bishop's Cleve as if she'd never left. No one but Uncle Jasper will ever have to know anything about the whole foolish escapade."

Clara, despite her reservations, promised with a full heart to do all she could to keep the knowledge of Ada's presence from her cousin and her true identity from everyone else. "I'll help you buy yer passage on the stage. But I'll tell ye frankly, Ada, that I'll miss Ada Surrey when she disappears. I ain't 'ad a friend like you ever afore."

They embraced tearfully. "Nor I you, Clara. Not ever."

Later, waiting for sleep to come, Ada went over her conversation with Clara in her mind. She was glad she'd finally revealed herself. It would be good to have someone to confide in. The only thing she'd held back from Clara was the story of her relationship with Lord Mullineaux. The feelings generated by her two encounters with his lordship were still too new and fragile to be spoken of aloud.

She twisted about under the coverlet in discomfort. Her emotions, when she thought about Griff Mullineaux, were so chaotic that they frightened her. She knew what those emotions signified, of course. She had read so much about the emotions of love that she'd recognized her symptoms at once. Even at the inn she'd known the name of the illness that had struck her. What she didn't know was the cure.

Love was something she'd dreamed of often. She'd always wanted to fall in love. She'd imagined the sort of man he would be: gentle, soft-spoken, wise, patient. She had seen him in her mind quite clearly. He'd be fair-haired and clear of eye, with a smooth, high forehead, a serene expression and a ready laugh. She supposed he'd be a vicar or a country squire with a small estate, someone whose social obligations were modest and whose friends were not fashionable, so that he wouldn't be embarrassed by a wife who was absentminded and a bit of a bubblehead. Even in her wildest dreams, Ada hadn't imagined falling in love with a dark-eyed, devilishly attractive rake of low morals and high income, who would kiss her before he even learned her name and who would decide, before they'd been acquainted for an hour, that she was a completely unsuitable consort for a man of wealth and fashion.

So love had struck, as she'd heard it so often did, with blind inaccuracy. Now she would have to face the dire consequences. One of those consequences might be being forced to watch (from this unfortunate position below stairs) cousin Cornelia, in her green *peau de soie* gown, catch Griff in her net. That would be a painful experience indeed. Her only hope was to arrange to leave this house *before* a romance between her cousin and Griff Mullineaux had time to develop. It was true that she'd decided, only a short time ago, that she wanted to remain here as long as possible, to be close to this man who had somehow, without warning, taken possession of her thoughts. But after tonight (after experiencing the feeling of being discovered, and realizing that things would have been much worse for her if the discovery had been made, not by Clara, but by Cornelia or her ladyship) she knew she had to get away. And soon.

Feeling stifled, she threw off the covers and crept out of

bed. She climbed up on a chair to reach the tiny round window which was the room's only source of fresh air. She pushed it open and peered out into the black, starless night. Yes, she thought sadly, she would leave soon. She would have to endure the night of the ball, of course—that was to occur in only two days' time—but with the receipt of her month's wages and with Clara's help, she might very well manage her escape a few days later. Once she was home again, far from Griff Mullineaux's dynamic presence and the scene of what would undoubtedly become Cornelia's triumph, she might begin to find a cure for this terrible disease that had so unexpectedly overwhelmed her.

Chapter Sixteen

Aubrey was hanging about again. He had tried on three separate occasions to arrange for an introduction to the magnificent Miss Haydon, but his timing was always off. The first time she was out shopping; the next time she was taking tea with Sir Nigel Lewis, and Aubrey was reluctant to interrupt; and the third time she was occupied with her ladyship's seamstress who was fitting her ballgown. "Where is she today?" he demanded of his friend as they sat at the breakfast-room table lingering over their coffees. "I'm determined to accomplish this mission today."

"I don't know where she is," Griff said irritably. "I can't be expected to keep track of her comings and goings."

Aubrey glared at him. "You're not trying to keep her for yourself, are you? That wouldn't be playing fair."

"Don't be a clunch. I've already told you that the girl doesn't interest me."

"Yes, so you did, but I think it's all a hum. Trying to pretend that you're smitten with another girl! The day that Griff Mullineaux is so smitten with a female that he's blind to the charms of someone like Miss Haydon will be the day I give up my tailor."

Griff gave a reluctant laugh. He was in a vile mood, and he didn't feel up to exchanging pleasantries with Aubrey this morning. He hated having to admit to himself that his mood had anything to do with his confused emotions about the young lady working in his library. It was less bothersome to attribute this depressed state to the news Finchley-Jones brought to him this morning. But Aubrey had accidentally put his finger on a strange truth—if this Miss Haydon was really such a diamond, how was it that he, the notorious libertine, had never noticed? Something was decidedly wrong with him. "I know how much Weston's tailoring means to a man of your girth, old fellow, but if you're going to make rash statements of that sort, perhaps you'd better start looking for someone else to cut your coats," he muttered glumly.

"What? Are you still pretending to be infatuated? With the same female you told me of? The maggoty one?"

Griff threw his friend a look of disgust. "I don't want to talk about it. Do you think I have nothing on my mind but females and tailors and suchlike fripperies? After what I learned this morning, your problem concerning Miss Haydon is the last thing on my mind."

"What did you learn this morning?" his friend inquired curiously.

"You wouldn't be interested. It's about my library."

"Your library? This pucker you're in is caused by your *library?* I don't believe it."

"You may believe what you like, Aubrey. Only go away and let me brood in peace."

Aubrey ignored the order and simply reached for another biscuit. "Very well, I'll believe you. What's so troublesome about your library?"

"I've just been told that my Tottel is missing."

"You don't mean it!" Aubrey cried in mock horror. "Lost your *Tottel?* That's dreadful! Tragic! Cataclysmic!" Then, calmly buttering his biscuit, he asked, "What on earth is a Tottel?"

"Not what, you gudgeon. Who. Tottel was a publisher in the sixteenth century. He published a collection of verse known as the *Miscellany.* Have you never heard of Tottel's *Miscellany?*"

"No, can't say I have." He paused in the act of bringing the biscuit to his mouth and peered at his friend in sudden, quite sincere alarm. "I say, Griff, you're not going to tell me you're turning bookish!"

"I've always been 'bookish.' I hope you won't be too badly shocked to learn that I've managed, in the past few years, to gather together a very commendable library. The Tottel was the gem of my collection."

"Good God," his friend said, aghast. "I wouldn't have believed it of you. Griff Mullineaux, bookish!" He took a quick bite to steady his nerves. "I *am* badly shocked, I must say. This is quite upsetting news to learn about someone you thought you knew well . . . someone you considered your very best friend in the world. I don't mind your confiding this piece of information to *me,* old chap, because I'd remain fond of you no matter what aberration appeared in your character, but I wouldn't say anything to anyone else about this if I were you. Wouldn't do to have it bruited about that you were bookish."

"Damnation, Aubrey, don't talk fustian," Griff muttered, dismissing Aubrey's raving with a mere toss of his head. "You don't realize what this loss means to me. A Tottel is a rarity. Collectors may search a lifetime without finding one. Try to imagine the blow it is, after having tasted the joy of acquiring it, to have it disappear!"

"Books don't disappear," Aubrey responded with bland indifference, looking under the covered platters to discover if any more of the smoked fish lurked beneath. "The thing is bound to turn up somewhere."

"I hope so. I've sent for Symonds and Mrs. Mudge to see what can be done about locating it. You're welcome to stay, old man, but I don't think you'll find the interview entertaining."

"Oh, yes, I shall. This view of Griff Mullineaux as a man of books is *vastly* entertaining. I wouldn't miss it for the world."

"Perhaps you'll be rewarded with the arrival of Miss Haydon at the end, eh?"

Aubrey shrugged. "After putting up with all this talk of literature, I *deserve* that reward."

Symonds and Mrs. Mudge both presented themselves to his lordship when his breakfast was finished. He explained what had happened very carefully. "I don't wish you to give the staff the impression that they are under the slightest suspicion of theft," he explained. "Theft of such an object, when there are many other articles about the house of equal or greater value, like her ladyship's jewelry, is quite unlikely."

"That's right," Aubrey put in. "It's only a book, after all."

Griff threw him a silencing glare. "It is my conviction," he went on to the heads of the staff, "that the book has somehow been misplaced. It is lying somewhere, in some out-of-the-way corner, unnoticed and forgotten. I know that I'm giving you both an enormous task—there are so many rooms, closets, niches and cubbyholes in the house in which a book may lodge. But, dash it all, it must be found!"

"Yes, my lord," Symonds said. "We shall make a thorough search. But I hope, my lord, that you'll be patient with us.

There *is* the ball tomorrow, you know."

"The ball?" Griff winced in annoyance. "Oh, damnation, I'd forgotten for a moment about the deuced ball." He rubbed his forehead disconsolately. "I suppose you must do what is necessary to make ready for it. Naturally, that must come first."

"Not first, your lordship," the butler said sympathetically, "but at least simultaneously. We shall manage to search while making the party preparations."

"Thank you, Symonds."

"Beg pardon, your lordship," Mrs. Mudge asked timidly, "but p'rhaps you can describe the book, so's we know what we're searchin' for."

"Yes, of course I can. It has a reddish-brown cover of tooled leather, somewhat worn at the corners. The pages are hand-cut, which means that the edges are rough and a great deal yellowed. On the spine are the words *The Songes and Sonnettes*, in gilt letters, spelled the old-fashioned way, with the *e* on Song and the *double-t* and *e* on Sonnet. That's about all I can think of."

"That's quite enough, I should say," Aubrey observed with amusement. "If ever *I'm* misplaced, I hope you can describe me half so well."

Aubrey lingered for another hour, but his "reward" did not appear. He took his leave, vowing to return as soon as possible for another chance. "I must have an introduction to her before the ball, or I shan't be able to find the opportunity to inscribe my name on her dance card!" he said worriedly before departing.

Griff saw him to the door and then set off down the hall toward his study. Aubrey's remark about the ball had set him thinking. His friend was looking forward to the ball but he was not. The house was already at sixes and sevens, with servants dashing about making ready, with deliveries of chairs and china and champagne and potted greenery, and with his mother preoccupied with preparations. And it would be worse tomorrow. His mother had already told him that the Corinthian manner of making a brief appearance, dancing one dance, sampling one pastry and one glass of champagne and then making off for a gaming hell would not do. He was expected, this time, to remain for the entire evening, to dance every dance, and to

escort the guest of honor to the buffet. He would obey his
mother's request, of course, but he could anticipate nothing
enjoyable about the experience.

However, there was one way the ball might be made as
interesting for him as it evidently was for Aubrey. If he, like
Aubrey, could sign the dance card of a young lady who'd
captured his eye, the evening might be saved. The ball might
turn out to be an exciting event if Miss Ada Surrey were present.
Why not? he asked himself. His mother would not object,
would she, to giving a card to the librarian's assistant? What
would be so wrong with that?

At that moment, as if she'd materialized from his thoughts,
Miss Surrey appeared down the hall. She had evidently taken
her luncheon in the servants' hall and was returning to the
library by the back stairs. He hurried his step. "Miss Surrey?"
he called.

She turned round with a start, peered uneasily into the gloom
of the hallway and then recognized him. "Good afternoon, your
lordship," she said with a little bob of a curtsey.

"I was just thinking of you," he admitted, catching up with
her.

"Were you?"

"Yes." He grinned down at her. "I was wishing you would
permit me to sign your dance card."

"My what?"

"Your dance card. For tomorrow's ball."

"Is this some sort of joke, my lord? Or is it the fashion
among the *haut ton* of London for the nobility to dance with
the servants at their balls?"

"No, unfortunately it's not the fashion, though I can think
of many fashions that have much less to be said for them.
However, you, my girl, will receive a card for the ball this
afternoon. Tomorrow night you will attend the festivities as a
guest, not a servant. I hope that answers your question. Now
that we have that matter cleared, I wish an answer to *my* question. May I have the first dance with you?"

Her eyes flew to his face. Even in the shadows of the rear
hallway, she could see the eager gleam in his eyes. Her heart
bounced up in her chest. How lovely it would be, she thought,
to appear at the ball and walk onto the dance floor on Griff
Mullineaux's arm for the very first dance. The blood sparkled
in her veins at the mere thought of it. "It is most kind of you

to ask me, my lord, but you're being impetuous, are you not? Won't you be escorting the *guest of honor* for the first dance?"

His face clouded. "Damnation, I didn't think of that. I suppose I shall have to." He frowned down at her in sudden suspicion. "For a librarian's assistant, you're very well informed on the rites and customs of the *haut monde* galas, are you not?"

She hoped that, in the hall's dimness, he wouldn't see her flush. "Well, I . . . I read a great deal," she explained lamely.

"That answer, ma'am, is a weak attempt to flummery me, I think. But it did me no good to quiz you before, and I expect I would get no better results now. So let us return to the subject I introduced earlier. Your dance card."

"I thought the matter was closed."

"No, not at all. Only the matter of the first dance. We shall now discuss the *second* dance. There can be no objection to my dancing *that* one with you, can there?"

"There certainly can, but we needn't go into that, for I won't be there."

"But I just explained to you that you *will* be there."

She shook her head. "I'm afraid, my lord, that it's quite impossible. It is not my place—"

"Hang it, girl, must you be so rigidly conventional? You were not so at our first meeting. Listen to me, my dear, and try to believe me. Once you've received an invitation, then it's as much your 'place' to attend the festivities as any other guest's."

"I do thank you for asking, my lord—"

"Griff. Call me Griff. I can not enjoy waltzing with anyone who calls me my lord."

She held up her hand as if to ward off an attack, but her expression was adamant. "I do thank you for asking, *my lord*, but if I have the right to be invited, I must also be given the right to refuse."

He caught her raised hand in his and brought it to his lips. "Don't refuse me, girl," he begged urgently. "The evening will be unbearable without you."

"Don't!" she whispered, a catch in her throat. "You shouldn't . . . you promised you wouldn't . . ."

"Wouldn't what?"

"Wouldn't flirt with me."

"I never made such a ridiculous promise."

"Yes, you did," she insisted, struggling to free her hand. "You said you . . . never fondle the housemaids."

"You're no housemaid. And this isn't fondling. I'm merely holding your hand. Even this . . ." He pulled her to him and encircled her waist with his arm. "Even *this* cannot be called fondling." Putting his cheek against hers, he hummed a strain into her ear and led her in a waltzing turn down the corridor.

She felt positively light-headed, floating down the length of the rear hallway in his arms. She had danced the waltz twice before, once at a Bishop's Cleve assembly and once at a private party. Each time she'd tripped over her partner's feet. This time she felt as if she were dancing on air. Every step was right. He whirled her about as easily as if she were a phantom, insubstantial, graceful and completely weightless. For a moment she lost her sense of time and place. They weren't master and servant or even Ada Surringham and the Viscount Mullineaux. They were Cinderella and the Prince, Juliet and Romeo, Eve and Adam. She didn't want the moment to end.

He didn't stop until they'd come to the dark end of the hall. And when he ceased dancing, he didn't release his hold on her. Breathless, they seemed to cling together. "Come to the ball," he whispered in her ear. "Please."

"Oh, Griff," she breathed against his chest, unable to return to reality.

"Does that mean yes?"

She forced herself back into the present. She would not behave like a bubblehead with him, if she could help it. "No, of course not. You know I mustn't—"

"I know nothing of the sort. Why not?"

"I have no gown, for one thing—"

"Mama will find one for you."

"I couldn't ask her to . . . besides, she would never . . . and Mrs. Mudge would have apoplexy . . . and the whole staff would take offen—" But he kissed her before she could finish.

He hadn't intended to do it. He hadn't intended to do any of the foolish things he'd done in the past few minutes. She was a dithering, maggoty, bubbleheaded female who was, on the one hand, too innocent to be taken advantage of but who, on the other hand, was too impossibly unsuitable to consider courting seriously. He'd known from the first that he should have nothing to do with her.

But every time he looked at her, something happened to his

common sense. It collapsed, dissolved, completely deserted him. One look in those eyes of hers and he lost his resolve. He realized now that for days he'd yearned to hold her in his arms and kiss her like this. She was soft, light and completely pliant in his hold. It was the most damnable pass! Never had he met a girl with whom he was so ill-matched, yet never before had a girl felt so right in his embrace. If he let himself go, as he was doing at this moment, he might forget himself enough to make the girl an offer! This strange, mysterious, absentminded, unbefitting creature might reel him in as no girl had managed to do before.

He'd better get hold of himself before there was real harm done. This girl was not for him. Slowly, with painful effort, he eased his hold on her. "Now, *that*," he said as he let her go, trying to hide his breathlessness and appear casual, "might be called fondling."

She sensed, at once, the change in him. She'd been carried away, blissful and dizzy, into a place that was completely new to her. She'd never felt so happy. She wondered if perhaps she were dreaming all this, although the excitement of her feelings was stronger than ever she'd experienced in a dream. But if this were real, she wouldn't have the courage to permit herself to waltz like a wraith in Griff's arms and to surrender—and respond like an eager little tart—to his kiss. Why, from the way he was embracing her, she could almost believe he cared for her. So this *couldn't* be reality. She simply couldn't believe this was really happening to her. Reality never turned out this way—not for her. Therefore, this was merely one of her dreams, though an especially thrilling and vivid one, and she might as well relax and enjoy it.

But it had turned out to be reality, after all. She knew it as soon as she felt him stiffen. He had kissed her, true, but all too soon he'd thought better of it. "Yes," she said, turning away so that he couldn't see the extent of her disappointment, "I think you might . . . call it f-fondling."

"I am sorry," he said in a subdued voice. "I *did* promise not to—"

Far away, down the length of the hall, someone opened the front door. The sound jarred them both. Griff was quick to notice how Ada wheeled about in terror. Footsteps appeared to be approaching. Griff looked over his shoulder. "It's only Mama's guest, Miss Haydon," he said soothingly. "You've no need to be embarrassed; we haven't been seen. Besides, even if we *had* been seen, the embarrassment would all be on my side, not on yours."

"Nevertheless, I must go," Ada whispered uneasily.

"There, you see? She hasn't even noticed us. She's going to the front stairs."

Ada felt so agonizingly deflated that she almost didn't care if Cornelia spotted her or not, but she had to get away from Griff's painful proximity. "Good day, your lordship."

"Wait!" He caught her hand again. "What about tomorrow?"

Cornelia, at the foot of the stairs, heard a sound from the shadows. "Griff? Is that you back there?" she asked, peering into the darkness.

"Damnation," he cursed softly under his breath, tightening his hold on Ada. "Well?"

"No, not tomorrow." Ada pulled her hand free and flew to the back stairs. "Please," she whispered tearfully as she disappeared from his sight, "don't ask me again."

Chapter Seventeen

The day of the ball dawned darkly, the sun obscured by a heavy covering of black clouds and the air heavy with an icy wetness. By six a drizzle began to fall with a cold persistence that seemed to promise a long stay. But not only the weather was forboding; human circumstances, too, were not propitious. The day began badly for almost everyone at Mullineaux House.

The first of the residents to receive bad news was Ada. The news was signaled by an urgent knocking at her door just as she'd arisen, a little past dawn, and begun her ablutions. It was Clara. "Ada, open up," she whispered nervously. "I 'ave somethin' t' tell ye."

Ada, shivering in the cold of her room, padded barefoot to the door. One look at Clara's face told her there was something very wrong. "What on earth's the matter?" she asked, stepping aside to let the housemaid enter.

"The book," Clara whispered dramatically as she shut the door. "That one in the corner, that ye said ye'd been usin' t' prop up yer mirror . . . I think it's the missin' treasure."

Ada stared at her uncomprehendingly. "Are you speaking of the book that Mr. Finchley-Jones has been searching for?"

"*Everyone's* searchin' fer it now. Even Mrs. Mudge. She tole the entire staff first thing this mornin' that 'is lordship ordered the place combed from top t' bottom. Mrs. Mudge explained what the book looked like an' said how we was all t' keep our eyes open fer it—"

"But, Clara, that book on the floor isn't the one. It *couldn't* be. The missing book is Tottel's *Miscellany*. Whatever made you think—?"

"That ain't the name Mrs. Mudge tole us. It was like the name you said the other night. Songs an' . . . an', ye know . . . those poems."

"Sonnets?" Ada asked in dawning horror.

"That's it. Sonnets with a double-*t* an' a *e*."

"Good God!" Ada dashed across the room and fell to her

knees, groping under her little table with trembling hands. She picked up the book, sat down on the floor and opened it to the title page. "Oh, Clara, it *is* the one! Here's the name Tottel large as life at the bottom of the page! I never even *noticed*. How could I be so featherbrained?"

"The question is, girl, what t' do now?" Clara said worriedly. "Mrs. Mudge is bound t' think ye filched it."

"*Filched* it? Oh, heavens! Will she believe I'm a *thief*?"

"I don't know, Ada. Prob'ly will. I think she's more likely t' believe ye a thief than a featherbrain."

"I'm not at all sure I wouldn't rather she *did* think that," Ada mumbled ruefully. "Oh, dear, I don't know what to do! Shall I just take this down to the library and confess to Mr. Finchley-Jones? He'll surely sack me when he realizes I've had this treasure all this time."

"'E might at that, even if it breaks 'is 'eart t' do it. Arfter all, it'll go 'ard with 'im t' face Lord Mullineaux an' tell 'im that 'is assistant 'as been usin' that precious book t'—"

"To prop up her mirror!" Ada finished, shuddering. "Oh, my God! How could I have done it?" She ran her hands over the book's leather cover to ascertain how much damage her carelessness had done to the binding.

"I think ye should keep yer clapper tight behind yer stumps fer a while," Clara said thoughtfully. "Today ain't the best time fer confession."

"You mean say nothing?" Ada asked, wide-eyed.

"Fer the time bein'. Now, while things is so skimble-skamble on account o' the ball, they might be real short with ye, t' get the matter over with and out o' the way, ye know. But if ye wait 'til the ball's done with, things'll be calmer an' tempers won't be as likely t' boil over."

"You're probably right, Clara, but I don't think I can bear waiting. How can I keep my mouth shut about so serious an offense? I'll *really* feel like a thief if I say nothing."

"It's only fer a day. Take my advice, Ada. Keepin' still is the smartest thing t' do fer now."

So Ada nodded her agreement, Clara went off about her business, and Ada finished with her dressing. But when she reported to the library to begin her day's work, she could hardly look Mr. Finchley-Jones in the eye, so uncomfortable was she in her hidden guilt.

Her ladyship also started her day with bad news. No sooner

had she opened her eyes than her abigail informed her that a dreadful scene was taking place in the kitchen. The lobster for the patties (which were to be the highlight of the buffet) had failed to arrive, and Monsieur Albert, the French chef, was having a tantrum in the kitchen over it. He'd spent the past half hour, the abigail reported, screeching to the undercooks and the gaggle of scullery maids who were gaping at him in frozen alarm that *"il est trop tard pour changer le menu,"* and that if her ladyship could not do something *"immédiatement,"* he was going to his room *"pour faire mes valises."*

Her ladyship sighed in resignation as she pulled herself from her bed. It was going to be one of those days, she told herself glumly, that made one wish one could escape to the Indies.

Cornelia's bad news came somewhat later that morning. It was during a mid-morning breakfast that the realization broke upon her that, in spite of all her efforts, she was not making an impression on Lord Mullineaux. She had come to breakfast early in order to encounter his lordship there, and she'd worn her most magnificent morning robe for the occasion. It was a rose-colored masterpiece in lacy *point de tulle* worked in a most intricate pattern, through the holes of which a white satin underdress could be detected. She'd tied the overdress tightly under the breast and let the neck edge fall low on her shoulders. She knew it made the most of her dewy morning skin. In addition, it rustled when she walked and emphasized her tall, willowy grace.

But she'd done even more to her appearance before descending to the breakfast room. She'd let her hair fall loosely to her shoulders, and she'd brushed a smidgeon of blacking on her lashes. Every little touch was calculated to suggest a sleepy informality that was bound to be enticing to any man of normal appetite. Both her mirror and her abigail had told her that she looked delectable.

She found his lordship at the table, as she'd expected. He was alone. She stood posed in the doorway for more than a minute before he looked up, but he was apparently engrossed in perusing a sheaf of papers which seemed to be nothing more than neatly copied lists. When he *did* look up, he rose politely, held a chair for her, murmured something about its being a shame it was raining on the day of the ball, and returned to his lists. She tried three times to engage him in conversation, but she received mere monosyllables in response. "I've wasted my most fetching robe on you," she muttered irritably at last.

"What's that?" he responded, looking up. "Did you say something about a fetching robe?" Then, realizing what she meant, he threw her a somewhat abashed grin. "I'm sorry, Cornelia. It *is* fetching. I should have said something."

"If you truly think it fetching, why don't you pay some attention to me? Why is it so difficult for me to hold your eye?" she demanded, pouting.

"Because, my dear, my library work demands my attention, too." Without a touch of guilt, he returned that attention to his papers. He was quite familiar with the tricks of accomplished flirts, and he was not in the least susceptible to them. Suddenly, he looked across the table at her with a glimmer of amusement in his eyes. "However, Cornelia, if you linger over your coffee just a bit longer," he suggested, "my friend Aubrey will be dropping in. Aubrey has been most eager to make your acquaintance. There is no one in the world who would appreciate the charm of your most becoming *dishabille* more than Aubrey."

Cornelia rose from her chair like an angry hawk rising with a flapping of its wings from the limb of a tree that had been shaken by a sudden squall. She felt as if she'd been doused with cold water. Never before in her life had a gentleman tried to palm her off on someone else! That his lordship wanted to do so was quite the last straw. Without another word she'd stalked from the room in a sulk. The incident threatened to ruin her joy in the entire day.

His lordship watched her departure with a touch of mischievous merriment in his eyes. The girl was self-centered and spoiled, and he'd found the temptation to give her a set-down quite irresistible. He didn't think he'd been too unkind. If he'd wrenched her from her complacency and disturbed her mood, the upset would only last a little while. When tonight's festivities were over, and she'd become the belle of the *ton*, she would completely forget his little slight.

Of course, he was well aware that he'd spoiled her morning. What he didn't know was that his own morning—and afternoon and evening as well—were to be filled with disturbances a great deal more wrenching than the one he'd dealt his mother's guest.

The first of those disturbances occurred a short time later, with the arrival of Aubrey. The fellow was in a belligerent mood, declaring that he would not vacate the premises until he was given an introduction to the young woman of his dreams. Griff felt a flush of sympathy for poor Aubrey, knowing how often the fellow had made the attempt to meet Cornelia, and he was perfectly willing to oblige, but he feared that he did not stand in Cornelia's good graces because of what had happened in the breakfast room only a short while earlier. Thus he decided that the best way to arrange the introduction would be through the good offices of his mother.

He searched for his mother high and low, finally tracking her down in the kitchen. He tried valiantly to convince her to come upstairs and oblige his friend, but Lady Mullineaux was too preoccupied to take the time. "I'm sorry, dearest, but I haven't yet discovered what has happened to the lobsters, so I must remain available to keep Monsieur Albert calm. And when the lobsters *do* arrive, I shall have to solve several other problems—an insufficiency of champagne glasses, for one. Clark and Debenham's delivered only half the number I ordered. We cannot serve champagne in wine goblets, you know; we'd be the laughing stock of London. Furthermore, Symonds tells me that the Regent has sent a message that he will honor us with his presence after all; that means I must completely rearrange the seating for supper. I am quite at my wit's end, dearest, so please go away and deal with Aubrey's problem yourself."

Griff tried his very best, sending Symonds to plead with Cornelia to come downstairs for only a brief quarter hour, but the girl adamantly refused. After the incident that morning, Griff was not surprised. But Aubrey, who knew nothing of the little contretemps at the breakfast table, could not understand why the girl had refused to make an appearance. "Can she have taken me in dislike without even knowing me?" he asked uneasily. "Has she heard something disgraceful about me, do you suppose?"

"I say, Aubrey Tait, what disgraceful thing have you done?" Griff teased. But reading the frustration on his friend's face, he changed his tone. "I think she's just too busy preparing for this evening," he added, trying to be comforting.

"Preparing for this evening? But it's not even noon!"

"Oh, well, you know how women are. They can fuss over their gowns or their coiffures all day."

Aubrey dropped into a chair in the drawing room and sul-

lenly refused to leave. "I shall wait," he declared stubbornly.
"I shall wait if it takes *hours!* After all, she ain't likely to
remain upstairs closeted in her room all day. Sooner or later
she's bound to make an appearance. And when she does, I'll
be here."

Griff shrugged. "Suit yourself, old fellow. Make yourself
at home for as long as you like. But I hope you won't mind
if I go about my own business."

His first order of business was an interview with his librarian. While Aubrey settled deeply into his chair, put his feet
up on a hassock and indulged in a desultory perusal of the
Times, Griff and Mr. Finchley-Jones put their heads together
over the shapely Sheraton table that was the jewel of the drawing room and went over the now completed list of books on
English history. Mr. Finchley-Jones made suggestions for needed
additions (which he read to his employer from still another list)
and wrote notations beside those works whose purchase his
lordship approved. When their business was completed, and
Mr. Finchley-Jones rose to leave, Lord Mullineaux held up a
hand to detain him. "I was wondering, Mr. Finchley-Jones, if
you would like to attend tonight's festivities."

Both Finchley-Jones and Aubrey looked up, startled. *"I*,
my lord?" the librarian asked, his lorgnette slipping from his
nose in his surprise.

"My mother and I would be pleased if you came...and
Miss Surrey, too, of course."

Finchley-Jones flushed with pleasure. "Why, your lordship,
I...I'm overwhelmed! Such an invitation is quite unprece-
dented. I do thank you, and Lady Mullineaux, too, most sin-
cerely. I...We shall be honored to attend."

Griff was aware that Aubrey was watching the scene with
curiosity, but he went on anyway. "I know you cannot speak
for her, but do you think Miss Surrey could be persuaded to
join you? I have the impression that she might be too diffident
to—"

"I'm quite *sure* that I can persuade her," Mr. Finchley-Jones
said with what Griff felt was a rather obnoxious self-assurance.

"Are you indeed?" he asked, his tone suddenly growing
chilly.

Finchley-Jones looked down at the spectacles swinging on
his chest like a pendant and smiled complacently. "You see,
your lordship, I am fortunate to be able to announce to you

that Miss Surrey has recently consented to become my wife, so I—"

"*What?*" Griff felt as if someone had landed a hard blow to his midsection. "What did you say?" he asked again, frozen-faced.

"I don't blame you for being surprised," the librarian said, keeping his eyes lowered modestly. "You are thinking, I suppose, that I am somewhat advanced in years for this sort of change in my way of life—"

"I am thinking, fellow," Griff interrupted curtly, trying to keep his voice level and his temper even, "that I can't have heard you properly! Did you say that you asked *Ada Surrey* to *marry* you?"

The tone of voice in which the question was asked, though not loud, had such a timbre of angry shock that it disturbed not only Mr. Finchley-Jones but Aubrey. Both heads came up abruptly. "Yes, I did," Mr. Finchley-Jones said, his smile dying. "Doesn't your lordship approve of—?"

"Of course I don't approve!" his lordship barked, jumping to his feet. "Are you trying to pretend the girl *accepted* you?"

Mr. Finchley-Jones, although as impressed as anyone in his station with the awesomeness of rank and wealth, was not a milksop. He drew himself up to his full height and raised his lorgnette to his eyes. "There is no need for me to *pretend,* my lord," he said proudly. "She *did* accept me."

"I don't believe it! Why wouldn't she have *told* me—?"

"Told *you,* my lord? Why *should* she have—?"

Aubrey leaned forward in his chair. "I say, Griff," he asked in amazement, "this chit you're speaking of . . . she ain't the *one,* is she?"

"The *one?*" the librarian echoed, looking round at Aubrey in confusion.

"You know," Aubrey persisted, ignoring the librarian and keeping his shrewd eyes fixed on his friend's face, "the mag-goty one you told me of."

"Shut up, Aubrey," Griff snapped. "Stay out of this."

"I don't understand, your lordship," Mr. Finchley-Jones said uneasily. "Other than meeting her in the library, are you *acquainted* with my betrothed?"

"I'm more than 'acquainted' with her! I know her well enough to know that what you say is ridiculous." He leaned on the table with one hand and pointed a threatening finger at his librarian with the other. "So don't refer to her as your 'betrothed' ever again!"

Mr. Finchley-Jones stuck out his chin stubbornly. "Miss Surrey *is* my betrothed, and I shall refer to her as such so long as it remains true," he declared bravely. "And when it is no longer true, my lord, I shall refer to her as *my wife!*"

Griff glared at the fellow, fighting an urge to throttle him. Then he threw up his hands in frustration. "I think, Finchley-Jones, that you've *lost your wits!*"

"I hope you'll pardon me for saying this, my lord, but perhaps *you* have lost *yours!*"

"Well, let's find out, shall we?" His lordship strode to the bellrope, but before he could pull it, the butler appeared in the doorway. "I'm sorry to disturb you, my lord, but—"

"Not at all," Griff said. "You're just the man I wanted. Find Miss Surrey and tell her she's wanted in the library. *At once,* mind!"

"Yes, my lord," the butler said, looking uncomfortable, "but first I must tell you that there's a . . . a certain someone at the door."

"A certain someone?" He glared at the butler in irritation. "What kind of announcement is that?"

"A certain . . . lady." That Symonds disapproved of the "certain lady" was obvious.

"Has everyone gone mad today?" Griff growled. "The lady has a name, I presu—"

Before he could finish, the sound of rushing slippers and the rustle of a cloak drew all their eyes to the doorway. Julia Alcorn came running in, her rain-spattered cloak billowing behind her and its hood slipping down to reveal a head of disheveled hair. "I couldn't wait, Griff," she cried tearfully, dashing up to him in complete disregard of the others in the room. "He's coming! With his *pistols!*"

"Oh, good God!" muttered Aubrey. "Here we go again!"

Chapter Eighteen

Griff groaned in impatience. "Julia, what have you done now?" he asked disgustedly.

"Don't be angry with me," she said with a hoarse catch in her voice. She looked quickly around the room like an actress surveying the audience, and, as impervious to the presence of Aubrey and Finchley-Jones as an actress would be to a full balcony, continued with her scene. "I had to tell him, dearest. I *had* to."

"Tell him what?"

"He threatened to send me back to his mother if I didn't! Oh, Griff, you don't know how that threat cuts into my soul! Life with his mother is...*unspeakable*. So,...so I admitted it."

"Yes, my dear, so you've told me. But *what* is it that you admitted?"

"That I ran off with you when you went to Wales."

"But that's not true! He knows it isn't true. Confound it, Julia, you went back home with him, didn't you? He saw me at the Black Boar with..." Griff hesitated, not willing to go further in this ill-assorted company.

"You're referring to the girl in the inn, aren't you?" Julia asked.

His brows snapped together. "How did you know about her?"

She gave a careless shrug. "Giles Alcorn doesn't keep secrets from his wife. He told me all about the incident at the Black Boar."

Griff's eyes burned with fury. "He did, did he?"

"I told him that that was all a pretense, that the girl was probably some lightskirt you'd hired for the performance. You must have played your part magnificently, Griff, for I had a great deal of difficulty convincing him that I spoke the truth."

"It's why you *wanted* him to believe it was a performance that I don't understand," Griff muttered, wondering what had ever possessed him to become involved with this troublesome woman in the first place.

"Because she'd rather throw *you* to the wolves than face her mother-in-law, that's why," Aubrey said, as disgusted as his friend by this latest turn of events.

Griff put a hand to his forehead. "Very well, ma'am, you've warned me. I am obliged to you for coming, but I think it would be best for all concerned if you would now return to your home."

"But Griff, you're not going to remain here and *wait* for him, are you? We may still have time to—"

"To do what, my love?" came a voice from the doorway. Everyone looked up to see Alcorn standing there, face white and pistol case under his arm. "To make off together to Wales again? Did you really think I wouldn't follow you to Wales?"

"Good afternoon, Alcorn," Griff said drily. "It wanted only your presence to make this party complete. Come in, come in."

"I think, my lord," said Alcorn, "that I am not in the mood for a party. Can you rid us of all these onlookers?"

"That's a bit high-handed of you, isn't it?" Aubrey demanded, rising from his chair and stepping forward. "This ain't your house."

"True, Tait, too true," Alcorn said with a pained smile, "but I nevertheless have an aversion to having my private affairs discussed before strangers."

"I shall be glad to withdraw, my lord," Finchley-Jones offered stiffly. "Do you wish me to return at a later hour?"

"No, I don't wish you to withdraw at all," Griff said shortly. "We have an important matter to conclude. Alcorn, if you don't wish to discuss private matters before strangers, you can take your wife and go. You may come back to continue the discussion at another time, if you find you still wish to do so."

"Oh, no, Mullineaux, you won't be rid of me as easily as that. I've come here to settle matters with you once and for all."

"And how do you intend to that, eh? Have a duel right here in the drawing room?"

"Griff, no!" Julia cried, throwing her arms about his neck in the manner befitting a true Cheltenham tragedy. "I won't let you shed blood over me!"

"How touching," Alcorn said bitterly, sneering at his wife.

"Very cleverly phrased, too, my dear. With those words one can't be sure if you're protecting your husband or your lover. If only you'd thrown your arms about *my* neck when you said them, I might almost have believed it was *my* blood you wanted to protect."

"*Your* blood ain't going to be shed, Alcorn, and you know it," Aubrey said furiously.

"No? I'm flattered, Tait, that you think so highly of my prowess with the pistol."

"I *don't* think highly of your prowess, you gudgeon. I happen to know that Griff won't shoot you. He intends to delope."

"That's enough, Aubrey," Griff said curtly. "Sit back down in your chair again and don't upset yourself. There isn't going to be any duel."

"I should hope not, indeed!" This was said by a new voice. All eyes turned to see Lady Mullineaux entering the room briskly. Julia backed away from Griff and self-consciously adjusted her cloak to cover her décolletage. Aubrey jumped up from his chair again, and Finchley-Jones made a stiff bow. Only Lord Alcorn failed to alter his position to acknowledge her ladyship's arrival.

"Welcome to this *ménage*, Mama," Griff said, throwing her a rueful grin. "Perhaps your presence will restore some semblance of sanity."

Her ladyship surveyed them all with thinly disguised disdain. "How can you—*all* of you—be so thoughtless as to stand about like this, babbling on about *holding duels in my drawing room*, when I'm expecting guests to begin to arrive before three more hours have passed? Really, Julia, my dear, have you no sense of time? I sent you and Alcorn a card, did I not? Why aren't you home dressing?"

"I believe, Mama," Mullineaux said, looking at Alcorn pointedly, "that they were about to leave to do just that."

"Ha! Do you think I have dancing on my mind at a time like this?" Alcorn ranted. "I've come to demand *satisfaction*, and satisfaction is what I shall have!"

"Very well, Alcorn," Mullineaux said with a helpless shrug, "if you insist on acting the fool, you may have your duel."

"Oh, how delightful," Lady Mullineaux said with ironic disgust. "Is that the sort of sanity you were referring to a moment ago?"

"Don't worry, Mama. The duel will not take place here."

"So you say," Alcorn muttered threateningly.

"So I say, Alcorn. Not here and not now. If there is to be a duel at all, it must be done properly. Aubrey will call on your second (if you can find someone idiotic enough to second you in this foolishness) tomorrow to make the arrangements."

Julia gave a terrified shriek. "No, Griff! You mustn't!"

"Be still, Julia," Lady Mullineaux said curtly. "If you had only learned to exercise some discretion and a touch of self-control, matters might not have come to this."

"They would have come to this in any case," Lord Alcorn said, his manner becoming a little more calm. "A man can not be made a cuckold without taking measures."

"Yes, but he needn't carry on like a looby so that the whole world knows it," Aubrey put in.

"That's *enough*, Aubrey," Griff ordered.

"Very well, Mullineaux, my second will call on Tait before nightfall tomorrow," Alcorn agreed, and then turned to the Countess with a stiff bow. "Your ladyship, I hope you will forgive us this untimely intrusion. Come, Julia. We shall take our leave."

He held out his arm to his wife, but the lady recoiled. "I'm not going with you!" she cried. "Never!"

"Oh, Julia, *really!*" Lady Mullineaux said in disgust. "Must you make a scene in my drawing room? And today, of all days? Do, please, behave like a sensible woman and go home."

"You don't *understand*, your ladyship," Julia quivered. "If I go home with him, he'll send me to his *moth—*"

"I beg your pardon," came a voice from the doorway. "Excuse me for this intrusion, your lordship, but be assured I wouldn't interrupt if this were not a matter of the utmost importance." In came Cornelia, still clad in her "fetching" morning robe and leading a red-faced, angry Clara by the ear.

"Damnation!" Griff muttered under his breath. *"Now* what?"

"Griff," Aubrey whispered to his friend excitedly, his eager eyes drinking in the ravishing vision, "it's *she!* She's come down! At last I'll have my chance!"

"Gracious!" the Countess exclaimed, striding across the room and releasing Cornelia's hold on her housemaid. "What is happening here?"

"I believe," Cornelia announced importantly, speaking directly to Griff, "that *this* is the thief who stole your missing treasure."

The librarian, who had been observing these proceedings with the fascination natural to someone who spends most of his life in the somnolence of bookrooms, gave a start, his lorgnette dropping from his nose again. "Are you referring to the *Miscellany?*" he asked eagerly.

Griff's eyebrows rose. "My *Tottel?* This girl stole it?"

The entire company, whose attention had been captured by Cornelia's extravagant beauty, now turned their eyes to the flushed, unhappy housemaid. "How unpleasant," Julia murmured, "not to be able to trust one's servants."

"But what Miss 'Aydon says . . . it ain't *true*, m' lord," Clara declared, glaring at Cornelia belligerently.

"Of course it isn't," Lady Mullineaux said soothingly. "Whatever made you think, Cornelia, that Clara—who's been with us for *years*—could be the culprit?"

"It's as plain as day, your ladyship," Cornelia said confidently. "She was assisting my abigail in readying my costume for tonight, when I noticed a leather-bound volume in the corner of a shelf in the wardrobe in my room. You know the wardrobe, my lady. The painted oak, with double doors—"

"Yes, I know the one. Do go on."

Cornelia nodded and turned back to face his lordship. "Of course, I thought immediately that it must be your missing book. 'Climb up, girl,' I said to this creature here, 'and get that volume down. I think it may be Lord Mullineaux's treasure.' And do you know what she said?"

"No, of course we don't," Griff said impatiently. "That's what we're waiting to hear."

"She said, 'No need to bother. That isn't the one.' She turned out to be right, of course. It was only a circulating library copy of Matthew Lewis's *Bravo of Venice*, which some forgetful guest must have left behind and which some careless housemaid—like *this* one, I have no doubt—had pushed aside. Now, I ask you, Griff, if this chit's remark isn't an incriminating one. How can she have known it wasn't the missing volume if she didn't have information to the contrary? I've been questioning her for the past half-hour, but I've not been able to get a further word out of her."

"*Do* you know something about the missing book, Clara?" Lady Mullineaux asked gently.

Clara looked at her mistress miserably for a moment, and then her glance dropped to the floor. "Can't say, m' lady."

"*Won't* say, you mean," Cornelia snapped.

"See here, girl," Griff said, crossing the room and peering at the housemaid closely, "if you know something about my Tottel, it will go better with you to confess openly. If you took it without realizing what it was, or if you found it somewhere and became frightened..."

"'Tain't nothin' like that, m'lord," Clara said nervously. "'Tain't my tale t' tell."

"Then whose tale is it?"

But Clara refused to answer.

"*I* might be able to answer that," Cornelia offered. "My abigail says that this creature and your librarian's assistant are thick as thieves. An apt expression in this case, I believe. It seems quite plain that the two of them plotted the theft together."

"*My* assistant?" Finchley-Jones took a nervous step forward. "Miss *Surrey?*"

Cornelia looked at the librarian coldly. "I assume, by that question, that *you* are the librarian. Well, you can't expect *me* to know the name of your assistant, now, can you?"

"Dash it all," Griff muttered furiously, "why does Miss Surrey's name crop up in every household crisis?"

"My lord, you can not believe *my betrothed* had anything to do with stealing the Tottel!" the librarian said, appalled.

Finchley-Jones's repeated use of the appellation "betrothed," added to the other nuisances that had beset Griff this afternoon, caused his temper to explode. "Confound it, Finchley-Jones," he thundered, "*stop calling her your betrothed!*"

Lady Mullineaux stared at her son in amazement. "Griff! What on earth's the matter with you? How *can* you speak to Mr. Finchley-Jones in that manner?"

"There's nothing wrong with my manner, Mama. The fellow insists on making the ridiculous claim that he's betrothed to my... to Miss Surrey."

"I don't understand," she said, puzzled. "What has that to do with *you?*"

"That is exactly what I was wondering, your ladyship," Finchley-Jones put in.

"Asked him the very same thing myself," Aubrey said, his eyes gleaming mischievously with the certainty that *he* knew the real reason for Griff's extraordinary behavior.

Griff felt a flush creep up from his neck to his ears. "I have my reasons," he said awkwardly. "It seems to me that—"

"My lord?" It was the long-awaited Symonds who stood in the doorway this time.

"Ah, Symonds," Griff said with relief, "there you are. I was beginning to wonder if you were neglecting your duties."

"You know better than that, my lord," the butler replied complacently.

"But, dash it, I don't see Miss Surrey with you. Where is she?"

"I can't seem to find her, my lord. But—"

"Did you look in the library?" Finchley-Jones spoke up nervously.

"Of course. First thing. She's not there, nor is she in her room. But, my lord, there's something else . . ."

"I hope, Symonds, you've not brought us *another* crisis," the Countess remarked. "I don't think I could bear it."

The butler looked at her with as much sympathy as he could appropriately show. "I'm not certain, my lady. It's a pair of callers."

"Callers?" Griff groaned in disgust. "Send them away, man. We can't deal with callers now. Just send them away and go to find Miss Surrey."

"But they insist on seeing her ladyship," the butler said. "They are quite adamant."

"Who are they, for heaven's sake?" her ladyship inquired. "Do we know them?"

"They said that their names will be well known to you. The gentleman is a Sir Jasper Surringham and the lady said you would know her by the name of . . ." He hesitated for a moment, his mouth giving just a hint of his distaste at having to say the word. ". . . Doro."

"Good heavens!" Cornelia exclaimed. "It's *Mama!*"

"Your mother and Sir Jasper!" The Countess clasped her hands together in delight. "Oh, how lovely! They must have come for your ball. Hurry, Symonds, you must fetch them here to us at once. Don't keep them waiting!"

"Yes, my lady," Symonds said, bowing.

But before the butler could leave, Griff's irritated voice stopped him. "And then, Symonds, continue to search for Miss Surrey. I don't want to see you again until you've found her and brought her here! Is that clear?"

The butler bowed again and departed. For the first time

since the Alcorns' arrival, a silence fell upon the party. It was an appropriate time for the Alcorns' and Finchley-Jones to take their leaves, but somehow they made no move to do so. Clara, however, edged nervously toward the door. She understood that matters were about to reach a dramatic climax for her friend, and she anxiously watched for an opportunity to slip out of the room so that she might dash up to the servants' quarters and warn her.

Aubrey, meanwhile, realized that this might finally be his opportunity. "I say, Griff," he muttered *sotto voce*, "do you think that, while we're waiting for the new arrivals, you might introduce me to—?"

"And where," the object of his adoration said nastily to the housemaid at just that moment, "do you think you're going?"

"I beg pardon, ma'am," Clara responded nervously, "I didn't think ye wanted me round no more. Might I be . . . excused?"

"Not yet, young woman," Griff said abstractedly. "Just stay where you are." Unwilling to let anyone guess the turmoil churning within him, Griff remained leaning on the Sheraton table, a picture of outward calm. But he felt like a lion who was chained to his place in a cage and unable to pace about. His reaction to Finchley-Jones's claim to be betrothed to *his* Ada was more violent than he was willing to admit. His mother and his friend had asked what business it was of his, but he was reluctant to answer. The truth was that he couldn't bear the thought of her marrying Finchley-Jones (or anyone else, for that matter), but what right had he to object, unless he intended to marry the girl himself? Marrying her, however, was out of the question. She was impossible. Everything that was happening this afternoon seemed tied up in some way to her maggoty behavior. How could he marry so muddled a female?

The protracted silence roused Alcorn to the realization that he'd long overstayed his intention to depart. "Perhaps it is time, Mullineaux, for *us* to take our leave," he said. "It's quite plain, Julia, that this is not the time for you to air our problems. Let us go."

"No!" Julia said stubbornly. "I've already told you that I won't—"

But at that moment Lady Dorothea appeared in the doorway, raindrops still glistening on her bonnet. "*Cornelia*, my dearest!" she cried in relief, throwing her arms about her daughter's neck in an emotional embrace.

"Doro!" Lady Mullineaux held out a hand in greeting as soon as Cornelia had broken from her mother's arms. "How lovely to see you!"

"Celia!" Lady Dorothea cried, taking the Countess into a second embrace.

"Mama, for heaven's sake," Cornelia scolded after the usual expressions of delight in each other's appearances had been exchanged, "why didn't you *tell* us you were coming?"

But Lady Dorothea could only beam at her daughter and dab at her tearful eyes. "Oh, Cornelia," she murmured thankfully, "you *are* here!"

"What a strange thing to say," Lady Mullineaux remarked. "Of course she's here."

Sir Jasper, who'd followed his sister in and had stood waiting in the background during the exchange of greetings, could contain himself no longer. "You, ma'am, are the Countess Mullineaux, I take it," he said bluntly, making a quick leg before her and putting out his hand. "I'm Jasper Surringham. I don't like roundaboutation, so I'll ask ye straight out. What have ye done with my niece?"

The Countess smiled at him warmly and took the proffered hand. "Nothing dreadful, Sir Jasper, as you can see. She looks blooming, wouldn't you say?"

"Not *that* one!" he growled irritably. "My *Ada!*"

"Who?" Lady Mullineaux asked, not comprehending what he'd asked.

"Ada?" Griff asked, arrested.

"Ada?" Finchley-Jones echoed weakly.

"My Ada!" Jasper repeated impatiently. "Ada, your god-daughter and my niece."

"I don't know what you mean, Sir Jasper," her ladyship said. "I haven't seen your Ada since her birth."

Jasper's face paled. "Are ye sayin', my lady, that she *ain't here?* I sent her to ye more'n three weeks ago!"

"You sent her here? To me? But *Cornelia* is the one who came!"

"You see, Jasper?" Dorothea said triumphantly, embracing her daughter again in delight, "I *told* you it would be so. Cornelia doesn't lie."

Jasper's knees began to tremble. "But the letters..." he muttered, shaken. "She's sent me three letters, all from London. Can she have gone to the wrong house?"

Cornelia, following the conversation with growing amusement, gave a scornful laugh. "Don't tell me that my featherheaded cousin has lost herself again!"

"Isn't that just like Ada?" Dorothea murmured with the self-satisfied pity that comes from feeling superior to the one being pitied. "She's probably living somewhere not far from here and thinking that she's safe among the Mullineauxs!"

"Come now, Doro. You don't really believe the girl can have found a home among strangers without knowing who they are!" Lady Mullineaux objected. "Do you wish me to believe the girl is witless?"

"I'll have ye know, Celia Mullineaux, that my Ada has more brains—and more character, too—than any young woman I've ever known." Jasper glared directly at Cornelia and Dorothea as he spoke. "An' *present* company *ain't* excepted!"

Griff, his brows knit, looked over at his mother. "There *is* an Ada in this house, you know."

"Good heavens!" Lady Mullineaux's eyes widened. "You don't mean *the girl in the library!*"

A murmur rose in the room. Aubrey sank down in his chair agape. Clara groaned aloud. Mr. Finchley-Jones squealed. "Are you accusing my betrothed *again?*" he demanded in an injured falsetto.

"Damnation, man," Griff snarled, "if you call her your betrothed *once more,* I give you my word I shall land you a facer you won't forget."

"I think I'm becoming quite confused," her ladyship confessed. "Are you saying, Mr. Finchley-Jones, that, being betrothed to Miss Surrey, you believe her to be who she says she is?"

"Yes, your ladyship, I am."

"While on the other hand, you, Griff, believe her to be Sir Jasper's niece?"

"I think it more than likely." Throwing a dagger look at his librarian, he added, "And much more likely than the possibility that she's betrothed to this... this mooncalf!"

Finchley-Jones had had more than his nerves could bear. "You'll eat those words, my lord!" he yowled, waving a knobby, shaking finger under his employer's nose. "You wait and see!

You'll *eat* them! She'll tell you herself, as soon as she comes in—"

"If ever she *does* come in," Griff muttered, throwing an impatient look at the door. "Where on earth can she be hiding?"

"Let me find 'er, m'lord," Clara offered eagerly. "I think I might know where—"

"Not on your life," Cornelia said. "Don't let her go, Griff. She'll only take this opportunity to warn this Ada away."

Jasper had been following these exchanges with intent concentration. "Do I understand ye all t' be sayin' that my Ada *is* in this house?"

"Nonsense," Cornelia declared, feeling quite convinced that her innocuous little cousin and the librarian's assistant could not be one and the same. Ada Surringham could never have managed to create so much interest in her doings as this chit from the library seemed to have done. "If she were here, wouldn't I have seen her?"

"Not necessarily," Lady Mullineaux suggested. "You haven't visited our library since you arrived, have you? Since the girl works there—"

"My Ada? Works in yer *library?*" Jasper asked, horrified.

Celia Mullineaux looked at the elderly man guiltily. "I really don't know, Sir Jasper. If she does, it was without my knowledge or consent, I assure you."

"An' I suppose it was also without yer knowledge or consent that she's gotten herself betrothed t' that scarecrow there?"

"She's *not* betrothed to him!" Griff said through clenched teeth.

"She *is!*" Finchley-Jones insisted, close to hysteria.

"Oh, what a dreadful coil this all is," the Countess murmured.

"Please, m' lord, send me t' find 'er," Clara begged, edging toward the door again.

"I think it would be better—" his lordship began, but a movement at the door stayed his tongue.

It was Symonds in the doorway. "Miss Ada Surrey, my lord," he announced. "She would like a moment of your time, to confess something to you."

"Well, well," Griff said with a perverse satisfaction, "it's about time. Let her in, Symonds, by all means."

Symonds moved aside and Ada, a shabby leather-bound book clutched to her breast, stepped over the threshold. With her eyes lowered in fright she launched immediately into her confession. "I have something I must tell you, my lor—" Her eyes lifted. Gasping in shock, she whitened at the sight of the ten pair of eyes staring at her.

"Come in, Miss Surrey," Griff said with a spider-to-the-fly leer. "We've been waiting for you."

Chapter Nineteen

Her first thought was that a group of constables had gathered to arrest her for thievery. But then she saw her uncle. "Oh, my *God!*" she breathed, wincing.

"Ada!" Jasper gasped, half in relief and half in anger, while everyone in the room began to speak at once.

"Heavens, it *is* she!" Lady Mullineaux muttered to herself. "How could I have failed to recognize the likeness in her eyes? Her mother's eyes *exactly!*"

"Good Lord!" exclaimed Alcorn at the same time, coming to life in excited surprise. "It's the *girl from the Black Boar!* I say, Mullineaux, it's the outside of enough, even for one of your set, to keep your mistress in your own house!"

"Mistress?" Jasper said, his voice choking as he wheeled about. "Did that fellow say *mistress?*"

"No, of course not," Lady Mullineaux assured him quickly while throwing Alcorn a look of angry disapproval. "This is all some sort of mistake—"

"Dash it all, Alcorn," Aubrey said in an outraged undervoice, "hold your blasted tongue."

"*Ada Surringham!*" Cornelia said amid all the babble, striding across the room in a fury, "have you been hiding in the library *all this time?*" Her ire was caused by sheer jealousy at the overwhelming attention being paid to her dowdy, absentminded, innocuous little cousin (although she had no conscious awareness of this jealousy, being incapable of achieving the objectivity necessary to analyze the weaknesses of one's own character).

Meanwhile, Finchley-Jones dropped down on the nearest chair, his bravado completely deflated. "Then . . . she *isn't* really Ada Surrey, is she?" he mumbled to nobody in particular.

"Never mind all this," Griff said, silencing the uproar with tight-lipped authority and focusing his attention on the girl in the doorway. "It doesn't matter if you're Ada Surrey or Ada Surringham or the daughter of Mama's French cook. Just tell this jobbernowl here that you're *not* betrothed to him!"

Julia, who'd been staring in openmouthed astonishment not at Ada or at Griff but at her husband, spoke up at that moment. "What did you mean, his *mistress?*" she demanded of Alcorn. "I thought the girl at the Black Boar was only a *pretense!*"

Alcorn gave an evil chuckle. "Well, my dear, your lover evidently pulled the wool over your eyes as well as mine. Not only was it no pretense, but she's *still with him!* It is just as I told you when I brought you home from Oxfordshire; Mullineaux has replaced you with someone else."

Julia swung round to Griff, her eyes blazing. It was one thing to be given up in the name of honor; it was quite something else to be replaced, especially by a mere slip of a girl at least five years younger than she. "Is this *true,* Griff?"

"Julia," Griff responded wearily, "go home."

"Answer the question!" Jasper demanded in an agony of confusion. *"Have you compromised my Ada?"*

It was Alcorn who took it upon himself to answer the question. "I don't know who you are, sir, or why this should concern you, even if you *are* the girl's uncle," he said fatuously, quite enjoying the situation now that his wife was getting this much-deserved set-down, "but I can tell you with absolute certainty that Mullineaux spent the night in your niece's bedroom at the Black Boar. I saw him go in with my own eyes."

"You are a *mawworm,* Alcorn," Aubrey said with loathing. "If Griff doesn't fire at you in the duel, I might very well shoot you myself!"

"Oh, my Lord!" Jasper groaned, tottering toward the nearest chair. "Give me a hand, someone. I must . . . sit down."

"You needn't concern yourself any more about the duel, Tait," Alcorn said, cheerfully ignoring the blow he'd dealt the shaken old man. "I think, now that Lord Mullineaux's interests have turned in another direction, I'm quite ready to forgive and forget."

"Magnanimous of you," Griff muttered drily, trying to help Sir Jasper into a chair while keeping his eyes fixed on the wide-eyed girl still standing frozen in the doorway.

"Take yer damned hands off me, ye lecher," Jasper barked, pushing Griff away.

"Take me h-home!" Julia wailed, throwing herself into her husband's arms. "I want to g-go home!"

"Before anyone leaves," Lady Mullineaux suggested, giving

what she hoped was an encouraging smile to the sweet child standing so stiffly in the doorway, "shouldn't we let the poor girl speak for herself?" This was her goddaughter, and a pure innocent (if the expression in those remarkable eyes was to be believed). It was not possible that all the accusations being thrown at her head could be true. "I'm sure there are a few simple explanations she can make to clear everything up, aren't there, my dear?"

Ada's eyes flew from face to face in sheer terror before fixing themselves on Lady Mullineaux's countenance. "Wh-What is it you wish me t-to explain, ma'am?"

The frightened little question stirred a reaction in almost everyone present. "What do we wish ye t' *explain?*" her uncle roared, his voice booming over everyone else's. "*Everything,* that's what!"

There was such a babble of shouts and demands and questions that Ada recoiled. Griff alone said nothing. He knew more of the answers than any of the others in the room, but he was filled with so strong a sense of irritation that it choked him like rage. The girl was infuriating! How had she managed to get herself into such a coil? He told himself that he was positively *enjoying* watching her being tortured by these questions and accusations. She *deserved* to suffer, blast her!

After a moment, however, he held up a hand for silence. "One at a time, please," he ordered. "I'm sure Miss Surringham—it is Miss Surringham, is it not, ma'am?—will be glad to respond to everyone in due course."

"*I,* for one, have no need for questions," Cornelia said in a voice heavy with scorn, "except to ask my 'beloved' cousin if the reason she hid from me in the library all this time was simply because of her dithering, childish cowardice!"

"There are several questions *I* would like to ask, of course," Mr. Finchley-Jones said, forcing himself to speak calmly, although his voice quivered in a register much higher than his normal, nasal tones, "but the most troublesome of them must be answered first. *Did* you, my dear, have anything to do with the theft of the Tottel?"

"*What?*" Aubrey asked, amazed. "Is *that* what's most important to you, you cod's-head? Ain't you going to ask if she's *betrothed* to you?"

"I have no need to ask that," Finchley-Jones responded with pompous certitude. "I already know she is."

"B-Betrothed?" Ada managed, blinking at him.

The librarian paled. "Don't you remember? I know you are sometimes a little woolly-headed, but surely on a matter such as this . . . ! I asked if you didn't agree that we should suit, and you said you'd given it some thought and that you *did* agree. Please say you remember!"

Ada did nothing but gape at him.

"Please say *something*, girl," Aubrey muttered. *"Are* you betrothed to this book-fellow or *ain't* you?"

"Oh, who cares a fig about that!" Julia declared. "What I want to know is if Griff really did go to your bedroom at the Black Boar Inn!"

Sir Jasper nodded in agreement. "Ada, my love, tell us the truth," he begged, quite stricken. "He didn't do such a thing, did he?"

"Of course he didn't," Lady Mullineaux said, patting Jasper's arm soothingly. "My son may be something of a libertine, but I don't believe him capable of seducing innocent young girls."

"Nevertheless, Countess," Alcorn insisted, "I did see them embracing at the inn, and I saw him enter her room. It *was* you at the inn, wasn't it, Miss Surringham? I couldn't be mistaken about that, could I?"

"The question I find much more interesting, Ada, is why you didn't tell me the truth about who you really were," the Countess said thoughtfully. "Am I so forbidding that you had to lie to me?"

If there were any more questions, no one asked them. Every eye was fixed on the girl in the doorway. Ada, however, seemed incapable of speech. She merely stood transfixed in the doorway, her eyes darting from one to the other like a trapped animal watching its trappers, her book still clutched to her breast in terror.

"Well, ma'am, we're waiting," Griff said, fighting back an almost irresistible urge to lift her in his arms and take her away from this inquisition. *She deserves all this*, he told himself, hardening his heart. "You've heard all the questions. What have you to say for yourself?"

Ada stared at them all for a long moment, her eyes filling with tears. Then she took a deep breath and opened her lips to speak, causing everyone in the room to lean forward in rapt attention. "Yes," she said softly. "Yes."

"Yes?" echoed someone in disgust. "Is that an answer?"

A veritable torrent of disgruntled remarks followed. "Egad, is something *wrong* with the girl?" Alcorn muttered.

"What on earth does she mean?"

"What sort of response is *that,* I'd like to know?"

It was another uproar. Griff held up a hand to silence them again. "Surely, girl," he said, scowling, "you can do better than that."

"But th-that *is* my answer," Ada said, her lips trembling and tears running down her cheeks. "Yes, I am Miss Surringham, and yes, I did lie to everyone about that. Yes, my cousin is quite right about my cowardice . . . I *was* too cowardly to admit to her and to my uncle that I'd arrived here too late. And about the b-betrothal to Mr. Finchley-Jones, I must say yes to that, too. I don't remember his asking m-me, but I do remember saying that I agree with him . . . about something. I must have been woolgathering, but if he says that it was an *offer* which I agreed to, then I . . . I suppose it must be so. And if I agreed to his offer, then I must indeed c-consider myself his betrothed. As for the situation at the Black Boar, you know the answer as well as I, my lord. It is also yes. Yes, you *d-did* come to my bedroom at the Black Boar, as you v-very well know, and yes, it was I whom Lord Alcorn saw being embraced by you in the dining room of the inn. I . . . I'm sorry, Uncle Jasper, to have brought such sh-shame on you, but my answer is yes to . . . to everything having to do with the Black Boar Inn. And I must give a yes even to you, your ladyship. I *did* find you f-forbidding and was ashamed to admit to you that I had come all this way in Cornelia's wake. I should n-never have come. I should have known that I'd be in her wake th-this time, too. And . . . and the final yes, your lordship . . . I *did* take your book. Here . . . I've b-brought it back to you. The truth is that I thought the m-missing book was c-called the *Miscellany,* so I had no idea that this, being c-called the *Songes and Sonnettes,* was the Tottel. I know it was featherheaded of me n-not to have noticed, but if you th-think I f-filched it on purpose, I don't m-mind. I'd rather be thought a thief than a b-bubblehead, although with all th-these yeses, I know you m-must really judge me to be b-both!"

She dashed the tears from her cheeks with the back of one hand and thrust the Tottel into Griff's arms with the other. Everyone in the room was staring at her, stricken speechless.

She looked round at them one last time and then ran to the door. "Ada—!" Griff said, his voice hoarse. He took a step toward her.

She paused in the doorway and shook her head, keeping her face turned away. "Please let me g-go, your lordship," she said with a little, negative gesture of her hand. "I h-haven't anything else to s-say, except that if you are going to c-call the magistrates to take m-me to prison, they can find me w-waiting in my room." With that, and one last little sob, she was gone.

Chapter Twenty

After Ada's disappearance, no one moved. Each seemed to be experiencing a feeling of dismay, not at Ada's behavior but at his own. Although the girl's little speech had been filled with admissions of guilt, the aura she'd left behind was one of innocence. Everyone in the room, even Cornelia, wondered how much his or her conduct had contributed to Ada's obvious misery. Only Clara was not smitten with guilt, and thus it was she who recovered first. "Ain't ye all ashamed o' yersels?" she muttered, stalking to the door. "Drivin' the poor thing t' tears with yer questions! An' if yer sittin' there thinkin' that she's done anything out o' the way, yer touched in yer upper works. I don't care that she said yes t'all yer accusations. I wouldn't care if she confessed t' murderin' 'er grandmama. Anyone who knows 'er at all would know she couldn't do nothing bad. The worst thing ye can say she done was t' use that there book as a prop fer 'er mirror!"

Having spoken her mind, she flew quickly out of the room. She had no doubt that "deevine retribution" for her insolence would be delivered upon her head at any moment, but at least it would not be in the drawing room in front of all those strangers.

"That saucy chit should be sacked at once," Cornelia muttered as soon as she'd recovered her usual aplomb.

"That saucy chit," Griff said, leaning against the table, an abstracted expression in his eyes, "is quite right. Ada hasn't done anything wrong, and it was despicable of us all to set on her like that."

"Are you saying, old fellow, that the girl is *not* your mistress?" Alcorn asked nastily, trying (despite an inner instinct that told him he was wrong) to cling to his comfortable conclusions.

"Really, Lord Alcorn," the Countess said, "isn't it plain as the nose on your face that she couldn't be? A child like that wouldn't even know how to go about it!"

"You're right, my lady," Jasper said, rising from his chair, the ruddy color returning to his cheeks as his spirit recovered its normal resiliency. "I don't know what made me even *think* it could be true. I know my girl; she may be a bit absentminded at times, but she hasn't the nature fer subterfuge or indecency. I owe her an apology fer thinkin' otherwise."

"Then why did she admit to all that business at the Black Boar?" Julia demanded.

"To protect me, I think," Griff admitted. "She agreed to the *pretense* of an affair to help me prevent a duel, and when she saw Alcorn here today, she didn't want to undo what we'd done. I assure you, Sir Jasper, that that's all it was—a pretense. If I'd known her better, I would never have asked her even to *pretend* to such behavior. Forgive me for it. But she was not in the least compromised by the pretense. My valet can vouch for that. He saw me climb into the window of my own room only a short while after I entered hers."

"So *that's* how it was done! In at her door and out at her window, eh?" Lord Alcorn muttered. "I ought to put a bullet into you for that trick alone!"

"I've heard enough about bullets and duels," the Countess said coldly. "Take your wife home, Lord Alcorn. After listening to your blustering this afternoon without much comment, I think I've earned the right to offer some advice. Spend a little more of your energies in attending to your wife—in listening to her wishes and trying to please her—and a little less on trying to arrange duels. If you do, perhaps you'd find your life more satisfying."

"Yes, Alcorn, take me home," Julia agreed with a sigh. "I'm feeling worn to the bone. I think I'm becoming too old for these theatrics. Perhaps I shall go to your mother's after all. I shall sit near the fire with her all day, rocking and embroidering, trying to grow old with grace and serenity."

"You, old?" her husband said, tenderly placing the hood of her cloak on her head. "Never, my dear, never." As he led her to the door, he glanced back at the Countess with a questioning glance. The Countess nodded her approval. Pleased with himself, Alcorn leaned down and whispered in his wife's ear, "And I shan't send you to my mother, so you needn't worry about that. I don't intend to let you out of my sight again."

Julia looked up at him in surprise. Then, with a quick glance over her shoulder at Griff, she sighed in meek acceptance of her fate. However, even in this significant moment (which she was wise enough to realize was the start of a new life of obedient, compliant, wifely boredom), Julia was conscious of the audience's eyes on her and made the most of her exit. Resting her head prettily upon her husband's shoulder, she let him lead her from the room.

The Countess expelled a relieved breath at their departure. "And now, Doro, let me take you upstairs and show you to your room. You, too, Sir Jasper. We all must begin to ready ourselves, you know. I hope you haven't forgotten tonight's festivities."

"Oh, yes, Mama," Cornelia agreed, her face clearing for the first time that afternoon, "do come upstairs. You must see the gown I've chosen for the ball."

The ladies and Sir Jasper left the room. Mr. Finchley-Jones and Aubrey were the only guests remaining in Griff's company. Mr. Finchley-Jones took out a handkerchief, removed his spectacles and began to rub them briskly. "I think that perhaps I owe you an apology, your lordship."

"Whatever for?" Griff asked.

"It seems that I am not betrothed after all."

Griff shrugged. "On the contrary, the lady admitted that you are."

"The lady admitted to a great many things that apparently are not quite true."

"I'm glad you see it that way, Finchley-Jones," Aubrey put in. "It seems to me that it wouldn't be fair to expect the girl to live up to a bargain she wasn't aware of agreeing to."

"No, it wouldn't," the librarian agreed. He put his lorgnette back on his nose with renewed firmness and faced his employer once again. "But I must tell you, my lord, that I intend to renew my suit as soon as an opportunity presents itself."

"You must do as you think best," Griff said quietly.

"But you really don't approve, do you?" the librarian accused. "Why is that, your lordship? Do you think that the lady is too far above me in birth and station?"

"I have no right either to approve or disapprove," Griff told him. "And as for her station, I have known of cases where the disparity is far greater and yet the matches led to sound marriages."

"I say, Griff, you ain't *encouraging* the fellow, are you?"

"Are you, your lordship?" Finchley-Jones inquired, studying his employer dubiously.

Griff looked up at his librarian with what seemed to be an effort. His mind seemed to be preoccupied, and it was with great difficulty that he focused on Finchley-Jones's question. "I'm neither encouraging nor discouraging. I'm merely pointing out that you have every right to do as you wish in this matter."

The librarian frowned. "I see. Well, then, there's not much more to be said. I intend to pursue my suit at the first opportunity. I owe it to the lady... and to myself."

"Yes, I think you do," Griff agreed. "But you will understand if I refrain from wishing you good luck in that endeavor."

"Oh, yes. Quite well. I am not familiar with the ways of the polite world, your lordship, but I am not such a fool that I did not recognize the... er... feelings that exist between you and Miss Surrey... Surringham—"

"Clever of you, old boy," Aubrey muttered drily under his breath.

"I suppose," Finchley-Jones went on, "that I am unlikely to succeed in my suit. However, if I fail, I shall not repine. It became clear to me this afternoon that Miss Surringham is not quite what I thought she was."

Aubrey glared at the fellow belligerently. "I hope you ain't suggesting, you greenhead, that there's something *wrong* with Miss Surringham?"

"Never mind, Aubrey," Griff said in restraint. "I don't think it appropriate to discuss Miss Surringham's character at the moment."

"I quite agree," the librarian said. "I have my opinion, and discussion is unlikely to change it." He lowered his head and cleared his throat. "I trust, my lord, that this... er... rivalry ... will not interfere with our association in the library work."

"Of course it won't," his lordship assured him. "In fact, I wish you will take this damned Tottel and put it somewhere safe. I've had enough difficulty over it to last me a lifetime."

"Yes, my lord. At once." The librarian took hold of the book and glanced down at it with awe before taking his departure. One glance at the worn volume and all the afternoon's tension seemed to vanish from his face. With the Tottel in his hands, he was himself again. His touch and the way he looked at the book were more loving and tender than they would ever be toward a woman.

As soon as Finchley-Jones had left, Aubrey leaned back in his chair. "Whew!" he said, putting his feet up on the hassock. "What an afternoon! For a while, I thought we'd have shooting right here in the drawing room. That Alcorn is a damned nail!"

Griff, still abstracted, brushed his hair from his forehead with the back of a hand. "I must say, Aubrey, you were a brick throughout all that nonsense. Don't think I wasn't aware of your loyalty."

"Hummph!" Aubrey grunted in acknowledgment.

Something in the sound caught Griff's attention. "Is something wrong, Aubrey? You sounded gruff. I think this afternoon has been difficult for both of us. Would you care to join me in a madeira?"

"No, I wouldn't," Aubrey said frankly. "Not in the mood to drink with you today."

Griff's right eyebrow climbed up. "No? Why not?"

"Something on my mind. I'm going to say it flat out before taking myself off." He took a deep breath before going on. "I have a good mind to call you out myself, Griff."

"Call me out? Is this some sort of joke? Whatever for?"

"For calling that sweet chit a maggoty female!"

Griff turned to his friend, now fully attentive. "By the term 'sweet chit,' do you mean Ada?"

"Of course I mean Ada! Who else?"

"You liked her, eh?"

"Who wouldn't? You certainly weren't very kind to her. And how could you describe her as maggoty?"

Griff threw his friend a rueful glance. "Because she *is* maggoty. Using my Tottel to shore up her mirror! I should have wrung her neck."

"If I hear any more about that deuced book, I'll wring *your* neck! Maggoty indeed! If you ask me, you're damned lucky to have won the affections of a girl like that."

"Do you think I've won her affections?"

"Without a doubt. It's midsummer moon with her as far as you're concerned."

Griff frowned and turned away. "An expert in these matters, are you?"

"Not in the least. But anyone with half an eye could have seen it when she looked at you today. Even that clunch

Finchley-Jones saw it. Are you going to offer for her, Griff?"

"Offer for her? Are you mad?" Griff strode across the room, pushed aside the fireplace screen and gave the grate a vicious kick, sending a shower of sparks flying up into the room. "Dash it, I'm as confused as a schoolboy. I had all I could do to keep from taking her into my arms this afternoon when she made that brave little speech. But she *is* such a deuced bubblehead, you know. How can one wed a girl like that?" He stared into the flickering flames glumly. "Can you imagine what life would be like with her? I'd be spending my days listening to her answering questions I'd asked an hour before, watching her lose her spectacles for the tenth time in a day, or searching for my *Times* that she's somehow mislaid. I think, in those circumstances, I'd be bound to turn nasty. You know how little patience I have for maggoty females."

"Don't use that word in connection with her again, Griff, I warn you. If you do, I shall plant you a facer! I suppose she *is*, as your librarian said, a little woolly-headed, and I ain't saying that a woolly-headed female would suit Griff Mullineaux as a wife, but to call the girl maggoty is going too far."

Griff turned his head to throw his friend a contrite grin. "Very well, that word will never again cross my lips. Shall we send for the madeira and drink on it?"

"No, not for me." With a real effort of will, he pulled himself from the chair. "I'd better get home and change."

Griff had turned back to his melancholy contemplation of the fire. "I'll see you out, then," he said without turning.

"No need for that. I can see myself to the door." Aubrey crossed to a pier table near the door where he'd left his hat and cane so many hours earlier. Picking them up, he remarked, "It's been a most interesting afternoon. Can't remember when I've been so vastly entertained."

"Oh, yes. Vastly entertaining," Griff muttered bitterly. "Lives falling apart everywhere, but vastly entertaining."

"Nevertheless, it was as good as a play."

Griff again noticed something in his friend's voice. Turning, he peered at him in sudden suspicion. "You don't look as if you've been entertained," he said. "You look a bit down in the mouth."

"Do I?" Aubrey shrugged. "If I do, it's only because I'm not looking forward to tonight's affair with the eagerness I felt earlier."

"Confound it," Griff swore in annoyance with himself, "it's because of Cornelia, isn't it? I never managed the introduction! I'm a selfish clod. But cheer up, old fellow, I'll make it up to you at once. I'll get the girl down here if I have to drag her by the hair! Just wait right here—"

"No, Griff, don't bother," his friend said glumly.

Griff stopped in the doorway. "Why not?"

"I don't know." Aubrey put on his hat, adjusted the angle and strolled out into the hallway. "It's funny, but . . . after hearing her talk to her little cousin the way she did today . . . I seem to have changed."

"Changed? In what way changed?"

"It's hard to explain. She doesn't look the same to me."

"Are you saying, old man, that you no longer want to capture Cornelia's attention? I find that hard to believe. Less than an hour ago you were whispering to me that she was ravishing."

Aubrey shook his head, nonplussed. "Can't account for it at all, Griff," he said as he sauntered down the hall, "but the ravishing Cornelia don't seem quite so beautiful after all."

Chapter Twenty-One

Ada sat huddled in a corner of her bed, her knees up under her chin and her arms embracing her legs, staring out ahead of her with unseeing eyes, daydreaming. She'd made a complete fool of herself before everyone who mattered in her life, but she felt to drained to weep. When the bottom falls out of one's world, tears seem inadequate. Ada had only one way of coping with disaster, and that was to escape from the reality of it. She was very good at that sort of escape. In daydreams she always found comfort.

At this moment, she was imagining herself the heroine in a slightly altered world. In her dream, she was a self-assured, capable, sensible noblewoman—very much like the Countess, but younger. She was married to a handsome, dashing Viscount who happened to be named Griff, and she presided over his home with amazing competence. Her parties were always the talk of the *ton;* perfect down to the smallest detail, they were universally admired. A card for one of her galas was the most sought-after of all social invitations. Everyone from the influential Princess Lieven to the Regent himself found it remarkable that Ada Mullineaux's parties never suffered from the slightest disaster; her famous lobster patties were never overcooked, the champagne was never warm, the guests were never incompatible, the rooms were never too hot, and no one ever had to walk from his coach in the rain. In her dream, the Regent arrived at her door, kissed her hand and said, "How is it, Lady Ada, that the rain never falls on the evenings of your galas?"

Her husband, who stood beside her greeting the guests, looked down at her with unmistakable affection and took it upon himself to respond. "Didn't you know, Prinny, that my Ada is especially favored by the Almighty?"

"Yes, I know. You are a lucky dog, Griff Mullineaux. Everyone says that she—"

A knock on the door caused her dream to evaporate instantly. She knew that it *couldn't* be the magistrates—Lady Mullineaux would certainly not permit her son to send for them to arrest her very own goddaughter—but her heart hammered nervously in her chest anyway. "Wh-who's there?"

"It's I, my love, Celia Mullineaux. I've come to fetch you to your new room."

"New room?" Ada opened the door warily. "What new—?"

"You surely didn't think I would permit my very own goddaughter to remain in the servants' quarters, did you?" The Countess stood before the door, smiling at her fondly. Looming behind her was Clara, her ruddy face beaming brightly enough to light up the dark hallway. "Clara will help you move your things. You'll like having her as your own abigail, won't you?"

Ada could do nothing but gape. Clara, as she passed her coming into the room, hissed in her ear, "Say 'yes,' you noddy, afore she changes 'er mind!"

"Oh . . . y-yes, yes, of course, but . . ."

"I want to hear no buts," her ladyship ordered. "I'm quite put out with you already for hiding your identity. Now, don't look so stricken. I'm more put out with *myself* for not recognizing you immediately when I met you in the library. If only I had known who you were, I would have been able to present *you* tonight along with Cornelia. It would have made me so happy to be able to do so. But I won't permit you, you foolish child, to deny me any further opportunities to fuss over you. Come along, like a good girl, and don't argue. We have a great deal to do before the guests begin to arrive. I have a gown and a seamstress waiting in the lavender bedroom, where you shall stay as long as this visit lasts."

Her ladyship did not wait for a reply but merely turned and started down the corridor with a purposeful stride. Ada had no choice but to scamper after her. Clara tottered along in the rear, carrying as many of Ada's belongings as she could bear in her arms. "But your ladyship," Ada said breathlessly, trying to keep up with the energetic woman, "I can't—"

"You must call me Cecy, as your mother did," her ladyship threw over her shoulder."

"Oh, I couldn't *possibly*—"

"Of course you can," her ladyship assured her. "You must learn, my dearest girl, to overcome this distressing tendency of yours to belittle yourself."

"'Ear, 'ear!" Clara chortled from the rear.

Before she knew how it had happened, Ada found herself
standing before a tall mirror in the prettiest bedroom she'd ever
seen, being fitted into a ball gown of shiny, light blue lustring
trimmed with corded satin. The seamstress was nipping in some
seams to tighten the high waistline, but the gown otherwise
was a perfect fit. Clara assisted the seamstress by pulling out
pins when directed to do so, but when not thus occupied, she
passed the time by grinning in happy admiration at her friend
in the mirror.

"I knew it would suit you," her ladyship said, also looking
happily at Ada's reflection in the mirror. Lady Mullineaux was
overjoyed that the girl she'd liked so much in the library had
turned out to be her goddaughter. And she was very pleased
with herself for having found, in so short a time, the perfect
gown for her goddaughter to wear to tonight's ball. She could
do nothing about the fact that Cornelia would be the star of
the evening, but at least Ada would not be overlooked. Not
with the blue-and-silver creation which she'd managed to find
among her stored clothes. "I used to wear it when I was young,"
she said, admiring the way the full skirt fell away from a knot
of gathers at the rear, low-cut neckline, "but it doesn't suit a
woman my age, so it's been on the shelf for many years. I
assure you, no one will guess it's a hand-me-down."

"It is beautiful, my la . . . Cecy, but I can't take it. I
don't . . . wish to attend the ball in any case."

"But you *must* attend," her ladyship insisted. "My dear, you
must do it for me! Don't you know how long I've yearned to
have you here with me, to fuss over you and dress you and
show you off to my friends?"

"Me, your ladyship? But you have *Cornelia."*

"Cornelia is . . . well, let us not say what Cornelia is. She
is very beautiful, of course, and I've enjoyed having her with
me, but she is not as special to me as you are. Besides, she
has a very devoted mother of her own, while you have none.
And I have no daughter of my own. Won't you let me have
the pleasure of playing your mother?"

"But . . . you have a son—"

Lady Mullineaux laughed. "Yes, so I do." She studied the
girl's face in the mirror with a sudden intent interest. "What
do you think of my libertinish son, Ada?"

"He is not really libertinish, I believe," Ada said, coloring.

"It seems to me that he is... very kind and... m-manly..."

"Yes, I quite agree," her ladyship said, her curiosity satisfied. "But a son is not the same as a daughter, you know. Besides, it is many years since Griff Mullineaux needed mothering. So you see, my love, I *need* you. Will you say you'll come to the ball and make your godmother happy?"

"If you put it like that, my la... Cecy, how can I say no?"

Her ladyship tried to embrace her goddaughter and received a puncture with a pin for her pains. "Oh, well," she laughed, "first things first. There will be a time for embracing later." She remained in the room until the seamstress finished the alteration and draped Ada with the silver gauze overdress that gave the gown its finishing touch. "There!" her ladyship said, studying Ada with her head cocked. "You look lovely. And now I must rush off and ready myself. Clara, I shall leave it to you to dress my girl's hair. Take down that knot and let a curl fall over her shoulder. She's too young to wear her hair in so severe a style."

"Yes, m'lady," the beaming Clara promised. "I'll 'ave 'er brushed an' ready in a trice."

"And when you've finished, come to me in my bedroom. I have a string of pearls for Ada to wear tonight, so as soon as you're free, Clara, please come and fetch them. Now, now, Ada my love, don't open your mouth to object. They are a very special gift that I've been saving for you since you were born."

This time they *did* embrace. "Oh, Lady Cecy," Ada said, quite overcome, "you are being t-too k-kind to me. I d-don't deserve it."

"You see? You *do* need a mother," Lady Mullineaux said, her voice also choked with emotion. "You need a mother to tell you how very deserving you are."

After she took her leave, Clara let out a whoop of joy. "Ain't this the most wonderful pass?" she chortled, hugging her friend, gathering her up in a tight hold and whirling her about the room in a hilarious polka. "Did ye ever *dream* that things'd turn out s' fine?"

"I dreamed it, Clara," Ada said when she'd fallen down upon the bed to catch her breath. "In fact I'm not certain that I'm not dreaming now."

"I'll pinch ye, ye goosecap, an' then ye'll be certain." Clara, grinning, took her hand and pulled her up. "Come on, get up an' let me dress yer 'air. Oh, Ada, isn't that gown a wonder? Ye'll be the most beautiful girl at the ball, see if ye ain't!"

The thought of attending the ball caused Ada's glow to fade. She didn't want to go to the ball and face Lord Mullineaux again. The look on his face when she'd come in with his book was engraved on her soul like a brand. She could still hear the scornful irony in his voice when he'd said, *Come in, Miss Surringham. It is Miss Surringham, isn't it?* "Must I go, Clara?" she asked plaintively as she sat down at the charming ebony and brass dressing table topped with marble. "I shall only make a fool of myself again."

"Look at yerself, girl," Clara said firmly. "Look at the girl in the mirror. Are ye tryin' t' pretend she ain't goin' to be the belle o' the evenin'?"

Ada looked. The dress seemed to emphasize the color of her eyes, and the gauzy overdress made her seem wrapped in a cloud. Clara was brushing her hair into one long coil, and by the time she placed it over her shoulder (shockingly bare because of the low décolletage of the gown), Ada hardly recognized the girl looking back at her. That was not a country mouse in the glass but a very presentable young woman. Ada blushed at the unaccustomed feeling of looking pretty. "I hardly know it's I," she whispered.

Clara knelt down beside her. "Ye know, Ada," she said conspiratorially, "I think we were wrong about 'er ladyship wishin' fer Miss 'Aydon t' wed 'is lordship. I think she 'as 'er eye on *you!*"

Ada felt her heart constrict. "Don't even *think* such a thing, Clara! His lordship doesn't approve of me."

"Because of that *book?*" Clara stood up, laughing scornfully. "When 'e sees ye tonight, 'e'll ferget all about the blasted book. Y'know, it's my view ye'd make 'is lordship a *perfect* wife." She burst into a guffaw. "Better even than ye'd make fer Mr. Finchley-Jones! When ye wed 'is lordship, Ada, an' set up yer own establishment, will ye take me as yer abigail?"

"You can be with me forever, Clara, if you want to. But don't go on about my marrying his lordship. I don't think I shall ever marry anyone."

"That's rot. But I won't speak of it if ye don't wish it. Now, ye just sit tight an' wait fer me. I'm goin' t' fetch the pearls."

* * *

When the family and the houseguests gathered in the drawing room before the guests were due to arrive, Ada's entrance caused a pleasant stir. She had paused in the doorway, hesitating in nervous fear of facing the same people who had, only two hours earlier, been witnesses to the most humiliating scene of her life. The first person to notice her was her godmother. "Ah, Ada," the Countess said in delighted greeting, coming to the door and taking her in. She kissed Ada's cheek and nodded with approval at her appearance. Then she turned and announced to the assemblage, "See, everyone, what a lovely goddaughter I have!"

Her uncle beamed proudly at the picture Ada made, and he came over and whispered into her ear an apology for his earlier behavior. "We won't say anythin' more about yer hidin' in the library all these weeks, either. If ye'll forgive me, I'll forgive you."

Symonds, passing among the company with a tray of glasses of champagne, so far forgot himself as to gape at her transformation, and Lawrence, the underfootman (who Clara had said was enamored of her and who was stationed at the drawing-room doorway to open and close the doors), gasped aloud when he recognized her.

"Good heavens, Ada," Lady Dorothea exclaimed in grudging admiration, "you haven't a *thing* out of place. I'd almost not have known you."

But Ada hardly heard her. She was heart-stoppingly conscious of the fact that Lord Mullineaux himself was approaching. His lordship gazed down at her with an unmistakable glow in his eyes. "You take my breath away," he murmured and kissed her hand.

"Thank you, my lord," she said in a tiny voice, unable to meet his eyes.

"We *do* have an understanding about the second dance, do we not?" he asked with a grin.

But Cornelia chose that moment to make *her* entrance, and beside *that* everything else paled. The girl was truly magnificent in her green silk gown that whispered as she walked. Her eyes were shining, her manner was animated, and it was plain to everyone that the evening would be hers.

And so it proved to be. From the moment the ball officially began, when his lordship walked onto the dance floor with Cornelia on his arm to the first flourish of the music, Cornelia held every eye. She was surrounded as soon as the dance ended, and for the rest of the evening she was never without a circle of eager admirers.

Ada was asked to dance the first dance by a callow youth who looked to be not a day over twenty. He was not particularly adept at the movement of the dance, and Ada was not adept at avoiding his errors. As a result, her toes were mangled by the dance's end, there was a dark smudge on one of her stockings, and the fellow had managed to step upon the hem of her gown and tear a piece completely off.

She wanted to run off and hide, but she *was* promised to Griff, she supposed, for the second dance. She refused two other invitations while she waited for him, but he was nowhere to be seen. When the dancers had all taken their places in the sets and the music began, she felt sick with humiliation. Tears formed in the corners of her eyes. If they actually slid down her cheeks and were seen by anyone in the crowd, she knew she would die of embarrassment. To avoid that fate, she went quickly out of the ballroom amd down the hall.

She found herself in the back part of the hallway, just opposite the library. That room, she knew, was not open to the partygoers. If there was anywhere in the house to hide, that was the place. She opened the door and slipped into the darkened room. She knew her way about quite well and was able, without mishap, to find the lamp on her worktable and light it with the tinderbox she knew was kept on the mantel. But before she could sit down and take a deep breath, the door opened. "I thought I'd find you here," Mr. Finchley-Jones said.

He came in without being asked and shut the door behind him. Ada was surprised to see how elegantly he was garbed. The points of his shirt were as high as those of the greatest dandy, his neckerchief was beautifully tied, his coat was well cut, his ecru waistcoat was in the best of taste, and his dancing shoes bore a pair of dashing rosettes. "You look very fine, Mr. Finchley-Jones," she said. "Are you enjoying the ball?"

"Not very much," he said, taking a stance midway between the door and her table. "I've spent the past half-hour searching through the crowd for you."

"For me?" she asked, suddenly feeling uncomfortable.

"Yes, Miss Surringham, for you. There is something I feel must be . . . er . . . clarified between us."

Only then did she remember. "You're referring to the

. . . betrothal that was mentioned this afternoon, I suppose."

"Yes. I am sorry that we did not understand each other during our last conversation on the subject."

"It is I who should be sorry, Mr. Finchley-Jones. It's inexcusable for a woman to be woolgathering when a gentleman is . . . is making an offer."

"I, however, will be happy to excuse you, ma'am. I know your tendency to be absentminded. I knew it when I offered. Of course, I did *not* know that you are a Surringham and a protégée of my employers. If I had known, I don't think I would have presumed . . ."

Ada did not wish to hurt him. Having no experience in dealing with unwelcome suitors, she wondered what she was expected to say. "I do not consider it a presumption, sir," she told him, sinking down on her familiar chair. "Your having made me an offer is very flattering, I assure you. However, under the circumstances, I shan't hold you to it."

"Nor I hold *you* to it." He advanced a step closer to her. "I've thought it over very carefully since this afternoon, and I've decided that the only gentlemanly thing to do is to make the offer again, ascertaining quite particularly *this time* that you are attending me with full consciousness."

"I am attending you, sir, but—"

"But you do not wish to accept?"

She looked over at him in the room's dim light, feeling an unaccountable urge to laugh. "I have the distinct feeling, Mr. Finchley-Jones, that you are hoping I won't. Have the events of the afternoon affected your original intentions?"

She felt rather than saw him wince. "I did find the details of your . . . er . . . escapades . . . rather shocking," he admitted.

"And you would be relieved, I think, to hear me refuse you. Well, sir, you may be happy. You have been as gentlemanly as humanly possible, and I absolve you of all obligations to me."

There was a moment of awkward silence. Then Mr. Finchley-Jones gave her a low, formal bow and turned to go. At the door, he paused. "Tell me, Miss Surringham, if you had been attending the first time I offered for you, would you have accepted me then?"

She shook her head. "No, I'm sorry, Mr. Finchley-Jones, but I would not."

He sighed a sad, deep sigh. "I see. It is too bad. For a

while, I was so . . . joyful." Then he took himself in hand. He had been made a fool of, made to suffer and had been rejected. He would not retreat without a parting shot of his own. "You have someone else in your heart, I know. I feel quite sorry for you, Miss Surringham. The one you dream of is not for you."

Ada stiffened. "What can you possibly know of my dreams, sir?" she asked coldly.

"I am bookish, Miss Surringham, but not blind. But his lordship will not make the mistake I made, the mistake of offering for you. He thinks you a maggoty female. That was his very word for you. Maggoty. I myself heard him say it."

With that cruel shot, he turned about on his rosetted shoes and left her alone.

Chapter Twenty-Two

The rain had not abated all day, so not one of Lady Mullineaux's guests was able to come to the party on foot. By the time the Regent arrived, the crush of carriages outside Mullineaux House was dreadful. No lady wished to make her entrance with rain spattered on her best cloak or soaked into her carefully curled coiffure, so every driver was ordered to maneuver his carriage as close to the front door as possible. Thus it was that the Prince Regent's own carriage collided with that of Lord and Lady Somerset, causing irritation and ill feelings on both sides. Griff, called upon to untangle the coil and soothe ruffled feelings, was therefore not in the ballroom during the second dance. He and Prinny were on intimate terms, however, and after Griff had accompanied his highness up the stairs and across the ballroom (the entire party having divided itself into two rows and formed an aisle down the center of the room along which the Regent, his retinue, Lady Mullineaux and her son paraded, Prinny stopping to shake hands and exchange quips with the many guests with whom he was on easy terms) and finally ensconced him at one of the card tables in the card room off the ballroom, he was able to excuse himself without giving offense. He immediately went to look for Ada to make his apologies.

But he couldn't find her. He searched the dance floor, the dowager's corner, and along the sides of the room where the chairs and sofas were lined up. He looked behind every potted palm. She was not there. He even sent a footman up to her old room in the servants' quarters and her new room in the west wing, but she was not to be found.

It was Finchley-Jones who led him to her. The librarian had come up to him to say goodnight. "Thank you, your lordship, for inviting me," he said stiffly, "but it is time for me to retire."

"Nonsense, Finchley-Jones," Griff said firmly, "you must stay for supper. My mother has arranged a veritable feast which I'm certain you will find worth the wait. By the way, you haven't seen Miss Surringham anywhere, have you? I've been looking for her."

Finchley-Jones looked at him strangely. "I saw her a short while ago. I think you'll find her in the library."

"The library? Why on earth is she hiding there?" But he didn't wait for an answer.

He crossed the hallway almost at a run and threw open the door. In the faint light of the lamp he saw that her head was resting on her arms folded on the table. Was the girl *asleep?* "Ada?" he asked, his voice tentative.

She started, her head coming up abruptly, and he could see that she'd been weeping. "Your *l-lordship!*" she said in obvious alarm.

"I didn't mean to startle you." He came in and closed the door. "I only came to claim my dance."

She shifted round on her chair so that he couldn't see her face. "You m-missed your dance," she said, brushing away the wetness from her cheeks with one unsteady hand.

"Yes, I know. I do apologize for that. My duties as host prevented my appearing. Prinny arrived at just the wrong moment, you see, and—"

"There's no need to explain," she said in a distant, formal way that was completely unlike her. "I did very well without you."

"Did you indeed? Who was the bounder who took my place?" he asked, trying to lighten her mood. "I shall challenge him to a duel—swords, of course—and run him through."

She didn't laugh. "I didn't dance. I was here, receiving an offer of marriage."

"Oh?" He came forward curiously. "Has Finchley-Jones been at it again?"

"Yes, but he was . . . quite relieved when I refused him." She lowered her head, still keeping her face averted. "It seems that, when a gentleman becomes familiar with . . . with the quirks in my character, he realizes how fortunate he is not to have any connection with me."

He walked round her chair and stood for a moment looking down at her. Then he lifted her chin. In the dim light the tears on her cheeks sparkled like diamonds, and her eyes looked almost ghostly. "Finchley-Jones is an ass," he muttered, feeling a decided constriction in his chest at the sight of her.

"Mr. Finchley-Jones is a gentleman of rare good sense,"

she said. Her manner was strangely cold. "He knows better than to ally himself with a . . . a . . . m-maggoty female."

Griff drew in a breath and dropped his hold on her. "Maggoty?" He could feel his hands tighten into fists. "Did he call you that?"

"No, but I . . . Never mind. I don't wish to talk about it any more."

"But I'm afraid you must. You see, I intend to make an offer for you myself."

Her remarkable eyes widened in shock. "You?"

"Yes, I. Shall I get down on one knee and do it now?"

She put out her hands as if in terror. "*No!* If this is some sort of joke, my lord, I must tell you that I am not amused by it."

He stared at her in confusion. "You behave as if an offer from me would revolt you. You must know by this time that I love you, Ada. What makes you think I'm joking?"

"You *must* be joking! You've told me several times that you don't care for bubbleheaded females. And after today you're surely aware of how bubbleheaded I really am."

"I was beastly to you today. I admit it. It was because I realized how much I loved you . . . and I hated myself for it. I didn't want to love you, you see. Despite my reputation as a libertine, I've never really loved a woman before."

"No!" She held her hands up to her ears. "I don't want to listen to this. I don't want to be told that you l-love me *in spite of yourself!*" She jumped to her feet. "You told Mr. Finchley-Jones that I'm a maggoty female, did you not? Then surely you will thank me, when you've had time to think this over, for not permitting you make me an offer. Let it never be said that the notorious libertine, Ivor Griffith Viscount Mullineaux, attached himself to someone maggoty!"

She turned and made a dash for the door, but he caught up with her in two long strides and pulled her into his arms. "Maggoty you may be," he muttered, tightening his hold, "but you do make the most irresistibly trenchant speeches." He held her imprisoned against him with one arm and lifted her face tenderly with his free hand. "I love you, idiot girl," he said softly, "and I think you love me. Don't you realize that nothing else matters?"

He kissed her then, and for a long time nothing else did matter. She could only marvel at the singing in her blood, the dizzying magic of his nearness, the inexpressible superiority of his actual, physical closeness to her imagined dreams. The experience was too exciting to permit her to think of anything else.

But the moment he released her, the pain returned. She *was* a maggoty female, and as soon as he'd recovered from this temporary madness he would wonder how he'd forgotten that fact. It was her place to help him remember it. "Please," she said breathlessly, holding him off, "don't kiss me again. There is a great deal else that matters. You don't know what I'm really like. If you did, you'd never wish to—"

"Ada, *listen* to me! I don't care about—"

"You *must* care. We are speaking of wedlock, not a night in a country inn. If we were wed, I should drive you to distraction in a week. Do you know that I sometimes don't remember what day of the week it is? And I—"

"Is this going to be another of your trenchant speeches, my dear? If so, why don't we sit down, with you comfortably settled on my lap, and—"

"No. I don't want you anywhere near me. Stand over there, please, and listen. I am *worse* than maggoty. I am completely *impossible!* Ask Uncle Jasper. I start upstairs to get something from my bedroom, and before I've reached the first landing I've forgotten where I'm going and why. I trip over carpets that haven't got a lump. I knock over the sugar bowl when reaching for the scones because I'm thinking of something else and not looking. My uncle has been searching for *three years* for a map of his property that I misplaced! I mix up the pattern pieces for the simplest kind of clothing. I once put *sleeves* into a *skirt*. Speaking of skirts, the entire village of Bishop's Cleve is familiar with the tale of my dinner with the vicar. The vicar's wife had given me a brooch for my birthday, you see, and later, when we were invited there for dinner, Uncle Jasper reminded me that it would be unforgivable not to wear it. Well, the brooch had a broken catch, and I had to fuss with it endlessly to make it stick—with Uncle Jasper shouting from downstairs for me to hurry. I finally managed to close the clasp, I threw my cloak over me and ran out. When we arrived at the vicar's— with half the town present and watching—the maid took my cloak and there I stood wearing nothing on my lower limbs but my undergarments. I'd forgotten to put on my skirt!"

Griff choked. "Ada," he managed, trying not to guffaw, "there's no need for—"

"There *is* a need. There is! You can't love someone like me . . . not for long. Think about it! Think of the sort of life it would be. You'd miss one of your favorite books and find it, after months of searching, in my flower shed, stuck behind the compost pile. I'd jot down a message from your friend about a place to meet, and when you got there you'd find that you'd arrived at precisely the right location and hour but the wrong day. I'd stitch a wonderful new waistcoat as a gift for you, and you'd discover that I'd set in the watch pocket upside down. I'd give you a half-dozen healthy children, but I'd never remember their names. I'd pay the bills, some of them twice. I'd send invitations to our parties to all the wrong people. I'd misdirect your letters. I'd put salt in the sugar bowl or lemon in your coffee. I'd leave my embroidery stand in just the place for you to trip over in the dark. I'd come to breakfast wearing my lovely new robe inside out. I'd spend hours looking for my spectacles and find them either in the flour bin, the linen closet or sitting right on my nose. You'd be leaving on a journey, and at the door I'd hand *you* the list of household chores for the day and kiss the *butler* goodbye. Who can marry such a one as I?"

Griff laughed and pulled her to him again. "I'll endure it all . . . except the butler. I will *not* have my wife kissing the butler."

But she pushed him away. "I know it sounds amusing, but it's *not!* I'm really *like* that. You don't want to marry a maggoty female. You said so! *Admit* it!"

Griff shrugged and turned away. What she said was quite true. He wanted her with every breath he took, but he didn't know if he could really bear living the sort of life she described. It was the same stumbling block that had barred their path since the first day they'd met. "I love you, Ada," he said, "but I can't pretend that I'd enjoy the constant turmoil that you describe."

There was a moment of silence. When he looked round, she was standing at the door. "Thank you for your offer, Griff," she said, subdued and saddened. "I shall always remember that you l-loved me for a while."

He took a step toward her. "Don't refuse me, girl. We may

be able to adjust to one another." He gave her a quick, hopeful grin. "Besides, my mother thinks you're perfect for me, and her judgment has always been impeccable."

Ada shook her head. "She wanted Cornelia for you at first. Everyone below stairs said so."

"No, she didn't. She doesn't like Cornelia much. Neither do I, for that matter. It's you we want, both of us."

Ada's eyes filled as she shook her head. "Nevertheless, you should wed Cornelia, Griff. I know she's arrogant and a bit spoiled," she said in a choked voice as she went out the door, "but at l-least she has some *sense!*"

Chapter Twenty-Three

The day following the ball was, of course, a beautiful day. The sun shone in a clear, sparkling sky and there was the smell of spring in the air. But everyone at Mullineaux House slept late. Even the early spring weather failed to rouse the household. The ball had not ended until dawn, and everyone from her ladyship to the lowliest scullery maid was exhausted.

The servants, of course, were not privileged to stay abed until noon as the Countess and her guests were, and by nine they were busily at work tidying up the wreckage that two hundred partygoers had left behind. Thus it was that Mrs. Mudge discovered that Clara was gone. That led to a second discovery and then a third, and then Lady Mullineaux's dresser scampered down the hall to her mistress's bedroom and woke her up. Her ladyship yawned, frowned, looked at her clock and glared. "It is not yet ten, girl. Have you gone mad?"

The abigail merely held out a folded note. Her ladyship took it with knit brows, opened it, read it, put a hand to her head, read it again and leaped out of bed. Throwing on a flimsy dressing gown, she ran down the hall in her bare feet and threw open the door to Ada's room. It was true. The bed had not been slept in, the drawers and chests had been emptied, and nothing remained of her goddaughter but a blue and silver ball gown laid out on the bed, a string of pearls resting on a velvet cushion on the dressing table and one shabby little half-boot lying forgotten under a chair.

A quarter-of-an-hour later, now fully dressed and unaccompanied, her ladyship marched down the hall in another direction. She carried the ballgown over her shoulder, the pearls and the shoe in one hand and the note in the other. She came to the door of her son's bedroom and, without knocking, strode into the room. In unmotherly fury, she shook the sleeping fellow's shoulder roughly. "Get up, you gamecock, and tell me what you had to do with this!" she ordered.

Griff, roused from a deep sleep, rolled over, opened one

eye, winced and pulled himself up reluctantly to a sitting position. "Mama?" he asked thickly. "Is somethin' amiss?"

"Read this!"

Griff rubbed his eyes, ran a hand through a tangle of unruly hair and took the note his mother was waving under his nose. *Dearest Lady Cecy,* he read, *I hope you will find it in your heart to forgive me for leaving in this unorthodox way, but it seems to me the best thing to do. Coming here was my first mistake and remaining was my second. I do not want to make a third one. I belong at home in Bishop's Cleve. I don't seem quite so foolish there as I do everywhere else. Or at least there everyone expects me to make muddles, so the consequences don't seem quite so horrifying. It was so kind of you to try to salvage something from the disaster I had made, but you must remember that you originally wrote that escorting two young women through a London season would be too much for you. I cannot in good conscience force that burden on you.*

I have other reasons, too, which make it urgent that I leave, so please do not feel that it is in any way your fault that I've gone. You were so sincere in what you said about wishing to play my mother that, if other matters were not so pressing, I would have stayed merely on your urging. But please believe that it was impossible for me to stay, under any circumstances.

Uncle Jasper is, of course, happy to take me home. He always feels, when he is away from home, like a fish out of water. I must also tell you that Clara goes with us. She is very sorry to leave your employ without having given sufficient notice, but she hopes that, in the circumstances, you will forgive her. She and I have become such good friends that we do not wish to be parted.

It was wonderful to be your daughter, even for one night, and I shall never forget anything that happened during last evening. Thank you for the use of the gown and the pearls. But thank you most of all for the many kind words you said to me. I shall always remember you with the greatest affection. Your loving goddaughter, Ada.

Griff stared at the letter a long while after his eyes had ceased to read it. His lips were white-edged, and his mother thought there was something in his expression that indicated that a troublesome turmoil was going on within him. "So she's gone home," he said at last, his voice shaking with a tightly controlled fury. "What has it to do with me?"

"Do you take your mother for a fool, fellow? Assignations at country inns, quarrels over nothing taking on deep significance, meaningful glances exchanged in crowded rooms, blushes and palings at the mention of certain names . . . what do you think those things are symptoms of?"

"Are you speaking of *me*, Mama? Have I been showing such symptoms?"

"You and she both. What have you done to her to make her run away?"

"Nothing," he said, flipping angrily over on his side, burying his face in his pillow and pulling the cover over his head in dismissal. "Nothing at all."

She pulled the cover back. "Tell me!" she demanded.

"Very well, if you must know," he said, sitting up again, "I committed an unspeakable crime against her. I asked her to marry me."

Lady Mullineaux's eyes widened. "Really, Griff?" Her face lit up in delight. "Is this *true?*"

"Yes, but you needn't get out the champagne," he said gruffly. "She won't have me."

"That's ridiculous. The girl adores you."

"So it seems. All the girls who adore me run for the hills when I offer for them."

"Don't be a clunch. She must have had a reason . . ."

"Oh, yes. She had a very good reason. She knew I have little liking for bubbleheads."

"Good God, Griff," his mother gasped, appalled, "you didn't call her that, did you?"

"Many times."

"You *are* a clunch. *Why?*"

"That is an idiotic question. I called her one because she *is* one. One of the worst. Ask her. She'll tell you so herself. At length!"

Lady Mullineaux sank down on the bed, confused. "But if you found her so, why did you offer for her?"

Griff gave an exaggerated shrug of self-disgust. "Thus love doth make bubbleheads of us all," he muttered.

"And she refused you?" his mother asked in disbelief.

"She did indeed. In that, at least, she had better sense than I."

She looked at her son askance. "Are you trying to pretend you're *glad* she refused you?"

"I feel like the devil, if you want the truth. But I'll get over it. And when I do, I will get down on my knees and thank God for sparing me from making the worst mistake of my life."

"Will you indeed? I think you'll *regret* this the rest of your life."

"What are you saying, Mama? I hope you're not suggesting that I go after her."

"That's exactly what I'm suggesting."

"Then I'm sorry to disappoint you, but that's the last thing I intend to do. The girl's a damned bubblehead, and this damned note is but another bit of damned evidence—as if I needed *more* evidence than I already have—that she'll never change."

"Watch your tongue, you insolent make-bait," his mother chided, slapping his wrist. "If I were a girl to whom you'd made an offer, I'd refuse you, too."

"Thank you, Mama. It's always comforting for a man to know that his mother is so completely devoted to him." He threw himself back down upon the pillows and burrowed into them again. "Now go away and let me sulk in peace."

She stared at the lump under the coverlet that was her son, sighed, gathered up her things and started out. "She didn't even keep the pearls I gave her," she said sadly.

"Mmmmph," said the lump under the coverlet.

"And she left this shoe behind."

"Shoe?" He threw off the covers and sat up again. "What shoe?"

"This one," Lady Mullineaux said, tossing it over to him.

He turned the worn, shapely little half-boot over in his hand, staring at it as if it were a talisman. "It wanted only this," he said at last, disgust and unhappiness warring within him. "My final, romantic vision of my lady love: I can see her now, misty-eyed and ethereal, limping toward her carriage wearing the mate of this on one foot and only a stocking on the other. Who but my Ada could leave behind *one shoe?* Honestly, Mama, I think that girl will drive me mad."

Chapter Twenty-Four

A fortnight passed and then a month, but Griff did not "get over it." In fact "it" became worse daily. He felt like the devil all the time. Aubrey began to complain that he always seemed abstracted. "You haven't won at cards in weeks, because you don't have your mind on the game. And you let Sefton's nag beat yours last week, which you'd never have done in your right mind. At least a dozen of us are out of pocket because of you, Griff." He gave his friend a look of lugubrious sympathy. "It's that bubbleheaded girl you're thinking of, isn't it? I hate to say this, old man, but this thing's made you as bubbleheaded as she!"

There was something in what Aubrey said. Griff *felt* bubbleheaded. His days passed in a kind of grey fog, in which he heard people's voices as if from a distance or saw their faces indistinctly. His life had lost its savor, its sharpness, its clean edges.

Meanwhile, Cornelia, realizing that she would not win Griff's attention, gave up and became betrothed to Sir Nigel Lewis. The Countess found the news amusing. "Two dignified, self-absorbed, good-looking fribbles," she said to her son, laughing. "I think they will suit very well."

The signs of spring in the air were then becoming more pronounced. There was a smell of lilac on the breeze, and the wind, whipping around the corners of the streets, had lost its sting. The days were like wine, but to Griff every beautiful sign of new life was painful; he had no one with whom to walk or to share the sights and smells. When he could bear the days no longer, he capitulated. "I'm going to Gloucester, Mama," he announced one morning at breakfast.

His mother's face lit up in excitement, relief and anticipation. "For Ada?"

"If she'll have me."

"But I thought," Lady Mullineaux remarked, watching her

son's face with fascination, "that you couldn't abide bubble-heads."

"I thought so too. But since I've become so bubbleheaded myself, the prospect of wedding one seems not only bearable but almost desirable."

He threw a clean shirt and some linens into a bag and set out that very day, driving a curricle and pair. He drove all through the day and night and presented himself at the door of the Surringham house in Bishop's Cleve the very next morning. He was bursting with an eagerness he knew was appropriate only to very young boys, but his youthful excitement was doomed to be short-lived. Cotrell, the butler, struck him to the bone with the news that Miss Surringham was not home and was not expected in the near future.

Griff felt so cruelly disappointed that the shock made him positively weak in the knees. "Not expected?" he gasped, almost bereft of breath. "Where *is* she?"

"I'm afraid I couldn't say, my lord."

"Then who *can* say?" Griff barked in irritation. "Is Sir Jasper at home?"

It took an endless five minutes before he was led into Jasper's sitting room, and the greeting he received after the wait was scarcely what a civilized man might expect. Jasper gave him no welcome at all. Instead he greeted him with a scowl and a pointing finger. "This nonsense is all *your* fault, Mullineaux," he bellowed as soon as Griff appeared in the doorway. "If it weren't fer you, she'd never have done it."

"Done what? I don't know what you're shouting about, Surringham. What nonsense are you speaking of?"

"Ada's disappearance."

Griff paled. "Disappearance?" he echoed faintly, sinking into the nearest chair.

"Left me a note, sayin' she's goin' away fer a month. T' prove t' herself an' t' the world, she said, that she's as levelheaded and competent as anyone. Didn't take a penny with her, nor leave me an address where she can be found. Damned silly female. We were perfectly content as things were before. Then you came along t' turn her head, an' now look at the muddle. I'm so worried I can hardly sleep o' nights!"

Griff questioned the man for a long while, but it became increasingly apparent that he would learn no more. The old fellow had told all he knew. Griff finally said his adieux and went to the door in utter depression. He had not a clue as to where Ada might have gone. Where could he *begin* to look for her? If Sir Jasper couldn't 'sleep o' nights,' what was *his* fate to be? Was it really his fault that she'd run off like this? Had he, with his critical superiority, driven her to this?

He went down the steps of the house and walked to his waiting horses so absorbed in self-abasement that he didn't at first hear his name being called.

"Yer lordship? Lord Mullineaux?" someone was calling in a hissing whisper.

He looked round at last. Beckoning him from a corner of the house was a ruddy-faced young woman in an apron and mobcap. "Is it . . . Clara?" he asked, his brows knit. Then his forehead cleared. *Clara!* The very person who might help!

She dropped a curtsey. "Yes, m'lord, it's me. Y're lookin' fer Ada, I expect. I tho't ye might be comin' t' find 'er."

"Did Ada think so, too?"

Clara shook her head. "She wouldn't let 'erself believe it. And now she's gone to be a governess, y' see. She'll never speak t' me fer tellin' ye, but I can't bear t' see ye go without seein' 'er."

"A *governess?* She's working as a governess? But why on earth—?"

"'Tis on'y fer a while, see? To show she can do it without makin' a muddle. She said she wants t' show ye she ain't maggoty."

Griff winced. "This *is* my fault, dash it! I don't suppose she told you where she went?"

"She did. Do ye think she'd ever fergive me if I tol' ye?"

"I don't know, Clara, but *I'll* never forgive you if you don't."

Clara studied his face in a dither of indecision. "Tell me, yer lordship," she asked uneasily, "what do ye want t' find 'er *for?*"

"I'll answer *that* question, girl, when you've answered mine. Is it a bargain?"

Clara nodded. "She's at Willow Haven, 'bout six miles down the road. The lady who she works fer is Mrs. Upshaw. There, I've tole ye. Now, then, m'lord—"

"I want to find her to *marry* her, of course," he said, starting off at a run for his carriage. "That is, after I wring her neck!"

*   *   *

Willow Haven was a rambling cottage with a thatched roof, but its size, its appointments and its well-kept trimmings gave evidence that its owners were prosperous. Thus Griff was surprised to hear screams, shouts and the sounds of general confusion when he approached the polished oak door. Nevertheless, he knocked briskly. His knock was answered by a maid wearing a neat apron but a worried expression. From somewhere behind her a baby cried, a child whined, another shouted and a woman screamed. The voice of the screaming woman was not Ada's. "Yes, sir?" the maid inquired.

"Is Miss Ada Surringham within?"

The maid looked at him in surprise, bit her lip and shook her head. "No, sir, she ain't."

"Dash it," Griff cursed under his breath. "Can you tell me when she'll be back?" he asked the maid with ill-concealed impatience.

"She ain't comin' back. Do ye wish t' see the Missus?"

Griff shrugged. "I suppose I must."

The maid led him into a sunny sitting room and disappeared. In another moment a youngish, rather pretty but overweight woman came in. She looked distressed and harried, and she carried the crying baby in her arms. Clinging to her skirt was a sullen-looking little boy of five or six. "Were you asking about Miss Surringham, sir?"

"I was, and I am. I was told she was in your employ."

The woman's eyes filled with tears. "She was, sir, until a little while ago. I had to dismiss her."

"Bad Mama," the little boy pouted. "I want Miss Ada *back!"*

"Be still, Timmy," his mother begged. "The gentleman and I are talking. You mustn't interrupt." She looked up at her caller unhappily. "He behaved so much better when Miss Ada was here."

"Then, ma'am, why on earth did you dismiss her?"

"I hated to do it, really I did. She is the loveliest young woman. But when Rachel ran into the drawing room *stark naked,* just when I was serving tea to Miss Faversham and her mother—"

Griff eyed the woman with fascinated concentration. "Rachel?"

"My little girl. She's four. It's she you can hear whining in her cradle."

"Ah, I see. She ran out of her cradle naked, you say?"

"Out of the tub. Miss Ada was supposed to be bathing her, but Timmy came to her with a book, asking questions as he always does, and Miss Ada became so absorbed in telling him the story that Rachel climbed out all by herself and ran out to the drawing room. You can imagine how hideously embarrassed I was."

"I *like* Miss Ada's stories," Timmy declared. "I want Miss Ada *back*."

"Well, you can't *have* her back!" Mrs. Upshaw snapped. "Really, I'm at my wit's end. I don't know what I shall do without her, until I find someone else, of course..."

"So it was merely this one little incident which caused you to sack her?" Griff inquired.

"If you'd seen Miss Faversham's face, you would not say a 'little incident.' And her mother almost *swooned*. It was quite the last straw."

"The last straw?"

"I mean, after all, there'd been the business with the paste, too!"

"The paste?"

"I know it *looks* like porridge, but *really!* How can anyone have confused the porridge with the paste? The porridge was in a *bowl* and the paste in a *jar!*"

"She confused them, did she?"

"More than once. After all, one can't have one's children eating paste, can one, even if it's only flour paste? And that wasn't all, you know."

"It wasn't?"

"No. There was the time she filled the tub without putting the stopper into the drain. She kept filling it with kettle after kettle full of water without even *noticing* that it was running out the bottom and puddling up on the floor!"

The little boy laughed. "Puddling on th' floor!" he chortled, and clapped his hands. "Happy, happy, happy!"

Griff glanced down at the child, puzzled. "What does he mean, happy, happy, happy?"

"I don't know, exactly. He does that when he's pleased about something." The woman's tears spilled over and down her cheeks. "But I must say that's how things were with Miss Ada...happy, happy, happy. There was something about her, you know, that made you feel cheerful just to look at her."

She shifted the bawling baby to her other shoulder, pulled out a handkerchief with her free hand and sniffed mournfully into it. "I hated to let her go, really I did. But I knew, the day she walked the empty hand-carriage, that she wasn't fit for this sort of work."

"Empty hand-carriage?" Griff asked, unable to help himself.

"Yes. It's a little wagonlike thing with four wheels, for taking the baby for an airing. She took it out for a stroll one day and forgot to put the _baby_ in!"

"I see," Griff managed, choking.

Mrs. Upshaw mopped her eyes and, having relieved herself of some of her feelings of guilt by relating all these episodes to her visitor, became more calm. "Have you come to see her home?" she asked, really taking note of her visitor for the first time. "I asked her if someone was going to call for her, but she said she would walk. Perhaps she forgot about you. She tends to be a bit absentminded, you know."

The little boy emerged from behind his mother's skirts and ran to Griff. _"Bad_ man!" he shouted, punching furiously at Griff's legs. _"Don't_ take Miss Ada home! I want her _back!"_

It took several minutes more for Griff to extricate himself from Mrs. Upshaw and her noisy brood, but he was shortly tooling down the road, his heart again pounding in boyish eagerness. He didn't know how he'd missed passing Ada earlier, for he'd just come up this same road. Perhaps she'd sat down to rest behind a hedge, and he hadn't seen her. This time he would keep his eyes open.

Only a very few minutes passed before he did see her. She was struggling wearily along, her bonnet askew, the hem of her dress sweeping the dust of the road, and the large portmanteau she was pulling behind her scraping and bumping on the ground. From the rear she looked pathetic and silly and helpless and utterly beautiful.

He drew up alongside her. "May I offer you a ride, ma'am?" he asked.

"No, thank—" She glanced up, blinked, and dropped her portmanteau with a thud. _"Griff!"_

He leaped down and enveloped her in his arms before she could utter another word. They kissed hungrily for a long moment. "I think that perhaps you're glad to see me," he murmured breathlessly when he lifted his head.

The joyful look in her eyes faded. "No, I'm not," she said, turning her head away. "You don't kn-know! I'm an utter *f-failure!*"

"Are you? That sounds serious. You must tell me all about it." He picked up her portmanteau and tossed it into the curricle. "But first let me help you up."

"I shan't ride with you," she declared, pulling her arm from his grasp. "You've come to persuade me to change my mind, and I won't! I can't! You don't *know—!*"

He pulled her into his arms again. "I know one thing, Ada. When I look at you, I feel happy, happy, happy."

She gaped at him in amazement. "You saw *Timmy!* How—?"

"Never mind how. But if you're going to make one of your trenchant speeches about how you failed as a governess, you may save your breath. If I'd wanted to wed a governess, I would have advertised for one in *The Times.*"

"Nevertheless, I'm as muddleheaded as I ever was. So nothing's really changed."

"*I've* changed. I've decided I'm just like Timmy. I don't care how muddleheaded you are, for when I'm with you I'm happy, happy, happy. I find I can't be without you, Ada. I become muddleheaded myself when you're not near."

She looked up at him as if she couldn't quite believe what he was saying, but, seeing something unmistakably fond and warm gleaming in his eyes, she reddened, sighed, and hid her face in his coat. "You can't really wish to marry such a maggoty creature as I am!" she murmured.

"Yes, I can, as soon as it can be contrived. I intend to wed you with as much pomp and ceremony as befits the future Viscountess Mullineaux."

"Oh, G-Griff!" She gave a tremulous little laugh. "I shall probably trip over my bridal train, fall on my face, and embarrass you before all of London society."

He put his cheek against her hair. "No doubt you will. But I'm so besotted that I shall probably find your pratfalls utterly charming."

Eventually they were seated side by side in the curricle watching the horses amble slowly along toward home. Ada, filled with a joyousness so overwhelming that she knew she could not be dreaming, snuggled against his shoulder. "Imagine your coming all this way," she murmured blissfully, "just to offer for me again!"

"I didn't come for that purpose at all," he said blandly. "The offer was merely an afterthought."

She sat up in mock hauteur. "An afterthought, indeed! Then why *did* you come?"

"I came, my love, to even up the score. Once you made a noble sacrifice for my sake, remember?"

"I remember. You called it a splendid indiscretion."

"So it was. I shall always be indebted to you for it. So I decided to make a noble sacrifice for you."

"You don't say! What sort of sacrifice?"

"A sacrifice of time and effort on your behalf. I came all this way—at great personal cost, mind you—to deliver something you had left behind."

"Something I'd left behind?"

"Yes." He put his hand into the largest of his coat pockets and pulled something out. "Something you must have missed dreadfully."

"There was nothing I missed dreadfully...except you, of course."

"Thank you, my love, but this is something more practical and necessary to your daily well-being than even I am. I couldn't bear to think of you limping about without it. So here it is, with my compliments."

And, with a broad grin, he dropped the little half-boot into her lap.